The
EDGE
RULES

Books by Melanie Hooyenga

The Campfire Series
CHASING THE SUN
CHASING THE STARS
CHASING THE MOON

The Rules Series
THE SLOPE RULES
THE FRIEND RULES (short story)
THE TRAIL RULES
THE EDGE RULES

The Flicker Effect Trilogy
FLICKER
FRACTURE
FADED

Anthologies
LOVE ON MAIN
THE ART OF TAKING CHANCES

Praise for THE SLOPE RULES

"There aren't enough books like The Slope Rules out there in the world of romance. This is a can't miss for anyone who wants more sweet than spicy and needs their hearts thawed on cold winter nights. No one will regret spending time on this book." —*YA Books Central*

"A fun, romantic story with a likeable protagonist and a familiar, yet enjoyable dramatic storyline that will appeal to teen readers." —*IndieReader*

"Author Melanie Hooyenga tells it like it is in this remarkably honest coming of age story. The Slope Rules offers drama, action and age-appropriate romance all wrapped up in an inspiring, page-turning read." —*Children's Literary Classics*

"Both sporting fans and readers who love emotionally charged novels will adore The Slope Rules,... a great romance for young adult readers... that explores love, coming of age, and personal growth." —*Reader's Favorite*

"The prose is tight and enjoyable from the first paragraph until the very end. The author's descriptions are vivid and beautiful. Cally has a strong, self-confident voice and is a fully developed character." —*The BookLife Prize*

Praise for THE TRAIL RULES

Gold Winner (Special Interest: Sports) 2018 — *Children's Literary Classics*
Silver Winner (YA Fiction General) 2018 — *Moonbeam Children's Book Awards*
Silver Winner (YA Romance) 2018 — *Readers' Favorite*

"In a must-read book..., the hilarious yet drama-fueled book THE TRAIL RULES follows one girl's adventure into self-discovery and security, leading to a goose bump-inducing conclusion that will inspire young adults to take worthy risks in their own lives that could reap a handsome reward." —*IndieReader*

"A fantastic sequel from Melanie Hooyenga... A well-done portrait of life at it's finest—when things end to make way for new challenges and excitement. When love trumps disappointment. And when we find out just how limitless we really are." —*YA Books Central*

"Hooyenga gives us an expertly-written, well-paced narrative and a fascinating and well-developed cast of teen and adult characters. Mike is a very likable teen who hasn't yet found her own path or her inner courage. As she gains experience on the bike, she devises ten (plus one) "trail rules," which also help her face the challenges of life. ...this is an extremely positive and engaging story told in a very beautiful way." —*Readers' Favorite*

"Mike's story is solidly plotted and well paced, and it shows that a change of heart is only the beginning step in understanding who you are. The characters here ring true, especially Mike, whose evolution and growing self-awareness propel the story forward. The writing has an immediacy and works to bring readers inside of Mike's head. And while there are some melodrama moments, they never overwhelm the narrative, instead, they keep the emotions raw and honest." —*The BookLife Prize*

"Hooyenga continues to deliver an exciting story with page-turning plots and sub-plots and an underlying theme of genuine female characters who are likeably flawed." —*Children's Literary Classics*

The
EDGE
RULES

Melanie Hooyenga

Left-Handed Mitten
Publications

THE EDGE RULES

Copyright © 2018 by Melanie Hooyenga

Published by Left-Handed Mitten Publications
ISBN-13: 978-1727366143
ISBN-10: 172736614X

UPC

Book design, cover design, and ebook formatting by Left-Handed Mitten Publications. Author photo by Jenn Marie Photography.

Author website: melaniehoo.com
Email: melaniehooyenga@gmail.com
Facebook: facebook.com/MelanieHooyenga
Twitter: @melaniehoo
Instagram: @melaniehoo
Newsletter: melaniehoo.com/hoos-letter

Melanie Hooyenga
PO Box 554
Grand Haven, MI 49417

For my brother and sister,
for never making me feel like a Second.

one

I adjust my goggles and breathe in the cool mountain air. Snow clings to the spruces towering above, which border the edge of this run, preventing less-experienced skiers from tumbling down the side of the mountain. My grip tightens on my poles and I push off from where I was resting. Pierre, the exquisite French boy I met on the chairlift, smiles at me, and together we swoosh, swoosh, swoosh down the slope.

I'm not a flashy skier—I prefer to always be in control and have worked for years to perfect my form—but it still takes work to make it look effortless. My leg muscles flex as my skis glide inches apart, and I toss another smile to Pierre.

We round a bend and my breath catches. Lake St. Moritz stretches out before us, its clear blue water reflecting the clouds in the sky. Even after a dozen runs, this view never gets old.

Pierre slows next to me. "It is pretty, yes?"

I nod. "Yes." A lump forms in my throat. I never want to go home. Everything about this moment is so wonderful and—

Pierre slaps his pole against mine, making a loud clanging noise.

"What are you doing?"

"Brianna." His sexy French accent slips away and he sounds angry. He hits my pole again and the sound echoes off the trees.

I reach for his hand, panic fluttering in my chest. "Stop. You're ruining the moment."

"Miss Vines!" His voice comes out a growl and I jump. Then my eyes open and the Swiss mountains fade away, replaced by a cold cement room flanked with metal benches on three sides. Floor to ceiling metal bars make up the fourth wall, and that's where a very irritated-looking guard is glaring at me.

I scramble to my feet.

"Your father is here."

I sink back onto the bench. Facing Dad requires strategy, a plan, and the only thought looping through my head is how stupid I am.

The guard shakes his head. "Nope."

Cold from the bench seeps through my jeans. Another hour in this filthy cell is better than having to face my father and the horrible things he's going to say. All of which I deserve.

"He posted your bail. Time to go."

My legs shake as I stand, and he opens the door with a clang. I always thought they added that sound to movies for effect, but it made that horrible noise when they put me in here two hours ago. Right after they took my glamour shot—I refuse to call it a mug shot—and my fingerprints. Which wasn't too long after a cop unceremoniously shoved me into the back of a police car a block from the Pearl Street Mall in downtown Boulder, after that screechy storeowner caught me with a handful of necklaces and a few other things that may have bypassed the cash register and found their way into my purse.

My heart gallops as the guard leads me down a dingy green hall, through a locked door, and into the main room where I first came in. I'm the queen of entrances, but it takes every ounce of strength to keep my face composed and conceal the tremor running through me. Dad pushes away from the far wall when he sees me, and my breath stops. I take a step back, bumping into the guard.

Frank Vines isn't a large man, but his presence commands respect. From his power suit to his two-hundred dollar haircut to his piercing blue eyes that are currently pinning me to this spot, he is not a man to be trifled with.

Edge Rule #1: When balancing on the edge of right and wrong, know which way you want to fall.

"Good luck," the guard murmurs, then walks away.

Normally I'd already have an excuse prepared, but this is beyond normal. With Frank Vines you only get one chance for vindication, and since I've yet to come up with the perfect explanation, silence is best.

I force my feet to carry me forward. Just get it over with. He can't say anything I haven't already thought. That I'm ungrateful, spoiled, a disappointment.

His glare hardens as I approach and a cold sweat breaks out over my skin. His cologne hits me first, and for a second I'm five years old, sitting on his lap eating breakfast while he reads the morning paper, but the moment is gone and he takes a step toward me.

His voice is low, carefully trained to not be overheard. "I will never do this again."

My head bobbles. "Yes, sir."

He gives me one more heart-stopping glare before stalking out of the Boulder Police Station with me on his heels. His sleek Mercedes is parked in the lot and he doesn't wait for me to climb in. The engine is already running by the time I fasten my seatbelt.

"Dad, I'm sorry." My voice comes out whiny—something not tolerated in the Vines household—and I cringe. Apologizing again would only make this worse, but the words dance on my tongue.

His head shakes from side to side, but his eyes stay on the road.

My pocket burns where the necklace was. I don't know why I took it. Or why I've been taking things. It's not like we don't have the money to buy anything I want, and I don't even wear what I've stolen. But the adrenaline that rushes through me when my fingers wrap around whatever shiny thing catches my eye outweighs the consequences of getting caught, and it always ends up tucked in my pocket. At first the jewelry sat in a pile on my dresser, reminding me of my poor judgment, but as the pile grew, I pushed it into the top drawer. Today's haul was just another conquest after another miserable day.

Dad still doesn't say anything as we turn into our neighborhood. At one point he mumbles "tonight of all nights," but when I steal a glance at him out of the corner of my eye, his jaw is clenched and his lips are firmly shut.

We glide past mega-mansions still tastefully decked out for Halloween—pumpkins, corn stalks, and ridiculous scarecrows in worn flannel shirts—and he pulls through the gate that's always open and up the long drive. Lights blaze from the downstairs windows but our porch is pumpkin-free. Mom hasn't done much in the way of decorating since the flowers last summer, and those lie withered in window boxes and the pots that line the sidewalk.

Dad walks ahead of me, and the car locks as soon as I close the door, telling me he's watching from inside. My feet refuse to move. Dad is the tyrant of the family, but Mom's no pushover and she's going to lose her shit over this. My only chance to get through this in one piece is to hold my head high, like they've taught me. Convince them that this is beneath me and won't happen again.

I step into the foyer, expecting an ambush, but they aren't there. I shut the heavy door and the sound of the metal lock catching throws me back into the jail cell. Panic grips me and my breaths come faster. How could I be so stupid?

My shoes click on the tiled floor, echoing through the oddly silent house. I'm tempted to race up the stairs and hide in my room for the next year, but Mom's voice calls out, stopping me.

"Brianna, come to the den."

Not the living room or family room, the den. Our house is amazing and I brag about it to anyone who will listen, but sometimes it feels like we rotate which room we sit in just to say we use all the rooms. I pause in the open doorway. Bookcases line three walls and overstuffed leather chairs form a seating area in the center of the room. They're sitting across from each other, waiting for me.

Mom smooths a piece of her shoulder-length blond hair and crosses her legs. She's still in a suit, and based on the lack of drink in front of either of them, she hasn't been home long. "What—" her voice is clipped, "—were you thinking?"

I sink into the leather chair facing the door. They're like two well-coordinated hunters circling their prey before the attack. Seeing the exit makes me feel a little less trapped, even though escape is futile. The leather begs me to curl up and let it end quickly, but I sit straight with my hands folded in my lap. "I'm sorry."

"That's not what I asked."

"I don't know."

"That's not an answer."

I take a deep breath. "What do you want me to say?"

She narrows her gaze at me. Between the two of them, it's no wonder I mastered that look by junior high. "I'd like to know why our daughter, who has been provided everything she has ever asked for and more," she points a manicured finger at me, "found it necessary to steal cheap trinkets from a store—"

"Just one," I whisper, and immediately regret it. Arguing semantics never goes well, plus it's not even close to true. One peek in my top drawer and they'll realize the jewelry today is just the tip of the cheap trinket iceberg. I glance at Dad, expecting a lecture on talking back, but I don't think he's breathed since I sat down. I get that he's upset, but he's a businessman to his core and never lets anger control his emotions.

Something more must be going on.

But Mom's not finished. "Tomorrow you will go back to that store and apologize to the owner. Tell her you didn't realize you had the necklace."

I squirm beneath her glare but force my chin up.

"What?" she asks.

"It's just that..." It feels like I'm ten yards down a black diamond when I meant to take the blue square. It's too late to turn around and it's only going to get worse, but I've already committed so I'm going down with my head held high. "I already offered her money to ignore it." And it was a lot more than just a necklace.

"Then offer her more."

I shake my head. "I don't think that'll work with her. She's more of a hard-ass than the others—" The look on her face stops me. Cursing isn't permitted in the Vines household, at least not by me, but that wasn't my biggest mistake.

"What. Others?" Her words are crisp and staccato, like she's giving a lesson in enunciation.

My head drops.

"Brianna, answer your mother."

I can't look up. It's one thing to lie to myself—to insist I can stop whenever I want and that I'm not hurting anyone—but admitting it to my parents is like letting out every awful secret I've buried deep inside.

Mom's voice is almost a whisper, but it drips with venom. She leans toward me and I fight the urge to burrow into the chair. "How many times have you done this?"

Stolen or been caught? Let's go with option two. "Only a couple times."

"Two," Dad says. "So one other time."

"Two other times," I say.

"In addition to the Calliope notebook last spring," he says.

I'd almost forgotten about that.

A red flush creeps up his neck until the tips of his ears burn bright. The same thing happens to me when I'm mad and for the millionth time I curse whoever's in charge of picking which genes children get from their parents. Mom's face only gets red when she's been in the sun too long.

"I can't look at you any longer," he says.

I start to stand, but wait for Mom's nod. Dad may be the tyrant, but walking away from Miranda Vines before she's said her piece can be equally destructive.

"We'll finish this later," she says. "Consider yourself grounded for the foreseeable future."

I hurry away before they change their minds. My social life is already over so the only punishment they have left is taking away my physical things. *Please not my 4Runner. Or my skis.* The season's just starting and I live for skiing, to be outside, gliding over the mountain with the sky stretching overhead.

The only saving grace from this punishment is they don't know that grounding me won't make a difference because I no longer have any friends.

*****

I turn the page of my history book but it may as well be filled with Egyptian hieroglyphics for as much as I'm understanding. There isn't a test tomorrow—thank goodness—but that won't stop Crusty Ray from calling on people to see if they've done the reading. I flip back to the previous page and don't remember any of it. This is pointless. I give it a nudge across the white duvet and it slides over the edge of the bed and lands on the floor with a satisfying thud.

My fingers itch to text someone, but there's no one left. Kenzie made sure of that. Mike might reply, but she's somehow found a backbone lately and I'm not in the mood for attitude. At the beginning of the school year, half the student body would've been thrilled to hear from me, but after losing Homecoming Queen, it's like my world crumbled around me.

I roll onto my back, and my Ethics book stabs my side. It's ironic that I'm doing well in that class. Miss Simpson will have a field day when she finds out what I did.

What I've been doing.

How could I be so stupid? Of all the things I've taken, I'd never be caught dead wearing those gaudy pieces of gold-plated junk. I mean, hearts dangling from a cheap chain? Right. The leather and bronze bracelets from last month are at least trendy. I don't know if I'm more embarrassed at being caught, or that I was caught with that particular necklace.

Necklaces. Plural.

And bracelets.

I yank the book out from beneath me and open it to the assigned chapter, but the words swim.

I was in jail.

Jail.

And I was arrested. Like really arrested. Not some stupid rent-a-cop thing where they put you in an office until your parents come get you. My skin crawls imagining the other people who've been in that cell and a shiver of disgust rushes through me, but as horrific as it was in there, this feeling of self-loathing is new. I changed clothes when I came upstairs, but I still feel dirty all over. And I don't know how to make that go away.

I toss the book on the floor—there's something about that thud that makes me feel a tiny bit better—and pad across the thick carpet to the bathroom that's attached to my room. Once the water's as hot as I can stand it, I step into the shower and wait for the shame to wash away, but it never does.

I'm drying off when shouts carry from downstairs. They've been fighting a lot lately—which I keep telling myself is better than the usual silence because at least they're talking to each other—but this time is different because it's about me. At school I show no fear. If someone even breathes the wrong way in my direction I tear them down with a withering glare, but at home I try my best to keep them from noticing me.

I crack the door to listen while I get dressed, but can only pick out the words like "family" and "bastard." So not much different from any other night.

I've got one leg in my fleece leggings with a bunny on the hip when something shatters downstairs. Everything comes into sharp focus. The books on the floor, the white canopy suspended over my bed, the piles of clothes bursting from my closet. Yanking on my leggings, I stumble to my door.

Mom's crying downstairs.

Dad's voice booms through the house as I reach the hallway. "This is not a negotiation! I've already made up my mind!"

My pulse roars in my head. I knew he was mad, but I didn't know he was this mad. I back into my room and am closing the door when the front door slams. A high-pitched keening sound drifts up the stairs but I can't move.

I can't breathe.

What did he decide?

I take the stairs two at a time but stop short when I reach the bottom. Mom's crumpled in the middle of the floor, her head in her hands. The base of one of those squat glasses Dad drinks Scotch from lies on its side against a wall, the top shattered. Broken glass reflects the light from the chandelier and amber liquid pools against the baseboard. But that's not what stops my heart. In my almost seventeen years, the only time I've seen Mom on the floor was for yoga or a family portrait.

Never like this.

It's like whatever Dad said sucked the life out of her and all that's left is her deflated shell.

"Mom?"

She shifts so she's sitting cross-legged but doesn't respond.

I move closer, unsure what to do. Miranda Vines prides herself on always being in control and projecting an image of superiority, "even when you're not feeling it." Imitating her is how I became the head Snow Bunny and the most popular girl in school.

Correction: formerly most popular.

Whatever happened with Dad has broken her.

"Mom," I say again, a little louder this time.

She takes a shuddering breath, like the effort is too much. "Your father left."

Obviously. But he leaves all the time, especially after they argue—not fight, "argue." Because "civilized people don't fight." Besides, you don't run one of the biggest craft breweries in Boulder without spending a lot of time there, even when it's inconvenient for your family. "Yeah, so?"

She looks up at me and my insides twist. Her normally perfect makeup is smudged beneath her bloodshot eyes and tears stream down her face, dampening her formerly crisp blouse. "No. He left." The energy she puts into the last word makes her sink farther inside herself.

"Left?" Alarm bells clang that *Something is Wrong! Something is Wrong!* but my brain refuses to catch up. "To go to Mischief." It's a statement, not a question. His brewery is open late so he's always there at odd hours. Because if what she's saying is true—

"Brianna, your father has left us."

two

My alarm wakes me from a dream that I was back in that jail cell and every classmate I've ever tormented leered at me through the bars, throwing ugly necklaces at my face and taunting that this is all my fault. Last night, Mom didn't say anything else about Dad, but she did find the strength to tell me I'm grounded for the rest of my life.

There's absolutely no way I can go to school. It was hard enough after I lost Homecoming Queen to that weird girl with purple hair in my Ethics class. I managed to hold my head high after Kenzie usurped me as head Snow Bunny and banished me from the group that had been mine since middle school, but too much has happened in the past twenty-four hours.

My second alarm blares and I turn it off. I have no idea where Mom's head is, but maybe she'll take pity on me. I text her.

Can I please stay home?

Her reply immediate. *Fine.*

That's good enough for me. I drag the covers back over my head and close my eyes, but sleep won't come. I keep replaying the moment when the storeowner, a graying, wrinkled woman with arms like a praying mantis, grabbed my shoulder. My stomach dropped before she said a word.

My phone buzzes next to me. *You'll make yourself useful today. Clear the dead flowers outside and put the empty pots in the garage.*

I type *That's why we have a gardener*, then remember she fired him over the summer. Sure, the dead flowers are embarrassing, but my chores usually involve cleaning up after myself and putting the groceries away. Yard work is hired out.

But I'm in no position to argue. I type *Ok* and climb out of bed. Maybe a latte will help.

*****

Four hours and three lattes later, my back feels like it belongs to an eighty-year old and I can barely grip my phone. Not that anyone has texted to check on me. There was a time when they'd send a search party if I didn't show up to school—which made skipping class a bit more difficult—but now it's like I don't exist.

I shove the final ceramic pot next to the others in the corner of the garage and stretch. I'm no stranger to exercise, but this manual labor crap is degrading. Everything aches, and not in a I-just-had-a-killer-workout way. My neck pops as I tilt it from side to side, and I rub my shoulder before I remember my dirt-stained fingers. "Crap." I brush dirt from my clothes, but it's pointless.

I've still got a couple hours before Mom will be home from her fancy-pants job as a buyer at a big-name tea company, and it feels like my last moments of freedom. They didn't take my car keys or phone, and I'm tempted to hop on the highway and just drive. Maybe hike a nearby trail for a couple hours. Anything's better than being trapped inside the house.

After Mom's declaration that Dad left, I expected there to be a shift in the universe, some seismic schism marking a clear line between the two parts of our lives.

Before and After.

If he really means it—if he's really leaving us—that decision will forever be tangled with my arrest. I'm not stupid enough to think my lapse in judgment made him leave, and it's unlikely to have any real effect on how he remembers last night, but I'm not sure Mom will be able to separate the two. Nothing is ever her fault and it's only a matter of time until she blames me for him leaving.

I skip the road trip and head upstairs to shower, careful not to leave a trail of dirt along the way. Petra, our housekeeper, is technically still employed, though I don't think she's been around in weeks. For a while I thought Mischief wasn't doing well and money had become an issue, but Mom's made a few comments about Petra's attitude so it must be nearly time for a new face. It's like the changing of the guards—Mom slowly builds resentment toward whoever's tasked with keeping our lives running smoothly, then fires them in a burst of anger and complains for the next several weeks until she hires a replacement.

After my shower, I flip through movies on my laptop until I find a mindless rom-com to distract me. I could do homework, but I'm already planning to stay home tomorrow so I'll have all weekend to catch up. My chest tightens at the thought of being alone for three more days, but it's not like anyone talks to me at school. At least this way I can wallow in private.

When the front door opens, I snap my laptop closed and sit up. My arms feel heavy and the lattes churn in my stomach. Mom may have fallen apart last night, but she's had a day to pull herself together, which means whatever was left unsaid after Dad walked out is about to be hurled in my face.

My door's open, and when she appears, we lock eyes.

She crosses her arms and looks down her nose at my messy room. "Is this all you've done today?"

I straighten my back. "Did you not notice the flower boxes?"

She glances at the window as if she can see down to the first floor. Her steely bravado wavers, but her back remains ramrod straight. "No."

I cock my head. Miranda Vines is a stickler for detail. How did she not see the work I did? I hold up my aching hands. "Dead plants are gone. Pots are in the garage." My voice is emotionless, but inside I'm a swirling mess. On the surface she looks like her usual polished self, but it's as if the fire that burns in her eyes has been snuffed out. "Are you okay?" I ask. We don't do emotions here, but maybe enough has happened…

She clenches her jaw. "I'm fine."

I almost say "seems like it" but catch the words before they escape my mouth. My lack of filter is usually a point of pride for me, but not when I'm facing the woman who taught me everything I know. She can rip me to shreds with only a handful of words.

"Can I stay home tomorrow?" I'm careful to sound bored. If she knows how terrified I am to face everyone she'll force me to go to "build character." Never mind that I've got enough character for half the junior class.

She sighs and leans against the doorjamb. The stoic resolve falters, revealing tired eyes and a disappointed frown. That's the closest to a concession as I'm gonna get.

"Thank you."

"But just tomorrow. After this weekend, you go to school." She closes her eyes and I want to know what she's thinking. Is she disgusted with me? Ashamed? Embarrassed? Or am I barely a blip in her thoughts? When she opens them, her mask is back. "Your father will be here for dinner, so please be dressed." Then she turns on her heel and walks down the hall.

The childish part of me that hides in the corner of my mind clings to the hope that last night was a mistake. That he isn't really leaving. They'll scream it out, then make up like they always do.

But the cynical part, the side that dominates my world these days, points out that she didn't say he'd be home, just that he was coming for dinner. As if he's an invited—if not unwelcome—guest.

*****

Dad arrives with take-out from the Mediterranean place down the street from Mischief, and for a moment, everything is normal. Silent and tense, but normal. But halfway through the Kalamata chicken, Dad points his knife at me and I drop my fork.

Here it comes.

"Your hearing is Monday. I called in a few favors and you've got a judge I've been assured is lenient, which should mean community service. But no guarantees on clearing your record." He cuts into his chicken and takes another bite while the room crashes around me.

Blood roars in my ears and my vision blurs. This is real. I was really arrested and put in a police car and locked in jail. His words ping-pong through my head.

Hearing.

Judge.

Record.

As in the permanent record you're warned about as a child, but by the time you reach high school is nothing more than a joke. But this isn't a school record that gets thrown in a closet after you graduate. This could follow me for the rest of my life.

I rest my elbow on the table and drop my face in my hand.

"Elbows off the table," Mom says.

I lower my arm and temper the glare that comes naturally. I'm in no position to argue.

"The hearing's at eleven. Your mother will meet you there."

Mom glances at him, and there's a flash of uncertainty in her eyes.

It's like someone flipped the table and I'm picking apart everything that's been left unsaid. Dad being here now, talking about Monday like he won't be here the rest of the weekend. Him passing the responsibility of their delinquent daughter to his wife, when legal matters and anything resembling a negotiation has always fallen on his shoulders. The subtle tremor that keeps Mom from saying anything more than she has to.

"What else is going on here?" I ask.

Dad closes his eyes and takes a deep breath, like he'd rather be anywhere else.

I know how he feels.

"What's going on here is I'm putting my neck on the line for my daughter who doesn't seem to grasp the severity of this situation. What's going on here," his voice grows louder and I wish I could curl inside myself. "Is I'm being forced to clean up your mess while you hide in your room."

Mom catches my eye but there's no apology in her gaze. Some kids have an alliance with one parent against the other, but my darling mother has always made it clear that she stands by her husband and his decisions. She may be the one who let me stay home from school, but it's him I must answer to.

"Do you understand how it looks to my associates when my daughter is arrested?" Dad shouts. "People will start to question my ability to run a business if I can't keep order at home."

"Is that why you're leaving?" I don't mean to say the words out loud, and based on how quickly his face turns fuchsia, he didn't expect it. "I mean—"

He silences me with a hand in the air. "I wasn't going to do this today, but since you asked." He smiles at me, but it's cruel and calculating and anything but fatherly. Then he looks at Mom. "My apologies for doing this with an audience, but we're a family, right?" He emphasizes "we're a family" like he's repeating her words from an earlier argument. He leans back in his chair and crosses his arms over his chest—his power position. "As I told your mother last night, I'm moving out. My lawyer is finalizing the divorce documents and I expect this to be settled promptly."

He got the divorce papers without warning Mom? I know he's cold-hearted, but that's low even for him. But it also keeps her from striking first.

"The part I didn't share last night is my future plans."

Mom's watching him like a deer in headlights. Clearly she thought the divorce was the worst of it.

"I'll be staying across town in Broomfield."

Her nose crinkles. "Broomfield? But you hate it there. You drive out of your way to avoid it."

Everything moves in slow motion. It's like when you're watching a movie and the bad guy's about to reveal how he pulled off the crime but you figure it out two seconds before everyone else. Except this is my father and the people he's deceived are his family.

I clench my jaw, determined not to give him the satisfaction of a reaction.

Edge Rule #2: Don't let your emotions get the best of you.

"I'll be living with a woman named Susan. She and her daughter have become rather important to me." He drops his gaze for half a second—all the remorse we'll get from him.

"How long have you been seeing her?!" Mom slaps a hand on the polished table, her normally level voice a shriek.

Dad puts on a show of counting in his head. "Piper will be seven next spring," he meets Mom's gaze. "So roughly eight years."

If it's possible to hate someone in an instant, I do.

The color drains from her face and her hands drop beneath the table. She catches my eye and we reach the same conclusion in the same breath.

He has another child.

He pushes away from the table. "I hate to eat and run, but I've got to get home to my family." The slap of his shoes echoes through the foyer, and as the door opens and closes, it feels like he's walking out of our lives forever.

Disbelief and shock suck the air from the room as our food grows cold, the tick-tock of the grandfather clock in the hall counting the interminable seconds. Mom stares at her hands, which grip the edge of the table. I feel like I should say something, but acknowledging this will make it real and as long as we sit in this bubble, the truth will hover over us like a storm cloud waiting to unleash the rain.

The minute we breathe, it'll all come crashing down.

But I can't hold my breath forever.

I push my plate away. Mom looks up at the sound, but it's like she doesn't see me.

The same thought repeats in my head, punctuated with each tick of the clock:

I have a sister.

three

Monday morning, Mom's waiting for me at the bottom of the stairs, and based on the way her eyes narrow, she doesn't approve of my appearance. Skinny jeans, kitten heels, and a high-necked flowy blouse felt appropriate, but her eyebrow is cemented to the middle of her forehead.

"You're not wearing that to see the judge."

My stomach turns. It's not that I forgot that my hearing is today, but every time that worry worked itself to the front of my brain, I swatted it away like an annoying underclassman.

"And your hair needs work."

My hand flutters to my hair, which I painstakingly straightened. Whining won't help me. I need to present a solution, even if it's not what she wants. "What if I bring a jacket to wear to court, and pull my hair back before I get there?" I smooth a hand over the front of my shirt. "If I show up at school dressed for court, people will suspect something."

Her eyebrow lowers. Appearances are everything—that's what she's always taught me—so playing to those sensibilities are my best chance. "Fine. Your black blazer with the ruffled lapel. And be sure you have a hair tie."

My Business Meeting Blazer. The one she makes me wear whenever we join Dad's partners for dinner.

I sprint up the stairs in my heels—a skill I mastered the summer before freshman year—and grab my BMB from the back of my closet. Mom's taste in fashion is more conservative than mine, and the ruffly "bit of flair" is about as risky as she gets.

Her scowl softens when I return. "Leave school at ten. Not a minute later."

We walk side by side through the garage to our cars, back out together, and I'm following her out of the drive when it strikes me that it's just us now. This is my family. Panic grips my chest at all the unknowns, especially this daughter Dad so casually mentioned in the middle of dinner—my sister. How could he drop that on us like he's talking about the weather?

Mom turns the opposite way of my school and beeps her goodbye.

I wave, even though it's still dark out and she can't see me, then shake my head. Dad can't occupy my head-space today. I need to prepare for the kids at school and whatever torment they've prepared for my latest fall from grace. Over the years, I've perfected my queen bitch persona to the point that anyone but my friends are terrified to speak to me, and until a month ago, it's served me well. But since things have started falling apart—with Mom and Dad fighting more often, then the shoplifting and losing Homecoming Queen, something I've dreamed about from the moment I knew it was a thing—even my friends have stopped talking to me. The kids I've treated like maggots will no doubt return the favor when word gets out that I was arrested.

I park in my usual spot and take an extra moment to compose myself. As hard as I try, I can't get Dad's bombshell out of my head. How do you keep a second family secret for seven years? Boulder's not that big. Someone had to know. His betrayal feels like shrapnel coming from every direction, and I fear we'll be nursing our wounds long after this week.

When I was little I wanted a sister more than anything in the world, but Mom always said that destroying her body once was barely worth it, so I stopped hoping. Now, I can't help wondering about this little girl. Is she blond and blue-eyed like me? I get my looks from Mom, so—I can't believe I'm even wondering this—she could look more like Dad.

A gaggle of sophomores pass by, their giggles slowing when they see me. I kill the engine and grab my bag, and they scurry up the sidewalk.

That's more like it.

The hallways greet me like any other Monday. I get a couple looks from randoms, but I'm used to that. It's what I've always wanted—for people to look at me and wonder, but not really know what I'm thinking. The rush I get from the fear in their eyes is usually enough to sustain me, but lately the looks have been more curious, less fearful.

But I can't let that slow me down now.

I'm almost to class when I stop abruptly, and a kid bumps into me from behind. I glare at him, but it doesn't stop the sinking feeling in my gut. My formerly on-again, off-again boyfriend Austin—who's now permanently off—is walking ten feet in front of me with his girlfriend Mia. They're holding hands like they're strolling through a park, not a crowded hall filled with kids rushing to class.

Shame washes over me. When I lost Homecoming, I was furious at the world for what felt like the ultimate injustice. As I stormed out of the gym, I saw Austin and Mia making out in the hall and before I could stop myself, my house key was scraping the length of his truck. He knew it was me, and I realize now how lucky I am he didn't follow through with his threat to press charges.

That would make the shoplifting a second offense.

They turn a corner and I blink as someone brushes my shoulder. "Watch it," I snap, digging deep for the strength to get through this day.

I coast through Homeroom holding my breath, and while History with Crusty Ray sucks, my secret seems to be safe. Kenzie is still ignoring me from her seat next to mine, and my former BFF Mike refuses to look in my direction. In Ethics, Miss Simpson greets me with a smile and says, "I hope you're feeling better."

I just nod and take my seat. Miss Simpson is a saint among teachers. Most everyone likes her, and even though she saw me at my absolute worst last year—when I meant to just shove Cally and ended up drawing blood—she still treats me like a decent human being, which makes me want to do well in her class.

Right now we're studying variations in morals of different societies, and how some things we consider completely atrocious aren't as shocking in other countries. I'm pretty sure stealing is wrong everywhere. A few weeks ago we talked about laws that are sometimes okay to break, and someone mentioned stealing to feed your family, but I have no excuse. I don't even wear the things I've taken—they just sit in a pile gathering dust.

The bell rings and Miss Simpson closes the door. "I assume you all read the chapter last night and are bursting with ideas. So let's hear them." She paces the front of the room, dry erase marker in hand. "What are societal norms that we consider wrong, but other countries may not?"

Several hands shoot up around me, and she points at Jasminda, the alternative freak who won Homecoming Queen. "I've heard they eat dogs in China."

Several girls gasp, and there are a few "awws."

"Unfortunately, yes," Miss Simpson says. Her face pales, and she swallows hard before continuing. "There are animal rights groups actively working to stop it. In particular, to stop an annual Chinese festival called Yulin devoted to the practice." She nods at Jasminda. "You hit one dear to my heart. What else?"

"What about killing your wife?" a boy shouts from the back. "Aren't there religions where that's okay?"

She nods again. "These are commonly known as honor killings."

"Doesn't sound very honorable to me," says Mike. Her eyes stay focused on the front of the class.

"I agree," says Miss Simpson, "and it's a perfect example of how things that feel like common sense to us—don't kill your wife—can be a gray area for other cultures." She continues pacing in front of the room, a stern expression on her face.

"That's not to say they're legal. Honor killings in particular are only performed by a very small portion of society. The majority of people agree that taking a life—any life, and for whatever reason—is wrong."

Kids throw out other examples, but my brain is stuck on Dad. Adultery isn't illegal, but most people agree it's wrong. Taking it to the level that you hide an entire second family from your wife and child is something that most would argue is borderline insane. As someone who takes pride in thinking through every detail, I keep getting tripped up on the logistics. How do you hide a child for seven years?

When the dismissal bell rings, I skip lunch and head for my locker so I can leave by ten and catch Mike and Cally taping balloons to a locker. I noticed Mike excuse herself a few minutes before class and didn't think much of it at the time, but Cally doesn't have our lunch period so I guess this is the only time they could coordinate.

I'm tempted to stop and ask what they're doing when I realize who's locker it is.

Blake.

Cally's boyfriend, my former friend and first kiss, and the boy I've declared my enemy since middle school.

Our birthdays are only a few days apart and of course Cally's decorating his locker. They pause when I stalk by, and no matter how hard I try, I can't help but check out their work. Balloons cover the front of the locker and streamers drift from the bottom. The flimsy paper won't last long once kids traipse through the halls, but for now, it looks festive. I start to smile at Mike, but she turns away.

I don't bother with Cally. She was part of the Snow Bunnies for a hot second when she moved here last winter, but instead of being grateful for being included in the most exclusive group at Monarch High, she decided she was too good for us. I could have overlooked that, but she didn't settle for hanging out with the loser Ski Bums and moving out of my life. No, she took Mike with her.

Now they're best friends and despite a few awkward conversations with Mike that tell me she hasn't completely written me off, they exist in their happy little bubble without a care in the world.

Not that I'm jealous.

I really don't care that much. Mike apparently has some new boyfriend who doesn't even go here, but I'm sure he's a total loser, too.

I take a deep breath, pushing down the familiar twinge of guilt that twists my stomach whenever I see Cally or Blake. At least they seem happy together.

I toss my books in my bag and head outside, pushing Cally and Mike and weird dog-eating cultures out of my head. I've got bigger things to worry about now.

four

The judge slams the gavel. "Next case."

My shoulders slump. It took less than five minutes for him to decide that I'd best learn from my mistakes with fifty hours of community service. If this is leniency, I'd hate to see a mean judge. My lawyer, a man my father's age but with gray hair and a big belly, stands and motions for me to follow him to where Mom's waiting in the front row behind us. While I'm dressed like a normal teenager, she oozes wealth. People glance at me as we walk by, no doubt wondering why someone with money felt the need to steal in the first place.

The first time was an accident. I'd slipped the leather bracelet onto my wrist to see how it felt against my skin, then forgot about it as I browsed the rest of the store. The stupidest part is I bought other things. I didn't realize it was still on my wrist until I got home, but instead of feeling embarrassed or ashamed, I felt a rush not unlike the high I got when I tormented kids at school.

But this rush didn't hurt anyone. At least not directly.

The next time was more of an experiment: different store, similar bracelet. I was more subtle when I tried it on and made sure to buy something so the woman behind the register didn't suspect anything. And why would she? I clearly have money to buy whatever I want, so it wouldn't occur to her to make sure I'd paid for everything I was wearing.

And it snowballed from there.

I always bought something—lingering at the jewelry display then rushing out would surely draw attention—and I made sure to chat with the employees. That added to the rush. Knowing I could manipulate them so easily filled the hole inside me that grew larger and darker each day.

The first time I got caught, my cheeks turned that awful red before I could sputter an excuse, so I played it off like I was the biggest idiot known to man and didn't realize I was still wearing it. I bought the item in question, plus a few other things, and backed out of the store dripping my deepest apologies.

The next time, excuses sprang to my lips, but I played the bumbling idiot, even forcing out a few tears when the man didn't seem to believe me. After I bought two hundred dollars' worth of jewelry I'd never wear, he quietly asked me to never return to his store.

So last week when the storeowner grabbed my wrist, I pulled out all the stops. I acted confused, let my cheeks turn pink, and was careful to keep my irritation in check. But she wasn't having it. She called the police while still gripping my arm and insisted they arrest me.

Panic nearly froze me.

When she hung up the phone, I offered to buy the necklace and a number of its friends, but she refused to change her mind. When the cops arrived, they asked the question I'd been dreading.

"Did you take anything else?"

I've never been above a good lie, especially when it's to save my own ass, but I must have hesitated a moment too long because the cop spun me around.

"Place your hands on the counter." I did, and he patted my sides, stopping at my jacket pockets. "Empty your pockets and place the contents on the counter."

And that's when I knew I was screwed. Because today one necklace hadn't seemed like enough. Kind of like drug addicts who need more and more to feel the same high. When I set five necklaces and half a dozen rings on the counter, the cop grabbed my purse and rifled through it. He pulled out two pairs of sunglasses, a handful of earrings, and the only thing I actually planned to use: a striped cloth headband.

They asked more questions, but I didn't hear them. All I kept thinking was that my parents were going to kill me. And not because I stole a bunch of cheap crap. No, they would kill me because this will embarrass them. The cop tugged my arms behind my back and the feel of cold metal on my wrists snapped me to attention.

"You're arresting me?" My tone was shrill and nasty and I couldn't stop the look of disgust that rolled over my face. "For a couple necklaces?"

The storeowner locked eyes with me and nodded once. "If it was just necklaces, I probably wouldn't press charges. But your obvious lack of remorse pisses me off."

They led me outside, where I shook my hair in front of my face to avoid the curious stares of the people on the sidewalk. Once I was in the backseat, I ducked below the window, my life officially over.

But now, standing in the hallway outside the courtroom, I know it's only going to get worse. My lawyer is talking to Mom, and something he says jumps out at me. "Wait, what did you say?"

Mom scowls. "I'm so glad you can be bothered to pay attention. This is your future we're talking about."

"Sorry, I have a lot on my mind."

"You and me both."

Mr. Lawyer clears his throat, and we both look at him. "I was explaining to your mother that if you finish your community service within the prescribed time frame and without further incidents—"

Mom rolls her eyes and I bite back a snotty comment.

"—then you'll have six months probation, after which your record will be cleared." He levels his gaze at me and my breathing stills. "You're fortunate Colorado considers under eighteen a minor."

"I'm not even seventeen yet."

"You will be in a week," Mom says.

As if I'm not aware.

"I don't think you're grasping the severity of your situation," Mr. Lawyer says. "Fifty-three weeks later and we could be looking at an entirely different outcome."

Heat floods through me at the realization of how bad this could have gone.

He hands Mom a brochure. "This has the community service options. Some are... ahh... better than others, but those tend to fill up first."

"What are you saying?" I ask.

"This isn't going to be like volunteering after school. Most of these projects are menial labor. Gross, dirty work."

Mom takes the brochure and flips through it. "Surely you can pull a few strings. Frank Vines' daughter cannot be seen—" she pauses with her finger on a picture— "debasing herself in this way."

"Well, ma'am," he says, looking at me. "She should have thought of that before she broke the law." He straightens his suit jacket and holds his hand out to me. "Good luck, Brianna. I hope we don't see each other again for a long time."

He leaves us standing in the hallway, Mom clutching the brochure and me gaping after him like he's my final lifeline and he's slowly drifting away.

*****

"I have to pick up trash?! On the side of the road?! Like one of those chain-gangs or something?!"

Mom did her best, but I want to get this over with as soon as possible and the only community service option accepting people immediately was trash duty. As in neon-jacket, long poky stick, and a bunch of delinquents meandering along the side of the highway while people who manage to get through the day without breaking the law drive by on their way to their non-criminal activities.

Activities that do not involve picking up trash every Tuesday and Thursday for the next couple months.

"Can't you arrange for me to work at your office or something?" I'm not one-hundred percent certain what she does as a buyer, but I guarantee anything in her building is vastly superior to roadside humiliation. "Stocking the warehouse would be better than this."

Mom shakes her head. "I'm sorry, but the judge was very clear. You have to complete your hours with the services listed in the brochure."

"I'd like to burn that brochure."

"Brianna."

"I'm sorry, but this is stupid. How is this even a suitable punishment?"

She narrows her eyes. "Would you rather spend fifty hours in jail?"

I clench my jaw.

"You broke the law. Now you have to live with the consequences. Your father and I—" her voice catches. "We can't always be there to bail you out. And it's time you learned that."

I want to argue. To scream and throw things and make her understand how absolutely unfair this is, but a tiny part of me knows she's right. When I got suspended last spring for hurting Cally, my parents were pissed but didn't ground or punish me in any way. Dad simply told me to make better decisions and that was the last we talked of it. Now, knowing all the lies he's kept from us, I realize he probably just didn't care. As long as my drama didn't affect him or the business, I could go about my life however I pleased.

And Mom's just as bad. She may still be here, but she's always made it clear that her number one priority is herself. If they think I expect too much, it's because that's what they taught me. To go after what I want, damn the consequences.

five

My secret is out.

From the minute I walk through the front doors of school, it's obvious people know. And with the way rumors spread here, by first period my crime will have morphed from shoplifting to murdering a family of cats. So I do what I do best—I hold my head high, glare at anyone who dares laugh in my face, and refuse to speak.

That gets me through Homeroom. When Kenzie stalks into History, my stomach plummets. She lifts her chin so she can look down her nose at me, and when she reaches her desk next to mine, she laughs. I've never seen her talk to the guy on her other side, but she leans toward him like they're best friends and whispers loud enough for the entire class to hear.

"Can you *believe* Brianna was arrested? I mean, I know everyone's ignored her since she lost Homecoming Queen, but this is *such* a pathetic cry for attention."

The guy fidgets in his seat like he's puzzled by her talking to him and terrified of saying the wrong thing. "Um, sure?"

She straightens, working for her audience. "At least I assume it's for attention." She faces me, her head cocked in curiosity. "Or are you so poor now that you have to steal?"

She reaches to touch the sleeve of my sweater and I yank my arm away.

"Did you steal this, too?"

Fury bubbles through me, but I will not let her bait me. I stare straight ahead and bite the inside of my cheek. I'm sure my face is horribly red, but I can't risk speaking and having my voice crack. Any sign of weakness will only make this worse.

I should know. I taught Kenzie everything she knows about humiliating people.

Mike twists in her seat and catches my eye, but I look away.

"So pathetic," Kenzie says, abandoning the whisper.

"Ladies, enough," Crusty Ray says. "Open your books to page..." He continues his lecture, but all I hear are the whispers around me.

Those whispers follow me through the hall to Ethics, where Mike tries to talk to me but I shut her down. At lunch I skip the cafeteria, opting instead to hide in the library, but I encounter pockets of students who seem horrified to see me. They aren't celebrating my fall from grace—they're still afraid of me. These are kids I've treated horribly, and now I'm trying to hide among them.

I mumble a "sorry" and wander the halls until my next class.

*****

Nothing I own is appropriate for picking up trash on the side of a highway. After tossing aside countless jeans and sweatshirts, I settle on the one pair of grungy jeans Mom's allowed me to keep "because you never know when you'll need them," and an old sweatshirt with the Snow Bunnies emblem over my favorite pink fitted T-shirt. No one else can see the T-shirt, but it feels like a shield as I head into the unknown.

A shudder passes through me when I park in the half-empty lot next to the non-descript brick building that matches the address in my GPS. It's like they purposely make government buildings as unwelcoming as possible. My eyes close as I take a deep breath.

You got yourself into this mess.

After another cleansing breath that does nothing for the knot in my belly, I face my fate. One of those short buses you rent for parties idles near the building, and a few kids my age wait near the entrance. A pixie-ish girl with brown skin and long dark curls that overwhelm her small frame is smoking a cigarette and laughing at whatever the blond Amazon next to her is saying. They glance my way, but go back to their conversation when I don't get out of the car.

My hands tighten around the steering wheel.

I can't do this.

More cars park around me, depositing the strangest mix of kids I've ever seen. An Asian girl with perfect skin, half her head shaved, and a tiny stud in her nose heads straight for Pixie and Amazon, but walks away after bumming a cigarette. A boy and girl who look like they could be siblings park next to each other and start talking the second they get out of their cars. They both have mousy brown hair and wear Army-green jackets over ripped jeans. The girl talks with her hands and he doesn't take his eyes off her, even when Shaved Head Girl joins them. Two jocks who look like they play football get out of a souped-up pick-up truck. They seem the most like me, but they keep to themselves and don't acknowledge the others.

What universe have I stumbled into where I am in the same group with these... these... losers isn't the right word, but it's close. They may look like kids from my school, but that doesn't mean I want to be friends with them. We have nothing in common—and yes, I realize I'm judging them entirely on their appearances, but so far it's proven to be a fairly reliable system. Besides, people project the image they want others to perceive, so I'm just following the rules of the game.

Then the biggest black man I've ever seen strides out of the building, the clipboard he's holding dwarfed in his hand. He scans the group like he's taking attendance, then glances around the parking lot like he's looking for someone else.

Me.

Our eyes lock through the windshield but he doesn't smile. He just stares at me until I feel like I'm going to vomit all over the dashboard.

Pixie stomps out her cigarette with a purple Chuck as the others file into the bus. *It's now or never.* I climb out, the crisp air cooling my face, and Clipboard Man watches me.

Edge Rule #3: Face your challenges head-on.

"You must be Brianna Vines." His deep voice booms over the parking lot and I instinctively look around to make sure no one heard him. He must see the embarrassment on my face because he cracks a smile, revealing a dimple that makes him almost pleasant. "You best get over that now. Everyone's equal here."

"Except me, right Bruno?" Pixie smiles up at him as she passes. She barely comes up to his chest but doesn't seem intimidated by him. She gives me a quick once-over and smiles before boarding the bus.

"You're always the exception, Drea." He returns his attention to me. "So, Miss Vines?"

I nod. "Yes."

He pulls a folded paper from his back pocket and hands me the clipboard. "I'm Mr. Shapiro, but call me Bruno. I take care of you kids while we're out." He crosses his arms and his neck disappears into his head. "I need you to fill this out before we go. We're only waiting on one more, so make it quick."

I take the paper and pen and prop the clipboard against my stomach to write. It's all generic information until the line above my signature that asks why I was arrested. The pen hovers over the page, and I imagine having to fill out job applications and confessing that I was arrested for stealing. How could I be so stupid? Tears burn my eyes as the future I'd always envisioned evaporates like the smoke from Pixie's—Drea's—cigarette.

A car rumbles into the lot and parks next to my 4Runner. Bruno smiles. "'Bout time. You done Miss Vines?"

My hand shakes as I scribble the word shoplifting, sign my name, and give it back to him. "All set."

"Good. Climb aboard. The Good Ship Lollipop leaves in two minutes."

I take a deep breath. Each step onto the bus feels like I'm moving farther away from the person I thought I was, like I'm losing a grip on myself.

A flutter of panic makes me pause at the top and I fight the urge to jump off the bus and never look back.

There are six rows of seats on each side with room for two in each, but several kids are sitting together. Drea and Amazon are in the back, the Army-jacket duo are across from them, then the others are spread out toward the front. Their eyes flick to me in unison, but only the Jocks' stares last more than a second. For once I'm grateful to not be the center of attention.

I take a seat across from one of the Jocks and stare out the window to deter any attempt at conversation.

"Hey, guys," a male voice says at the front of the bus. This must be the last person. I look up and my adrenaline jumps another level. His jet black hair's a little shaggy, there's a tiny silver hoop in each ear, and when his gaze lands on mine I feel like he looks right through me. His white waffle shirt is pushed up to his elbows, revealing a black tattoo that snakes down his arm. He smiles at the other kids, nods at the Jocks, then rests his hand on the back of my seat as he slides in behind me.

My senses hum. I can't remember the last time I was this aware of a boy—especially one I've never spoken to and who couldn't have seemed less interested in me.

The bus rocks as Bruno steps on. "Happy Tuesday." His voice fills the bus, commanding everyone's attention. "We're hitting Route 36 today. As always, you must buddy up. We've got a new addition today—Brianna," he nods in my direction, "which means one group will have three."

"Threesome," the Jock next to me whispers. His friend high-fives him and I make a note to avoid them at all costs.

"You know the drill. Remain seated until we stop. No smoking on the bus. And no funny business." His gaze lands on the couple in the back and I wonder what they've been busted doing. Bruno buckles himself into the driver's seat and we pull away from the building.

The group chats like they've been together for a long time, and I sink lower in my seat. Making new friends isn't my strength—alienating them is. Need to instill fear in someone, I'm your girl, but throw me in with people I have absolutely nothing in common with and I'm at a loss where to begin. From what Bruno said, I'll be paired up with at least one person, possibly two, so at least I won't be stuck wandering the highway alone.

Drea's laughter carries to me and I hate the part of me that wants to know what they're talking about. These aren't people I'll ever be friends with. I strain to hear the boy behind me but he isn't talking. I turn away from the window in the hopes that I'll catch a glimpse of him, but all I catch is Jock #1 staring at me like he's been waiting for me to look up.

A smile lights up his reasonably attractive face and he leans over the aisle. "Whaddaya say you, me, and Tommy partner up? There's slim pickings in this crowd." He throws a look at the back of the bus, clearing differentiating himself from the others—and including me with him.

I bristle, even though I'd classified them as the closest to my equal. I may be the queen of assumptions but I don't like it when others do the same to me.

Yes, I'm a hypocrite.

He's still watching me, waiting for a reply, so I shrug. "I hadn't thought about it."

He lowers his lids in what I guess he thinks is a sexy, bedroom-eyes look. "Well, start thinking."

Does this boy think I'm going to screw him on the side of the highway?

"Leave her alone, Toby." A low voice from behind me wipes the creepily seductive look off Toby's face and he leans back in his seat.

My pulse quickens. Was it Mystery Boy? I twist around to catch his eye but he's staring at his phone, so I turn my back to Toby and stare out the window for the rest of the ride.

A few minutes later, the bus slows and Bruno parks on the shoulder of the road. I'm not sure what I was expecting, but we're literally on the side of the highway. What if we have to pee?

Bruno stands and faces us, hands on hips. "Pinnies are in the box on the front seat. This is your only reminder that you may not remove it until you're back on the bus. No exceptions."

I follow the Jocks and grab a neon green mesh thing from the box on the front seat before stepping outside. The others join us on the grass that stretches twenty feet wide and as far along the highway as I can see and pull the green things on over their jackets. As I slip it over my head, trying not to breathe in, I can't help but wonder how on earth I ended up here.

six

It's like being the new kid on the first day of school—anxious and awkward—and I don't like it. The others pair off the way they were when we were waiting for the bus. Mystery Boy and Shaved Head stand together but are both on their phones—not that I care if they talk to each other—and I'm stuck next to the bus in a horrid green shirt that smells like smoke and sweat and old food. There's a reason I never permitted neon green as a Snow Bunny color. The only saving grace is we're miles from town and cars are going so fast no one should recognize me.

Bruno steps off the bus carrying long wooden sticks with a metal spike on the end and two small boxes tucked under his arm.

The Amazon and Drea each grab a stick, a trash bag, and what turns out to be those thin rubber gloves people wear at fast food restaurants. Thank god.

Drea smiles at me. "The first day is the worst," she says. She points at the blond girl. "I'm Drea. This is Heidi."

Instead of the carefully calculated response I normally give—a cool smile with a raised eyebrow—I smile at them.

And the world doesn't explode.

"I'm Brianna."

"Welcome to the Chain Gang." Drea laughs, and she and Heidi walk away.

"Take one of each," Bruno says from behind me. "Then pair up with someone."

Part of me hoped he would tell me where to go. Getting rejected from this crowd would be a new low. There's always the Jocks, but the way they keep watching me, I get the feeling I might need my stick for more than just picking up trash.

The only people who haven't wandered away are the army-green couple. I take a deep breath, then move closer and give them my most charming smile. "Can I join you?"

Up close they're even more similar. Same brown eyes. Wavy hair tucked behind their ears. They seem to weigh their options with an exchanged look, and the girl nods. "Sure, whatever."

I fall in step behind them, letting them choose where to go. "I-I'm Brianna."

"You don't want to hang with Toby and Tommy?" the boy asks.

A laugh escapes me. "I'm not really in the mood to fend off creepers."

The girl snorts, but neither of them tell me their names.

They lead me in the opposite direction of the Jocks, not far from Mystery Boy. I follow their example, stabbing wrappers and cigarette butts, then using the edge of the trash bag to slide them off. Bottles and cans have to be picked up by hand, and they seem to have an agreement that he does all the bending.

"I can't believe people just throw all this out here."

"People are assholes," she says.

Is that what they think of me? Usually I wouldn't care, but I'm forced to interact with them. It's not like I'm trying to be friends. My frustration grows the longer they ignore me, and after half an hour I'm biting my tongue to keep from unleashing a torrent of insults. Who do these two think they are, anyway? I was polite—I even tried to be nice—so why do they refuse to acknowledge me?

Doesn't feel good, does it? the little voice inside my head asks. She doesn't show up often, but when she does, she always calls me out for being a jerk.

"What's with the bunny?" the boy asks.

At first I think he's asking his girlfriend, but he's looking at me. I look around, expecting to see a small woodland creature at the edge of the trees, but his eyes are focused on my shirt. "Oh." I touch the emblem, and for the first time I feel a pinprick of embarrassment over the logo I helped design. I shrug. "It's just a thing my friends and I made."

Former friends.

He smiles, but it's not particularly friendly. "Life goals, huh?"

It's not the first time someone has compared the Snow Bunnies logo to the Playboy Bunnies—I'm not a complete idiot and know they look similar—but hearing it from this... this... nobody in a neon-green pinnie on the side of the fricking highway after everything else that's happened in the past week is about all I can take. My face warms and I'm sure I look like a whacked out Christmas display.

"I think you pushed a button," the girl says, leaning closer to him.

I shake my head to clear it. As much as I want to rip this guy a new one, I cannot cause a scene on my first day of community service. "Why don't you worry about yourself?" I turn away as they giggle, rage coursing through me. I lift my stick over my head and stab it into the ground as hard as I can. The metal spike sinks into the hard earth.

And stays there.

"Are you kidding me?" I mumble.

"Hit it sideways," the girl says.

I scowl at her over my shoulder, but do as she says. It slowly loosens, and I pick it up with one hand.

"I didn't mean to piss you off," she says, and I turn around.

"You didn't. He did."

He shrugs. "You think any of us want to be here?"

My mouth drops. How stupid of me. I've been so worried about poor me and how I don't belong here that it never crossed my mind that no one else wants this either. "I guess—it seems like you two don't mind."

She smiles. "We're a unique story. We'll be able to tell our grandkids we met picking trash."

He rolls his eyes but runs his hand over her back and for the first time since we got off the bus I feel something other than anger and humiliation.

"I'm happy for you?" I smile, and for once it's not forced.

She beams. "Thanks. I am too." Then she holds out her hand to me. "I'm Laina, and this is Crue."

I shake her hand. He gives me a small nod, but this small victory feels better than anything has in a long time. Of course, we still have another hour to go, but I feel like I got my foot in the door with this group. They may not be who I'd choose to hang out with—or even associate with—but like Crue said, none of us want to be here. We may as well make the most of it.

At the end of the shift, Bruno lets loose an ear-piercing whistle and we converge on the bus with half-filled bags. Drea's already removed her pinnie and is holding it and her trash bag with equal disgust. Mystery Boy collects the sticks while Bruno puts our bags inside each other, and Shaved Head grabs a bottle of hand sanitizer from next to the driver's seat and holds it out for the others. She pumps a generous dollop into their hands as they board the bus, and I give her a smile when it's my turn.

"Thanks."

"No one wants that nastiness on themselves any longer than necessary." Her voice is smooth and low and I can imagine her singing jazz in a club. Despite the weird hair, her skin is smooth and her brown eyes sparkle in the late afternoon sun. No wonder Mystery Boy paired up with her.

Inside, everyone takes the same seats as on the way here. While this wasn't as bad as I expected, I don't know if I can do this for forty-eight more hours.

Bruno gets in and starts the bus, but doesn't put it into drive. "Okay, whatcha got?" he asks.

I twist in my seat so I can see the others.

"Stuffed animal!" says Drea.

"Unopened can of beer," says Mystery Boy.

Bruno's eyes go wide. "I'll take that, X-Man."

X-Man?

"Already in the bag, sir."

"Condom!" Toby shouts.

"Dude, you always find a condom," Heidi says.

"I think he brings them himself," says Shaved Head.

"Brianna, what about you?" Bruno asks. "What's the most interesting thing you picked up?"

I try to think back, but I didn't pay much attention to what I put in the bag. "It was just trash."

"Just trash?" He places a meaty hand to his chest. "You're breaking my heart. You've got to look past the fact that it's garbage and find the story there."

I literally cannot think of anything I found that's worth sharing. "Sorry, it was mostly fast food cups and wrappers."

Bruno sighs like I'm killing him, then lets me off the hook. "Laina? Crue?"

I expect Laina to speak since she was the chattier of the two—if you can call her brand of non-conversation chatty—but Crue is the one who answers.

"A doctoral thesis on the life cycle of the pigmy goat."

Bruno's jaw drops. "I don't know what to say to that."

"Did you read it?" Heidi asks.

Toby snorts. "Like he can read."

I roll my eyes at him. On the ride here I probably would have laughed, but now that I've spent a couple hours with Crue, I realize he's not that different from anyone else here, he just likes to keep to himself.

Crue pats the front of his jacket and pulls out a CD with handwriting on the front. "Nah, left my laptop at home."

A low rumble shakes from Bruno and a wide grin splits his face in two. "You win." He tosses him something but it moves too fast to see anything but a flash of hot pink.

"What is that?" I ask Mystery Boy—X-Man?—but he's already looking at his phone.

"It's one of those little Troll dolls on a keychain," says Shaved Head. "Most creative discovery gets it until the next time."

"Do you have to hang onto the thing to win?" I ask. Keeping trash anywhere but at the end of my pokey stick does not sound like something I'd like to be a part of.

Mystery Boy looks up and meets my eyes. His are so dark they're almost black and for a second I forget where we are. "It's an honor system."

My pulse speeds up. "Honor among thieves?" I say the words without thinking, and I immediately wish I could take them back. For all I know I'm the only thief here.

But he smiles, a tiny curl of the side of his mouth. "Something like that."

"Put your seats in the upright position," Bruno shouts. "The Goodship Lollipop is taking off."

I don't know if it's the soft chatter around me, the two hours of fresh air, or the sense of relief I feel for making it through my first shift, but I can't keep my eyes open. My head rests against the window and the next thing I know we're back at the center. Everyone says good night to Bruno as they exit the bus and I head straight for my car.

Should I say goodbye to anyone? This isn't a party—this is court-mandated community service—but for the first time in my life I care what a group of strangers thinks about me. It's not that I'm intimidated by any of them—well, maybe Shaved Head a little, but I get the sense that she uses her appearance as a defense mechanism. Kind of like I do, just differently. While I try to appeal to the general population by looking as desirable as possible, she's taken the stay-the-hell-away approach. But she seemed nice enough on the bus.

As I open my door, a grinding squeal like fingernails on a chalkboard assaults my ears. I turn to see what the hell made the noise and freeze.

Mystery Boy's standing next to his car, the driver's door open, and our eyes lock. He rests his arm on the roof and his tattoo winks at me, and I catch myself wishing he'd push up his sleeves so I can see more. He nods his head, then unleashes a smile that really shouldn't be allowed in public. My insides warm and a thousand butterflies batter about in my stomach, but I have enough sense to smile back. And not my practiced come-hither smile. Just a regular, holy-crap-do-you-know-how-hot-you-are smile.

Then he gets in his car and starts the engine, and for the first time I really notice his car. The body says Subaru, but it's the junkiest one I've ever seen. Duct tape runs along the edge of the wheel wells, secures the bumper to the car, and covers the entire panel of the passenger door. Like there isn't a side to the door—it's made entirely of tape. And not the plain silver stuff. This has a dark green background with a smiling fox next to a tree. Over and over again. He pulls away and I'm left standing there with my hand on the open door, my heart racing.

But it doesn't take long for reality to come screaming back. While I've never have this kind of physical reaction from a boy, nothing can ever happen with him. He may be hot and make my insides tremble, but he'd never be allowed to set foot in the driveway.

To my parents, appearances are everything.

seven

This was supposed to be the best day of the year. I'd wake up to the scent of freshly baked pastries and French-roasted coffee and Mom and Dad would be waiting in the kitchen with the first of many birthday presents, then I'd float through the day as my adoring fans showered me with praise.

But the only scent coming from downstairs is the same coffee as always, and I doubt anyone's throwing me a parade at school. Nonetheless, I take extra time getting ready and based on Mom's smile when I join her in the kitchen, she approves.

"Happy birthday," she says, pointing at a mug of coffee next to a store-bought box of Danishes. "I know it's not what you were expecting, but there's a lot of that going around these days."

She already creamed and sugared my coffee, so I take a sip, hoping the artificial sweetness will rub off on my mood. Being disappointed that there aren't any presents for me makes me a spoiled brat, but it doesn't change how I feel. If they didn't want to keep up the tradition, they shouldn't have started it in the first place.

"Your father promised to stop by this evening."

Her emphasis on the word promised makes me wonder if he'll show. He may be a tyrant, but he comes through on his promises and if he says he'll be here, I have to believe he will.

"Don't be late."

"I don't have any plans."

She raises an eyebrow.

While she knows Austin and I broke up at the end of the summer, she certainly doesn't know that I keyed his car in a rage, or that he's already moved on with Mia. And while she's aware that Kenzie and I don't hang out as much—meaning never—I've managed to keep her in the dark about my shift in the social hierarchy. As in my plummet to the bottom. Even Mike, who was once my closest friend, barely looks at me.

"You said I'm grounded, right? I assumed there wasn't a furlough for special occasions."

Her eyebrow relaxes, and I breathe a sigh of relief.

"I've gotta run. Took too long getting ready this morning."

She smiles. "It shows." She means it as a compliment, but what I hear is that I haven't been putting in enough effort lately.

Edge Rule #4: Some days you have to work a bit harder to hold your edge.

When I get to my locker, I blink away tears and plaster on my nastiest expression. Since my eleventh birthday—the first year we had lockers—my friends have always covered mine with streamers and balloons and silly notes that told everyone how much they loved me. Sometimes it was a bit over the top, but I milked it for days. Seeing the bare yellow paint, just like all the other lockers, hits me in the gut.

As I grab my books, Austin walks by—without Mia for once— and pauses a few feet away. Our eyes meet for a beat longer than necessary, long enough for me to know he remembers it's my birthday, but before he can say anything, I turn away.

In History, I refuse to acknowledge Kenzie. She either takes pity on me or forgot it's my birthday, because she ignores me throughout class. I'm not so lucky in Ethics. Mike's already in her seat when I arrive, and based on the way she tracks me from the moment I enter the room, she hasn't forgotten.

I take my seat, determined to stare straight ahead, when something pokes my arm. Mike's holding out a small cardboard box with a hot pink tulle ribbon and the logo from my favorite chocolatier.

"I had a date there the other day and remembered how much you like their truffles so..." She sets the box on my desk. "Happy birthday."

Talk about getting hit with a feels-bomb. I finger the scratchy smooth fabric, unable to hide my surprise. This is the nicest anyone's been to me all week. But I shouldn't be surprised. Mike's never been super outgoing, but she has a good heart. It used to piss me off because she always put up a fight when I asked her to be mean to other kids for me, but I guess there's something to be said for standing up for yourself. "Thank you."

"I figured you could use something sweet."

If she's heard about the arrest, she's not letting on.

She smiles. "Do you have big plans later?"

My reflex is to lie, to tell her I'm having a party to end all parties, but I don't have the energy. Instead I find myself wanting to tell her everything that's happened. "No. My mom and dad split up and with everything else, I'm not in a very birthday-party-celebration mood."

Her jaw drops and I immediately regret saying anything.

"It's not a big deal. My dad's coming over later and—"

She silences me with a hand on my arm. "Bri, I'm so sorry. I had no idea."

I try to shrug it off but it's like I opened a portal to the tiny piece inside me with feelings. I force a smile. "I figured it's time I became a statistic, you know?"

She lowers her voice. "And with everything else..."

So she has heard. "I figured I'd start my seventeenth year with a bang."

Miss Simpson stands at the front of the room, our cue to stop talking. Halfway through the lecture, something Mike said jumps out at me. She had a date. I knew she'd broken up with Evan, one of the hottest, most popular boys in school, and has a new boyfriend, but this is the first time she's mentioned him to me. I hadn't put much thought into who he is, but now I sit up straighter, my senses humming, the potential for juicy gossip giving me a boost better than any cup of French-roast coffee.

*****

I refuse to become the kid who waits for her dad with her nose pressed against the front window. He's always worked a lot and kept weird hours with the brewery—although I'm now realizing a lot of that must have been with The Seconds, his other family. It's not like I miss him, or that I'm even looking forward to seeing him. Odds are he'll use this visit as an excuse to ride me about the arrest, but odds are also good he'll come bearing gifts.

It's dark by the time he arrives. His headlights cut across the front window and I fight the urge to run to the front door. Instead I sit at the dining room table, one leg crossed over the other, a bored expression on my face.

He enters the house in a rush, bringing the cold air inside with him. "Happy birthday, sweetheart." He brushes a kiss on my cheek and sits in the chair next to me. "Is your mother here?"

"She's in her office." She locked herself in there as soon as she got home, promising we'd celebrate once he leaves.

"I need to speak with her when we're done."

When we're done? Like I'm a checkbox on his list, not his only daughter—scratch that. Oldest daughter. I prop my elbow on the table and rest my cheek in my hand. Why did I think this would be different?

"Let's go in the study."

I follow him across the foyer to the bookcase-lined room that overlooks the front yard. When I was little and still enamored with my father, I'd play in here as a way to be close to him, imagining I was the CEO of a fashion empire and his business magazines were fashion magazines featuring my designs. But I stopped coming in here when he grew more distant. Now it feels cold and uninviting, like the man he's become.

Sitting behind his massive oak desk, you wouldn't know he's just left his family. He looks as calm and collected as always. Then again, Frank Vines is a master at keeping up appearances.

I take the seat facing him and wait. He wouldn't bring me in here without something important to say, but pestering him before he's ready to share will get me nowhere. I cross and uncross my legs and stare at the row of unread first editions on the shelf behind him.

"You're as bad as your mother with the fidgeting."

Okay then. I place both feet on the floor and concentrate on not moving.

"How was your day? Did you do anything fun?"

"Considering I'm grounded and don't have any friends, no." His eyes narrow and I press my lips together. I didn't mean to tell him that. I'm wound so tight trying to balance that line between being in control and exploding like a nuclear bomb that I can't help but snap at him. "Mom said we'd celebrate tonight."

He tilts his head, a slight waver in his stoic expression. "I'm not staying."

I lean forward, ready to pounce on his moment of weakness. "Mom and me, we. Not you. Or did you forget you walked out on this family?"

He leans back in his chair and rubs a hand over the back of his neck. "I know you're upset but—"

I roll my eyes.

"There's a lot you don't understand. When you're older—"

"Save it." I cross my arms. "This isn't why you brought me in here."

He rests his forearms on the desk, reclaiming control of the conversation. "Did you start community service this week?"

I nod.

"And when do you expect to finish?"

Fifty hours at four hours per week is, "almost thirteen weeks?"

He sets his phone between us and opens the calendar app. "It's the second week of November, so that has you finishing just before Valentine's Day."

"Of course it does." I started the week of my birthday, so why wouldn't I end on the most romantic holiday of the year?

Dad closes his screen and levels his gaze on me. "I'll make a deal with you."

Can he get me out of this? I sit up straighter.

"I'm planning a trip to Switzerland over spring break. If you finish your hours by Christmas—"

"Done. Not a problem." Switzerland is my absolute favorite place on earth. The skiing is like floating on a cloud, the boys are delicious, and best of all, I can be whoever I want to be.

"Let me finish. There's another caveat." He laces his fingers together, a move he makes when he's closing a deal, and his face twists into a frown. "It can't get out that you're picking up trash."

Dread fills my gut and I break into a sweat. "I don't plan on telling anyone, but I can't stop who might see me."

"If anyone bothered to look at those people, no one would believe it's you."

The knot in my stomach hardens. "I won't say anything."

"It's more than that. How do you think it makes me look that my daughter was, A)," he ticks off his fingers, "arrested for shoplifting, and B), is now wandering the highway with a bunch of criminals?"

Because this is all about him. Forget asking why I did it or wondering how I'm doing now that he's abandoned us, he's only worried about how this reflects on him. Never mind that he has two fricking families. I want to scream and ask if I'm allowed to tell people about *that*.

At least he didn't call me a criminal.

"So it's a deal?"

"This is my birthday present?" I suck in a breath. Frank Vines doesn't do talking back, and that came out bitchier than I intended.

He reaches into his suitcoat pocket and pulls out a small velvet box. "I'm not sure you deserve this, but I'd already bought it so..." He sets the box on the table between us.

I count to three before picking it up. Greedy hands are not tolerated. Inside, a diamond-crusted circle sits on a silk cushion, a silver chain tucked behind it. This hasn't been in style for at least a decade, but it looks expensive and based on the pleased expression on his face, he picked it out himself. "Thanks, Dad. I love it."

"Now you have no excuse for stealing cheap crap."

The tiny burst of happiness pops. He can't let me have one moment. I close the box and clutch it in my lap.

"There's one other thing."

I look up. How can there possibly be more?

"About the trip. This will be Piper's first time traveling abroad, so I expect you to show her the ropes."

Too many things crash through my mind. He's bringing *them*? I'm supposed to go on a trip with his new family like it's no big deal? What will Mom think? How can I do that to her? And finally, "Wait, you mean like a babysitter?"

"We'll worry about the details later."

So a babysitter. But still, it's Switzerland. I'll worry about how I'm going to complete fifty hours of community service by Christmas later.

"I expect you to keep me posted on your hours."

"What, like a spreadsheet or something?"

His eyes narrow at my tone. "A text is fine."

I fight the urge to salute him.

He stands and extends his hand toward me. I brush off the alarm bells clanging in my head and shake his hand—firmly, but not too firmly—and he leads me into the foyer.

"Could you please get your mother?"

I trot away like an obedient daughter and knock on her door. "Dad wants to talk to you," I say to the closed door.

When she steps into the hallway, she looks composed—hair styled like it's not the end of the day, clothes unwrinkled and flattering as always—but her eyes tell another story. Like it's taking all her energy to maintain the Miranda Vines mask. "What does he want?"

"Another power trip? I don't know. He's by the door." I lead her to where he's waiting and start to run up the stairs, but he stops me.

"Brianna, remember what I said."

I look down at him from a couple steps up. From here he doesn't seem as imposing, just another guy in an overpriced suit determined to make people think he's more important than he is. It used to impress me the way people cowered when he made demands. I dreamed of being just like him—it's why I became the bitch I am—but now, watching Mom fidget next to him, I wonder if it's worth it if you don't have anyone to be yourself with. Sure, he's got The Seconds, but I'd bet my 4Runner he treats them the same way.

If you have to demand love, what's the point?

I run my fingers over my lips like a zipper and go to my room.

Not much later, Mom knocks on my door. "Can I come in?"

"Sure." I push my homework aside and she sits next to me. I can't remember the last time we've sat like this, but strange times call for strange actions. "What did Dad want?"

She looks at her hands and tears spill down her cheeks.

My heart races. I can count on one hand the number of times I've seen Miranda Vines cry, and one of them was when the housekeeper spilled bleach on her favorite Gucci bag.

"He gave me the divorce papers."

"Oh, shit."

She laughs, but it's a sad, pitiful sound. "That was my reaction."

"So he's really doing this?"

"Seems so."

"Can I ask you a question?"

She looks at me, making no effort to wipe the tears from her face. It's like a stranger is sitting next to me, not my mother.

"Was the brewery ever in trouble?"

She shakes her head. "Paying for two families gets expensive. But he won't have that problem anymore." She looks defeated, like she played the game as best she could and has accepted her loss.

I sit up. "What does that mean?"

She pats my knee like I'm a little kid. "We'll be fine. He has to pay child support for another year and it's not like I'm unemployed. We'll be fine." She gives me another pat. "We'll be fine."

"The more times you say that the less I believe you."

The patting stops, but she leaves her hand on my knee. "This house…"

I push her hand aside and stand. My hands naturally fall on my hips, elbows out. I don't mean to look down my nose at her but years of practice makes it a habit. "What about the house?"

She looks around like she's seeing it for the first time. "It's so big. Do we really need all this space?"

I take a step back. "We have to move?! This is our home! I assumed that since he moved out, we'd stay here."

Her head falls forward and her shoulders slump.

I touch her shoulder. "Mom, you can't let him steamroll us. There has to be something you can do."

She lifts her head. Her eyes are glassy, like she knows I'm here but isn't seeing me. "I can hang onto the last shred of dignity I have. If I fight him on this, the entire world will know he's been cheating on me for half our marriage. Probably longer. And how will that make me look?" Her head wobbles to the side. "No, this is for the best. The money from the house will be more than enough to get us a nice condo."

"A condo."

She smirks, the first hint of my mother I've seen all day. "Are you planning to take care of a lawn?"

I shake my head, but there's too much rattling around to keep straight. From an ultimatum with Dad to chatting about our *condo* with Mom, this is by far the worst birthday ever.

She stands and lightly presses a hand to my cheek. "Order whatever you want for dinner. I'm going to bed."

eight

On Thursday, I take the same seat aboard the Goodship Lollipop and nod at the others as they work their way toward the back, ignoring the knot of worry in my chest. I'm more relaxed than the first day—if you consider sweaty palms and a nervous stomach relaxed—at least until a new guy steps on. He's not necessarily tall, but the way he glares at everyone as he makes his way to his seat, shoulders pushed back and jaw flexing as he grinds his teeth, makes it clear he considers himself at the top of the food chain.

It's the same way I used to enter a room.

Drea's behind him, her eyes practically bugging out of her head. She slides into my seat and leans into me. "Heidi's not here and that guy is terrifying. Buddy up with me?"

I nod, my eyes on him, and the knot in my stomach hardens. "Who is that?"

"He's been here a couple times. Hates the world and everyone in it."

While I understand projecting anger to keep people from getting too close, I don't think I ever came off as terrifying as he does. "Good to know."

He sits in the back, where Drea sat last time, and scowls at the rest of us. He catches me watching him and Drea smacks my arm, but I've never been one to back down from a challenge. I hold his stare, counting the seconds in my head. When I get to five, I roll my eyes and turn away.

"Are you fricking crazy?" Drea whispers.

I shrug, hoping she doesn't notice me wiping my sweaty hands on my jeans. "They wouldn't put him with us if he was dangerous, right?"

She peeks over the seat, then quickly ducks down. "My faith in the judicial system is not what you'd call high."

"I hear that."

She holds her fist up to me and I bump it like it's the most natural thing in the world. She doesn't need to know that until this second, I've only done that ironically with Austin when he was excited about sports.

"So what'd you do?" she asks.

My jaw clenches and my eyes narrow—my typical reaction when I feel like someone's trying to undermine me—but I force myself to take a deep breath.

She holds up her hands. "Hey, I didn't mean anything. It's a pretty common question around here."

I smile, and she relaxes. "I should probably get used to that, huh?" Shame washes over me as I think of the best way to say that I've been stealing things I don't need. But as I'm about to confess, Mystery Boy gets on the bus and my words evaporate. My lips purse and I raise an eyebrow, and he smirks at me as he passes.

Drea elbows me in the side and snorts. "Busted."

I giggle, and I'm surprised at how easy it is with her. She doesn't seem to give two shits about ulterior motives or saying one thing and meaning another—she seems to take everything at face value. "Was I that obvious?"

She nods. "But Xavier has that effect on girls."

Xavier. That explains the X-Man thing.

"Someone that smoking hot should not be allowed to have tattoos," she says.

I tilt my head at her, not following her meaning.

"It pushes him into another stratosphere." She holds up one hand, palm up. "You've got hot. Dreamy eyes, ridiculous body, and that hair. But you add tattoos and," she raises her other hand and lifts it over her head. "Stratosphere hot."

The urge to turn around and look at him almost outweighs the fact that he's sitting right behind us—and probably heard every word she said. "So you like him?" I ask.

"Nah. He's cool, but I've got a boyfriend."

Relief sweeps through me, followed by surprise. Relief because I barely know this girl, but if she likes him, I don't want to get in the way. And surprise because since when do I care about the feelings of a perfect stranger, especially when it comes to boys?

She leans her head closer to mine. "You never answered my question, so I'll go first. M-I-P. Got caught with pot for the third time. Got thirty hours. My only saving grace is it was right before my eighteenth birthday." She meets my gaze and nods, like she's trying to ease the words from me.

The bus shifts as Bruno climbs on board and the engine rumbles to life. "You know the drill. Remain seated until we stop. No smoking on the bus. No funny business." He watches us in the rearview mirror but since Laina and Crue aren't here, he doesn't call out anyone specific.

I wait until we're on the road to press my head closer to Drea's. "Shoplifting." My heart races, but somehow I'm still able to breathe. I open my eyes and she's watching me, a soft smile on her face.

"That wasn't so hard, was it?"

"I guess not. I'm just—" I break eye contact. "My life's kind of falling apart right now and this made everything worse."

She waits a moment to speak, like she's choosing her words carefully, and I'm struck again at how normal she is. Not a hoodlum or criminal like I expected from everyone here—she's just a girl who screwed up. "It's better than jail, right?"

"Longest two hours of my life." I shudder at the memory and her eyes widen.

"You were actually in jail?" Her voice rises at the end and I grab her arm, and she flinches. "Sorry." She looks over her shoulder. "No one's paying attention."

"Just until my Dad picked me up. It's not like I had an orange jumper or anything." I shudder again, this time for show, and toss my hair over my shoulder. "Orange is so not my color." I smile, unsure if we're at the jokey teasing level or if she's still testing the friendship waters. For whatever strange reason, I care what this girl thinks about me and want her to like me. And I don't want her to know my reputation, how I am in my normal life. This feels like a chance to recreate myself and I don't want to screw it up.

She rolls her eyes. "It's better than neon green." Then she holds out her fist for another bump, and I relax. "Thanks for buddying up. Heidi's cool but she barely talks."

For the first time since I was sentenced community service, I feel a glimmer of hope that maybe this won't be so bad.

Bruno parks alongside a warehouse and kills the engine. "No wandering off into the woods. Stick to the stretch between the warehouse and the road." His no-nonsense attitude is the same from Tuesday, but the underlying charm is gone.

"What's his deal?" I whisper to Drea.

"He's always tense when that scary guy's here. Like he's expecting something bad to happen."

"Great." I step off the bus and pull on my hideous pinnie. When I look up from straightening the hem—not like anything will make this look good—Xavier's watching me. My insides turn to Jell-O but fortunately I'm a master when it comes to concealing my true feelings. "At least they smell like they were washed," I say, and internally roll my eyes at myself. That was beyond lame.

He looks me up and down like he's trying to decide something. "Jail, huh?"

Heat flushes my cheeks and I curse the stupid green pinnie for making me look like a Christmas tree. I shrug like it's no big deal. "It was more like a waiting room."

He nods, but the smirk on his face shows he clearly doesn't believe me. "Right."

I start to protest, but stop. Why do I care what he thinks? He may be sexy as all get out, but liking him is completely pointless, which should make it easy to keep my distance. Except now I want to know why he's here.

Which means I definitely need to walk away. I grab a stick and bag and join Drea, who's watching Scary Guy with narrowed eyes.

"I don't think he's gonna do anything here," I say.

"You never know. I didn't get this far in life by ignoring my instincts."

I raise an eyebrow.

"Let's go the opposite direction of him."

Scary Guy starts walking away and Bruno hollers.

"Hold up!"

Scary Guy takes another step, then pauses.

"Jordan, you know the rules."

Scary Guy—Jordan—turns around and levels a soul-piercing glare at Bruno, then scans the group of us watching him.

The Jocks are already paired up and Shaved Head girl is inching closer to Xavier. "X-Man, you're with Jordan. Sarah, triple up with the girls." Meaning us.

"Great," Drea whispers.

"You don't like her?"

"She's fine, she's just really intense and only wants to talk about modern art and fighting the patriarchy."

"Interesting." I figured she was artsy based on her haircut and piercings, and the passion for women's rights usually follows close behind. Not that I don't think women deserve equal rights or anything like that, it's just not what I spend my time worrying about.

Sarah nods at us as she approaches. "You ready for another scintillating afternoon of picking up after our fellow man?"

Drea raises an eyebrow at me as if to say "see what I told you."

"You got a smoke?"

"Sorry, they're on the bus," Drea says.

"What about you? Brianna, is it?"

I nod and hold out my hands. "I don't smoke."

She smiles, and I'm struck again by her unconventional beauty. For as much effort as I put into my appearance, hers seems to come from within. "Good for you."

"Ladies, get a move on!" Bruno shouts.

"What crawled up his ass today?" Drea asks.

Sarah opens her bag and loops the drawstring around her belt loop, then ties it in a loose knot. "Jordan. You know that kid rubs him the wrong way."

"What's with the revolving cast of characters?" I ask.

Drea stabs a paper cup and drops it in her bag. "Some kids only come certain days of the week, or they miss for whatever reason. I'm finishing my hours as fast as I can. Trash duty sucks, but at least we're outside."

"Except you forgot the smokes," Sarah teases.

The time passes quickly—much faster than with Laina and Crue—and I learn more than I ever imagined about how the government is oppressing women and we need to fight for our inalienable rights. I also learned that while everyone is here because they broke the law, they're all normal kids. Maybe they're dealing with crap at home, like I suspect with Drea, or maybe like Sarah they're just misunderstood, but either way, they're just trying to get through each day the same way I am. I haven't shared any more about why I was stealing or the Dad and The Seconds saga, but they accept me anyways. It's kind of amazing—for the first time in my life I'm acting like my normal self without trying to manipulate anyone, and they actually seem to like me.

Maybe I've been going about this wrong.

I fire off a text to Dad. *2 hours plus 2 before = 4 hours.*

Four hours closer to swooshing above Lake St. Moritz.

On the bus, Bruno asks about our finds. I announce the box of cupcakes we found in a ditch, but Xavier wins with a license plate from California.

"I swear he makes his up," says Drea. "Who throws away a license plate?"

The back of our seat shifts and we turn to see Xavier smirking at us.

"If I worried what makes other people tick, I'd never get out of bed." His gaze bounces between us, lingering on my lips long enough for my breath to hitch.

We whip around in our seats and dissolve into giggles, not caring that he can hear us. With each exhale I feel a little bit lighter, like maybe this isn't the end of my world as I know it—things are just rewriting themselves a bit.

Drea nudges me. "Give me your number."

I tell her the digits without hesitation—another first for me—and my phone dings with a text moments later.

"So you can let me know if you won't be here," she says. "Or, you know, if you want to chat."

"That's cool, but—" I pause long enough for the smile to drop from her face. "I don't plan on missing any days." The promise of Switzerland is definitely motivation, but I'm not picking up other people's garbage any longer than I have to. "But what about Heidi? Aren't you two garbage buddies?"

She bites her lip. "Yes and no."

Two weeks ago, I wouldn't have thought twice about another girl's feelings, especially if it meant I got what I wanted, yet here I am feeling all squirmy at the thought of upsetting someone I met for three seconds.

"Yes on Tuesdays, no on Thursdays." She frowns. "Sorry, but I already promised her we'd team up until one of us is done."

I touch her arm and she jumps a little. I quickly pull it back. "Don't apologize for being a good person." *I could learn a lot from you*, I think to myself. "I'm sure I can find someone else for Tuesdays." My eyes drift to the back of our seat and she bursts out laughing.

"I'm sure you can."

We fall into a comfortable silence the rest of the way, and by the time we pull into the parking lot, I'm feeling content. It's too soon to know if Drea is truly my friend, but I enjoy hanging out with her, and right now that's enough. When Bruno parks, we rush off the bus to avoid Jordan and wave our goodbyes from across the parking lot. I'm halfway to my 4Runner when I realize the beat-up Subaru is parked next to me again.

I slow to a walk, hoping it doesn't look like I'm stalling, then not-so-accidentally let my keys slip through my fingers and fall to the ground.

A hand reaches around my foot, scooping up my keys. I straighten, expecting to see Xavier, but it's Jordan.

I jump back, then step forward again, shoving my hand out. "Those are mine."

"Finders keepers," he drawls, eyes shifting from me to my SUV.

"You know damn well they're mine." My voice shifts from friendly to menacing without missing a beat, and it feels good. I've been trying so hard to be nice that I'd almost forgotten how cathartic it can be to unload my anger on someone else. Especially when they deserve it.

His eyebrow quirks. He bounces my keys in his palm like he's testing their weight, and his eyes bore into mine. "How much they worth to you?" His voice is low and gravelly and would scare most people away, but I'm not most people.

I step closer. "Listen, asshole. I don't know who you think you are, but you will hand those over now or you'll be singing soprano for the rest of the week." I lift my knee to demonstrate what I mean in case he's too dense to understand, but he just laughs.

He tosses my keys across the couple inches separating us.

I snatch them in my fist and give him my deadliest Medusa glare.

"Watch yourself, rich bitch." He stalks away, leaving me trembling next to my car.

But I'm not trembling from fear. No, I wasn't ready for the argument to be over. There's still so much rage bubbling inside me and I need to scream or break something or—

"I was going to intervene, but you seem to have handled him just fine."

I whirl at the voice, my face a mask of anger and my fists clenched so hard my keys dig into my palm.

Xavier holds up his hands. "You okay?"

I relax my fists and rub a hand over the back of my neck. "If that dickweed thinks he can get away with treating me like that—"

He takes a step closer and drops his hands. Up close his eyes look like melted chocolate or toffee or some other delicious treat I could stare into forever. And let's not get started on the rest of him. His waffle shirt is fitted, showing off his muscular arms and a chest that won't quit, and his hair begs to be messed up with my fingers.

I shake my head and he tilts his head.

"I think I underestimated you."

"How so?" I cross my arms, which has the double bonus of making me look uninterested while also pushing up my boobs. But his gaze doesn't drift from my face.

He smiles, revealing straight white teeth. His tongue touches his lower lip and I almost come undone. "You seemed—cómo se dice?—a little unsure of yourself the first day."

My insides quiver when he speaks Spanish. It may not be French like my prison daydream, but there's something about a drop-dead gorgeous man whispering sweet nothings in another language that makes me want to pull him against me right here in the parking lot.

"Yeah, well, I guess I've found my sea legs, so to speak."

He laughs, a low sound that softens his features. He holds out his hand. "We haven't officially met. I'm Xavier."

I take his warm hand in mine. "Brianna."

We stand like that for what feels like an eternity, then I loosen my grip. I may be slowly turning over a new leaf with Drea, but I'm not ready to give the upper hand to a boy, no matter how much he makes me swoon.

"See you next week," I say.

"Until then." He touches my elbow, then moves around the back of his car and waits until I'm safely in the driver's seat.

When I pull into my driveway, I'm still thinking about Xavier. I've never met anyone like him—probably because I've never allowed myself to consider that something could happen with anyone not in the quote-unquote popular crowd. He's the exact opposite of everything I thought I wanted, yet I can't deny the way my body reacts to him.

Dad would kill me if I ever brought someone like Xavier home. From the tattoos to the earrings and the noticeable lack of a button-down or polo, he'd barely make it into the driveway before Dad would chase him away with his figurative shotgun.

But when I step inside and glance in his empty study, I realize it doesn't matter.

He's already moved out.

nine

As a lifelong gossip, it's torture not having anyone to tell my growing pile of secrets. While I never fully trusted Kenzie, we spent a lot of time together and I considered her a friend—even if I knew whatever I told her would end up all over school the next day. Mike might be willing to listen after her birthday peace offering, but if any of my secrets get out I'll be the laughingstock of the school.

All day Friday I feel twitchy, and the feeling is amplified when in the middle of Ethics someone shouts that it's snowing. And not just that flurry crap that barely makes it to the ground. Honest to goodness snow. Living in Boulder, you're pretty much forced to appreciate all four seasons since, as the joke goes, they can all happen in one day. Fall and summer are beautiful, but winter has always been my favorite. When fresh snow covers the world, it hides even the darkest mistakes and makes it feel like anything's possible.

Or at least the first real snowfall is like that.

It also makes my classmates act like they're high. The ski resorts have been making snow for a couple weeks, but real snow is an event worthy of school closing early. Of course, they don't actually close, but they may as well. First snow combined with Friday afternoon and the teachers have lost complete control.

As I head to my locker at the end of the day, kids I normally never speak to bounce by and smile at me. "Are you heading out?" Their excitement is contagious, but A) I'm not much of a night skier, and B) I'm technically grounded.

For now.

When Mom gets home, I'm ready with several plans of attack. If she's tired, I'll play to her sympathetic side, but if she's pissed off at the world I'll appeal to her need to burn off energy. She enters the house from the garage and dumps her purse and coat on the marble counter with a heavy sigh. Tired it is.

"How was your day?" I ask. "I was thinking sushi."

She collapses into a stool next to the island. "All this snow and you want sushi?"

I shrug. "We don't have to worry about it getting cold."

"Touché."

"Maybe watch a movie or something later?"

She raises an eyebrow. "What are you up to?"

I relax my shoulders and do my best to soften my expression. "Nothing. If your week was anything like mine—and I'm guessing it was—you could use a little distraction." I smile, and this time it's not fake. "I was thinking of the Channing, Gael, or Zac variety."

She drums her manicured nails on the counter. "Keep talking."

"Maybe some popcorn with real butter?" And a little wine once Mom gets into the movie and stops paying attention to me. One of the many drawbacks to my social life tanking is I haven't been to a party—and therefore haven't partied—in what feels like forever. I'm not a drunk or anything, but getting buzzed while watching some sexy man-meat in the living room might be the highlight of my week.

"Sold. Order whatever you want, just be sure to get me—"

"A seaweed salad," I finish her sentence. As if I could forget.

"Thanks. This will be good." She brushes a kiss across my cheek on her way out of the kitchen. "I'm going to take a shower."

I order several rolls and seaweed salads for both of us, then cue up my favorite Zac Efron movie and wait for Mom to join me. We're halfway through the movie when I make my move. "What are you up to this weekend?"

She takes a sip of her second glass of wine. "You're looking at it."

"Mom, that's not healthy."

She twists on the couch so she's facing me. "Now you know what's best?"

I pick at my leggings. "No, but staying cooped up on the first weekend since—" I wave my hand, unwilling to say the words arrest and Dad.

She raises an eyebrow. "And this has nothing to do with the snow?"

I press a hand to my chest. "I'm hurt."

"And I'm right."

"Maybe a little." I lean forward, closing the space between us like we're a couple of girlfriends, not mother and daughter. "Let's go skiing. It'll be like old times." When I was little, before I decided I was too cool to be seen in public with my parents, the three of us would go skiing almost every weekend. As much as I love traveling abroad, our trips around Colorado felt more special because they were spontaneous.

She grabs the remote and pauses the movie. "What's going on, Bri?"

I pushed too far. "What do you mean?" My eyelids start to bat on their own and I look down to conceal my mistake. That doesn't work on her.

"Since when do you want to do anything with me, especially on a weekend? Are you suddenly too good for your friends?"

If she only knew. "They're busy. And I thought it'd be nice to spend some time together."

She leans back against the couch. "I appreciate the sentiment, but I'll pass. If you really want to go, consider yourself ungrounded. There's not much point anymore."

I'm torn between exuberance that I get to go skiing and horror that I'll have to go by myself. For a hot second I consider pleading with her to go, but she presses play and the moment passes.

I can handle going alone. No one will realize I'm by myself as long as I keep moving, and that's kind of the point of skiing, right? The only time I'll have to be careful is if I take a break in the lodge.

I've gotten pretty good at lunchtime diversions, so how hard can a ski resort be?

*****

So far, so good. I ordered my season pass weeks ago so I don't have to wait in line by myself. I'm not wearing my usual hot pink outfit because when I pulled it out of storage, I discovered my cherry lip balm had melted all over my pants. Fortunately I had a pair of white snowpants from my pre-Bunny days, so while they aren't my preference, it's better than having to wear Mom's skin-tight black ones.

Carrying my gear solo was a little embarrassing—this is the first time I've missed having a boyfriend since Homecoming— but Dad always makes me carry my own equipment so it's not like I'm helpless. I step into my skis and skate to the nearest lift, and as soon as I'm scooped into the air, my problems fade away.

Until I get to the top and Cally and Blake are there.

They shouldn't be here. The ski and snowboard teams always have meets on Saturdays.

Cally sees me right away and her normally relaxed smile turns into a scowl. Nice to see our mutual hate-hate relationship is still going strong. I glide by them with my head held high and Cally watches me, no doubt waiting for me to say something horrible, but I don't have it in me. Seeing them together—and not boyfriend-girlfriend together, but hanging out like normal friends—hits me harder than I expected. I'm not sure how I miscalculated things so badly, but here I am, standing alone on the top of a mountain, jealous of the two people I banished from my life.

But all that fades away when my skis take over. I'm not a balls-to-the-wall skier like Cally is, so they'll no doubt pass me in a minute, but that's okay. Up here, surrounded by snow-covered trees, I can finally breathe.

I work to keep my skis parallel with as little space between them as possible. When I first learned to ski, Dad showed me videos of guys gliding down the slopes so smoothly it's like they were out for an afternoon stroll. Legs together, posture relaxed but upright, the only indication you're putting forth any effort is when one foot slides a little in front of the other when turning. It's like snow ballet with five-foot fiberglass sticks strapped to your feet—all grace and beauty.

But not everyone skis that way. A loud whoop echoes off the trees as Blake and Cally race by, snow kicking up in their wake. They give me a wide berth and don't look at me as they pass, and for a hot second I wish I could fly down the hill with their reckless abandonment. Cally's tucked in a crouch, her helmet cutting through the air, and Blake's a couple feet behind her, arms tucked to his chest and board pointing straight down the hill. As much as I want to hate them, they're perfect together.

I finish the run and take a different lift that's far away from the terrain park, where they're most likely headed, and finally start to relax. I've seen a couple kids from school, but they're all so terrified to speak to me that it's like I'm here by myself.

Which kind of sucks.

When I first set out to rule the school, I assumed dominance and cruelty were the keys to earning respect. A few harsh words here and a casual rumor there—with the help of Kenzie and Mike—and I quickly became known as the head Snow Bunny, she who was not to be messed with. And I loved it. Lashing out at people lessened the anger I felt inside, but it took more and more to release it. By the time Cally showed up and started her Brivolution—yeah, she thinks I haven't heard that, but I have—I was at a breaking point. Keeping up the reign of terror is exhausting, and when Mike walked away, my foundation started to crumble. Losing Homecoming was the final crack in my façade, and that's when the shoplifting got out of control. Despite how clever I like to think I am, I'm shocked it took as long as it did to get busted—really busted. And now here I am, completely alone.

The chairlift reaches the top of the run and I have to side-step around two girls on snowboards who are sprawled at the bottom of the ramp, apparently still learning the difficult task of riding a board with only one foot strapped in. I don't understand why anyone would choose boarding over skiing—having both feet strapped to one board makes it harder to stay in control, and you're constantly sitting in the snow. As a skier, I pride myself on never wiping out. There's no way it can be fun getting soaked every other run.

Case in point: a snowboarder's lying on his back fifty feet ahead of me, board in the air, goggles halfway between us. At least I think it's a guy. Between the helmet and unflattering black outfit it's impossible to tell what's underneath all those layers. I slow down to pick up the goggles, and not until they're in my gloved hand does it occur to me that this is the first time I've ever stopped to help someone. I'm not sure what made me do it—maybe picking up trash is starting to rub off on me—but now I have to talk to whoever's lying on the ground.

"You okay? I have your goggles." I come to a stop with my arm outstretched, hoping I can dump them and be on my way without a twenty-minute conversation with a rando.

The boarder rolls to one side, props onto an elbow, and looks up at me.

It's Xavier.

My breathing stills. Birds chirp in the distance and I swear I can hear the snow falling in the trees over the sudden pounding of my heart.

"Thanks." He smiles, and my knees nearly buckle.

Suddenly sitting in the snow doesn't sound so bad. What the hell is it with this boy and why do I have such a strong reaction every time he looks at me? "You okay?" I ask again. Maybe I should offer to check for injuries.

"Caught an edge. Haven't done that since middle school."

I'm acutely aware that he's still sprawled out in front of me while my brain is locking down bits of information. I'm still holding his goggles, but he makes no move to take them from me so I jab my poles in the snow and do the unthinkable—I bend my knees and lower to the ground next to him. Because of my skis, I have to sit with my legs pressed tightly together like some prissy lady from the last century, but aside from taking them off, that's my only option.

He pushes up so he's sitting, and I act like this is the most natural thing in the world.

Edge Rule #5: For every action, there's an equal and opposite reaction.

"That's why I ski. No nasty edges out to get me."

He laughs and runs a gloved hand along my ski, and you'd think he's stroking my thigh the way my insides heat up. "You've got twice as many edges."

"I suppose, but we use them differently, right? If one catches, I can just lift that foot and balance on the other one. With this," I point at his board, which is light blue with navy swirls, "you're all in."

The corner of his mouth lifts. "Not ready for that level of commitment?" His dark eyes stay on mine and I fear he might actually be able to hear my heart galloping away in my chest.

"I prefer to be in control. Lying on my back," I nod at him, "isn't my style."

"Noted." He watches me long enough for me to realize what I just said and my cheeks flush despite the cold. "So what would it take to get you on a board?"

"The second coming of Christ?"

He laughs, a warm sound that wraps around me. "What if I don't want to wait that long?"

"You tell me." The space between us suddenly feels smaller, even though neither of us have moved. Is he asking me out? Or has he realized that I can't turn down a challenge?

He brushes the snow off his boots, breaking the spell. "I've been told that I'm an excellent instructor."

I hold up his goggles and give him a look that says I don't believe him.

"Okay, this doesn't help my argument, but trust me."

"Why should I?"

His gaze flicks from my eyes to my lips, and I swear he does that just to throw me off. "Have I given you a reason not to?"

"Not yet." Based on how he carries himself, I'm sure he's an amazing boarder, but I'm not going to admit that to him. I literally know three things about him: he drives a horrendous car, he snowboards, and he did something bad enough to wind up on the Chain Gang. And that's not counting the fact that he's completely wrong for me.

So why can't I stop thinking about him?

He pushes to his feet in one smooth motion and holds out his hand to me. I hand him his goggles, but he grabs my wrist and hauls me to my feet. I let out a squeal—he's stronger than I anticipated and I wasn't expecting to be pulled up like that—and the next thing I know we're chest to chest. Well, chest to belly, since he's half a foot taller than me.

"Thanks." My voice comes out breathy but I'm too flustered to care.

"Thanks for grabbing my specs." We stand there for an impossibly long moment, neither willing to make a move or say goodbye. I never make the first move and it appears he doesn't either, which means we'll either be stuck on the side of the mountain for the rest of the day or—

I pull away gently. "My friends are probably wondering what happened to me."

He touches my arm, then lets his hand fall to his side. "Mine too."

"So," we say at the same time.

"I'll see you Tuesday?" I ask.

"Can I get your number?" he asks.

So much for assumptions. Every time I think I have him pegged, he surprises me. "I like your question better," I say.

He unzips his jacket and pulls his phone out of an inside pocket, and for the second time this week I give my number to someone I never thought I'd be friends with.

My phone chirps in my pocket and I smile.

"Let me know when you're ready to see what you've been missing."

That could mean so many things. "I will."

"See you around." He winks before securing his goggles over his eyes, then sets off down the mountain.

I take off after him, careful not to get too close so he doesn't think I'm following him, and I'm surprised when he doesn't make the turn for the chairlift, but instead heads for the lodge. I'm considering following him when I come to a quick stop, spraying snow in front of me.

Cally and Blake are on the patio near the fire pit and they wave when they see Xavier.

Even worse, he waves back.

Then joins them.

If he's friends with them, it's only a matter of time before they fill his head with all kinds of crap about me. All of which is true. Then he'll run away as fast as he can.

Not that I care.

I toss my hair over my shoulder and get back on the lift, determined to push Xavier and the Dynamic Duo out of my head for the rest of the day.

*****

That lasts about three hours. Now I'm home and I can't stop replaying our conversation. When we talked after my encounter with Jordan, I thought I saw a glimmer of interest but told myself that was just the sex appeal that seems to ooze from him. But now I'm not so sure. He wasn't shy about getting my number, and for some inexplicable reason I'm considering risking my pride and preconceived prejudice to take him up on his proposition.

But not without outside consultation. It's doubtful Drea expected this when she gave me her number, but I text her anyways.

I need advice. It's a thousand times more direct than I'd normally be, but if I want my plan to work, I need an answer fast.

You've come to the right place.

I have a boy question.

I figured this would take at least another couple weeks.

I laugh. *Me too.*

Spill.

Are you sure you're not busy?

Quit stalling.

I take a deep breath. *Saw Xavier skiing. He asked for my number and offered to teach me to snowboard.*

And where exactly does my advice come in? Say yes.

I can't tell her about Cally and Blake without admitting the reasons they'd tell him to stay away from me. Truth is, they could tell him about any number of things I've done and he'll avoid me all on his own.

I admit something I never have before. *I'm second-guessing myself.*

Well knock it off.

It's like she's channeling the voice inside my head—the one that normally keeps me from second-guessing anything. *So I should text him?*

Uh.... YES. You do not let a boy like that get away.

She has a point. *What should I say?*

Have you never asked a boy out?

Not exactly.

Technically he asked you, so you're just answering.

That doesn't make this easier.

Stop overthinking and just do it.

Now?

Yes. I'll wait. :)

I take a quick breath and switch to a new message, but my charm and wit seem to have flown out the window. What would I say if I saw him in person? I'd make a joke so it's clear this isn't a big deal, plus Drea is right. He asked me, I'm just answering.

I've been thinking about your offer.

No no no. Delete that.

You still think you can convert me?

What the hell is wrong with me? This is terrible. I clear the screen and switch back to Drea. *This is harder than I expected.*

SIGH. Just be upfront. No games. Tell him you want to ride his board.

Nice.

You know what I mean.

brb

I switch back to the blank message. *I'll go on one condition.* I hit send before I can think about it any longer, then switch back to Drea. *Done.*

Good luck. I've gotta run but let me know how it goes.

I will. Thanks for holding my hand.

:)

I cradle my phone, willing the physical contact to telepathically elicit a response from him. After several minutes—the longest I'm willing to wait around for a boy—I toss it aside. My gaze drifts out the window and I'm hit with a wall of emotion. We've lived in this house my entire life. This view of the trees and the backyard are all I've ever known and I can't believe we have to leave. It's doubtful any place we find will have a room big enough for my queen-sized canopy bed—and what else will we have to leave behind? Dad's study for sure, but what about the couch and kitchen table? They're the only places I ever let my guard down. It feels stupid to be so attached to physical things, but the more I think about it the harder it is to breathe.

And where will we live? This neighborhood is part of my identity. Mom mentioned a condo, but that could be anywhere.

A thought hits me like a sledgehammer to the chest and I sink onto the edge of the bed. What if I have to change schools? I can't start over with only a year and a half left of high school.

Although maybe that'd be better, the voice in my head whispers. *You've screwed things up so bad that a fresh start could be nice.*

I shake my head. Rule number one of being the biggest bitch in school is to never doubt yourself—there are plenty of people to do that for you. Admitting that I should have handled things differently would be like erasing my years of being at the top.

But look where it's gotten you. Alone in your room on a Saturday night, stressing over a boy who a month ago you'd never think twice about.

How would I even go about changing? I've put so much effort into perfecting my image that without the status and reputation, I don't know who I am. I flop back on the bed and am staring at the gauzy fabric of the canopy when my phone dings.

It's Xavier.

And what have you been thinking?

My stomach flips. *That I shouldn't say I don't like something if I've never tried it.*

I like where this is headed.

I blush. It's like he leads me into saying things with double meanings on purpose.

What's your condition?

Not at Eldora. I'm not embarrassing myself where I know everyone.

There's a pause, and I reread my message to make sure there's nothing to read into it. He wouldn't think I'm embarrassed about him, would he? True, we come from completely different worlds, but he doesn't know me well enough to think that's what I meant.

How about Echo Mountain?

I exhale. *When?*

Tomorrow?

I sit up. I figured he'd stretch this out for another week. *I can do that. Noon?*

You need that much beauty sleep?

You don't?

Is 10 okay? I've got stuff later.

I start to type *It's a date*, but quickly erase it. *I'll see you then!*

Sleep tight Brianna.

You too. I include a smiley face emoji, but just a regular one. No hearts or tongues hanging out, even though I'm drooling at the thought of spending an entire afternoon with him.

And for the first time in forever, I'm actually worried what someone will think of me. I always care about other peoples' opinions, but this is different. I barely know Xavier, but I get the feeling that he doesn't put up with the type of BS that I thrive on. How long will he stick around once he finds out who I really am?

ten

I wake up well before my alarm. I keep telling myself that nothing will happen because we're too different and my parents would never accept him and he'll hate me once he discovers the real me, but that doesn't stop the butterflies in my stomach. I dance through breakfast and wish I had a different outfit to wear, but most people wear the same jacket and snow pants all season. Besides, the bright blue sweater beneath my ski jacket makes my eyes look amazing and is a definite step up from my Chain Gang ensemble.

I knock on Mom's door and wait for her to answer. When she finally murmurs a response I say, "I'm going skiing again. Be home later." If she changes her mind about me not being grounded, I don't want to stick around to find out.

It feels weird to leave for a ski resort without my skis, and even weirder to have my four-year old, never-been-used helmet on the passenger seat. I made fun of Cally for wearing one the first time she skied with us, but that's because as a skier, I never fall. Strapping myself onto a snowboard guarantees that I'll wipe out. I grab a grande latte on my way out of town, then settle in for the drive to Echo Mountain.

The butterflies get worse as I get closer, and by the time I pull into the parking lot I'm borderline nauseous. Who AM I? I don't get flustered over the opposite sex. I'm the flusterer. And since when do I do anything outside my comfort zone for a boy? Snowboarding is the antithesis of everything I stand for—I've always thought of boarders as losers and slackers—yet here I am, about to risk my butt for a little attention from a boy I barely know.

I carry my helmet to the ticket line and freeze when I see him. He's decked out in the same black outfit from yesterday and has his helmet tucked under one arm. Most boys don't bother doing their hair since the helmet destroys it, but he definitely did his hair before coming here. He smiles when he sees me, and his entire face softens.

Oh lord, I'm in trouble.

"Hey," I say. My gaze drops to his throat and I get the incredible urge to brush my lips over his skin.

"I tried to borrow a board for you so you wouldn't have to rent, but everyone's heading out today."

I shrug like it's no big deal, even though I've never rented in my life. "Lead the way."

I fill out the form with my height, weight, and experience level, and I must make a face because he laughs.

"It's killing you to admit you're a beginner, isn't it?"

"No." I shove the lid back on the pen. "Okay, maybe a little. But I guess I need to get over that, huh?"

He presses a hand to his chest. "What if I promise to have you on a blue before we leave?"

"I thought you have to be somewhere later?"

He smiles, then grabs the paper from my hand and leads me to the rental counter. "She's a newbie, but can you give her something nicer than the beginner boards?" he asks the bearded guy behind the counter. He's not much older than us but right now he holds all the power.

I smile my sweetest smile, the one guaranteed to get me whatever I want, and Xavier smirks. "I promise to be extra careful." I even bat my eyes a few times for good measure.

The guy looks over both shoulders, as if anyone's paying attention, then leans over the counter toward us. "Okay. But if you trash this, you're buying it."

Xavier's lips get tight but I keep smiling. "Sure thing."

The guy sets a sleek purple board with big white letters on the counter, then grabs a pair of boots and adjusts the bindings. He gives Xavier a stern look before handing it over. "I'm trusting you."

"Thanks, man." Xavier grabs my gear and leads me to a row of benches, where I swap my regular snow boots for what look like giant moon boots.

It feels like I shoved my feet into oversized hiking boots. My ski boots are top of the line but they still dig into my calves after a couple hours on the slopes. I could spend all day in these. "Are all boarding boots this comfortable?"

The corner of his mouth turns up. "And these are rentals."

I peek at his boots—also black—and compare them to mine. His laces are in better shape and the sides aren't nearly as scratched. "I could get used to this."

He rubs the pad of his thumb over my cheek. "I hope you still think that after a couple runs."

My confidence dips once we're outside. He straps my front foot to the board and we do the awkward shuffle-hop to the chairlift, and while he glides easily into line, I struggle to keep up. The helmet is more comfortable than I expected, and it actually makes me feel a tiny bit better to know that I won't knock myself out if I fall, but it restricts my peripheral vision, making it hard to see other people until they're zooming into line around us.

"You doing okay?"

What was I thinking trying something completely new with a boy I barely know AND who I'm trying to impress? "I've seen enough boarders fall getting on and off the chairlift to know this may not end well."

He hooks his arm through mine. "You push, I'll make sure you don't fall. Deal?"

I nod, too nervous to answer because we're next in line and the chairlift is here and oh crap, oh crap, he's pulling me forward and I'm not sure if I can stop and ooh, the chair's hitting the back of my legs and we're sitting and we're in the air.

"Nice job." His arm is still looped through mine, not that I'm complaining.

"That was all you."

"The hardest part is next."

"Harder than actually boarding?"

He nods. "Most people bite it because they don't stay in control of their board. If you rest your back leg on the board and pretend it's strapped in, you can glide off no problem. If you try pushing with your free foot, the board will twist and you'll catch the edge you're so afraid of."

"And down I'll go." I try not to read into the fact that he's already figured out what scares me.

"Right."

"Got it." He makes it sound easy, but saying and doing are two entirely different things.

"When you fall, try not to catch yourself with your hands."

Not if, when. "Why not?"

"That's how you break your wrist."

I mentally curse my twelve-hour-ago self for ever agreeing to this.

"Want me to help?"

"A two-person pile-up will not make this better."

He purses his lips like he's considering that, and now I'm picturing us rolling around in the snow.

The top of the lift arrives too soon. "I'm having second thoughts."

He squeezes my knee and heat shoots up my leg. "Too late now. Remember to keep your back foot on the board and no flailing."

"No flailing?" My voice comes out an octave higher than normal but I don't care because we're at the top and the chair pauses like it always does but it's like I've forgotten everything I know about exiting a chairlift. My board hits the snow and Xavier's arm tightens around mine.

"You've got this," he whispers.

My left foot—the one strapped to the board—glides like it's supposed to, but my right foot comes down on the hard snow and I stumble.

"Put it on the board."

I do what he says and squeal as we drop down the incline. He points us away from the lift so the next people can exit, but as soon as he releases my arm, I pitch forward. I hit the ground fast, landing on my shoulder. Normally I'd be mortified to fall, especially at the top of the chairlift where everyone can see, but I'm so excited I didn't break my wrist that I'm not even thinking about that. "I take back every mean thing I've ever said about boarders who can't get off the chairlift."

"Over here," he calls. He's on his butt near the lip of the hill, already strapped into his board.

I shuffle-hop to him and drop to the ground as gracefully as possible with a giant piece of fiberglass swinging every which way. At least my feet are comfortable. I slide my right foot into the bindings and latch it in, then he runs his hand over my foot, checking my work. His hand stays there long enough for my pulse to pick up, and he meets my gaze.

"Only one thing left to do now."

Please let it be anything other than going down the hill.

In one fluid movement, he balances on an edge and stands, then hops so he's facing me with his back to the hill. I mimic his movements, and while I don't make it look nearly as effortless, I manage to get to my feet.

Skiers zip past us and shoot over the top of the hill. I stare longingly at two girls whose synchronized movements almost seem choreographed, reminding me of me, and for a second I panic. What if Kenzie's here? As far as I know, she's never been here, but she's got a new crew and maybe they're changing things up.

Xavier touches my chin. "Hey."

"Shouldn't we have started on the bunny hill?"

"Tow ropes are a bitch."

I peer over his shoulder. On skis this slope is nothing, but on a board it looks like a cliff. "Yes, but bunny hill."

"Take it ten feet at a time. Slide with your board parallel to the incline. Stop by lifting your toes so you're balanced on your heels. It's called a falling leaf because you drift back and forth across the hill"

"But not too fast or it's concussion city."

He taps my helmet. "That's what this is for. But yeah, if you catch the edge too fast you'll go down hard."

"Awesome."

"I think you're gonna surprise yourself. You've seen people board before, right?"

I stiffen, and immediately lose my balance. I catch myself on his arm. "Of course."

He gets me balanced and squeezes my shoulders. "Stay loose." He lowers his head so his eyes are inches from mine. The scent of mint gum and woodsy body wash hits my nostrils and I relax. It's like he has a chemical effect on me. "Ready?"

I smile. "No."

"You go first."

My eyes widen. "Why me?"

"Because I want to make sure you don't stay up here."

I don't admit that I've laughed at kids too afraid to push themselves off the top of the hill. I take a deep breath and push away the thoughts screaming at me that this is a terrible idea. "Wish me luck." He lets go of my shoulders and I slide past him to the top of the hill. *Ten feet at a time.* I twist my body so the board is facing downhill and I start to move. *Think leafy thoughts.* Adrenaline rushes through me and I get that same terrified and excited feeling that comes over me when I bypass the cash register with something shoved in my pocket. Then I pick up speed and have visions of barreling straight into the trees on the edge of the run and jerk my legs sideways to stop. Except that's how you stop on skis, not a board. My front edge catches and I smack face-first into the snow.

Snow is everywhere. In my mouth, in my hair, inside my goggles. But I did it!

Snow scrapes as a board stops next to me and I lift my head. Light blue board with navy swirls. He crouches next to me, a mixture of amusement and concern on his face.

"How'd that feel?"

"Amazing. Then cold." I laugh. "I think I destroyed my leaf."

He brushes snow off my face and smiles down at me. "Ready for more?"

I flip onto my back and sit up. Aside from being covered with snow, nothing seems to be broken. "Watch out for that first dip. It's a doozy."

He slips his hand into mine and pulls me to my feet. "Ten feet at a time."

This time, instead of pointing my board straight down the hill I keep my body facing downhill and slide on my back edge. *Yes! Be the leaf!*

Xavier swoops around me and comes to a stop twenty feet away, shaking his head.

I lean back until I coast to a stop. Without falling down! "Why?!" Yes, it comes out whiny but I went twice as far as his ten-feet-at-a-time thing and didn't fall down!

"I'm not letting you go down the hill like that. Would you snowplow the whole way on skis?"

"God no."

He smirks. "Well, that's the equivalent of snowplowing."

We may not know each other well, but he's figured out how to motivate me. "So what am I supposed to do?"

He hops toward me, uphill, and my mind lingers on the abdominal strength it must take to do that. He stops a foot away. With the slope of the hill we're eye to eye and I feel a rush of power at being almost taller than him. "A little of the first try and a little of the second."

I give him a half smile. "Without the face-plant."

His eyes twinkle. "Yeah." He hops backwards, then spins

around and looks at me over his shoulder. "Like this." He points his board at an angle and glides across the hill, then shifts his weight and crosses the other way with his opposite foot leading. He stops and smiles up at me.

"Oh sure, just like that." I take a deep breath and take a tiny hop, turning my board the same direction he did. I start moving slowly, tilting back to keep from going too fast. My arms go out on their own to help my balance. When I reach the spot where he changed directions, I shift my weight like he did, but it doesn't go as smoothly. My back edge catches and I land on my ass. Hard. But I'm still facing forward so I push to my feet and point myself in his direction. I wobble a little but stay on my feet— and slam right into him. His arms wrap around me, slowing me down, but my momentum is too much and he falls backwards. The next thing I know I'm lying on top of him, his arms around my waist and every inch of our bodies pressed together.

"Sorry!" I say at the same time he says, "That was great!"

As much as I'm enjoying the feel of him trapped beneath me, I roll uphill and prop myself on an elbow. "I'm two for two on spectacular crashes."

"That was pretty spectacular," he says. He stares into my eyes, and kill me now because his tongue slides across his lower lip and it's all I can do to keep from leaning in and kissing him. "Just keep doing that."

"The boarding, or knocking you over?"

He shrugs, and I sit up before I get sucked in any deeper. It's one thing to have fun with him, but this can't go anywhere.

And maybe if I keep reminding myself I'll start to believe it.

*****

Xavier turns out to be a pretty good cheerleader. His face lights up after each of my mini-runs and when I reach where he's waiting, he gives me tips on how to improve. Apparently I need to get over my love of facing directly downhill and become one with being sideways. But I make it down the hill without any more faceplants—just countless falls on my butt—and when I reach the bottom, I'm ready for a break.

"Just a quick drink of water," I tell him when his eyebrows crease. "I don't need a break after every run."

"You've earned it."

We lean our boards against a communal rack outside the lodge and I'm amazed again at how comfortable the boots are. "I think more skiers might convert if you shoved their feet into these," I say as he opens the door. He holds it open and gives me a soft smile when I pass him.

"You saying you're ready to convert?"

"Not yet, but it's not as bad as I expected."

He laughs a full, deep laugh that makes me want to bust out every joke I know. "Water fountain's over by the bathrooms, unless you wanted a bottle." His eyes drift across the room of half-full tables to the cash register, where the line is twenty people deep.

"Water fountain is fine. Be right back." I head in the direction he pointed and take a quick drink, then duck into the bathroom since I'm right here. When I'm washing my hands, I'm surprised at how pink my cheeks are. And not the garish red like when I'm embarrassed. This is a rosy, I've-been-exercising-and-having-fun-outdoors color and it's more flattering than any makeup.

I take another longer drink when I'm done, but Xavier's not there. I peek around the corner to the dining room and spot him talking to a girl with long red curls wearing an all-gray snowboarding outfit. Jealousy takes hold fast. My jaw clenches, my eyes narrow, and I feel like I could rip her head from her neck if I had to.

But I don't do any of that. He doesn't know that side of me and as much as I want to walk up and slide my arm through his, claiming him as mine, he's not mine. *Not that that's ever stopped me before.* But he's different, and I don't think he'd get off on two girls fighting over him.

The girl points at her leg several times and a look of horror darkens his face. Then he sees me and that beautiful smile is back. He says something and the girl turns and my stomach drops.

I know her.

She's friends with Cally and not only did I spread rumors about her and Cally kissing—they DID kiss, but it wasn't mutual—I was so horrible to her at Cally's party that she left early. That was the night Cally revolted against the Snow Bunnies with a huge screaming fight, and the same night I took her dad's brewery notebook. The night everything started to change.

Based on the way Redhead's smile turns into a glare, she remembers me too.

eleven

She recovers more quickly than I do. Her eyes narrow and her face pales, but her jaw stays clenched. Then she smiles, shakes her head at Xavier, and fist bumps his shoulder before heading back to her table.

She could have destroyed any chance I have with him—and rightly so—but she didn't.

Why?

Sitting at a table with her friends, she looks no different from anyone else here, so why was I so hell-bent on treating her like crap? One of her friends reminds me a little of Drea and I feel sick. Never in a million years did I think I'd make friends with the Chain Gang crew, yet the two people I've talked to the most in the past twenty-four hours—heck, the past week—are both from there.

Maybe I've been too quick to judge other people, too.

Girls' heads turn as Xavier walks my way, their gazes flitting from him to me and back to him, but I'm too anxious for my usual antics. If I ever caught girls checking out Austin, I'd make a big show of touching him, smiling and laughing and sometimes even kissing him to make it clear he was taken. But I'm too distracted by the fact that he seems to know all the people I've been horrible to.

And not just know them—he's friends with them.

He stands close enough that I can smell the body wash that does kooky things to my brain. "That was Amber," he says.

I smile and nod, doing everything I can to keep my face neutral. "You know people everywhere you go?"

"Snowboarding's like a family. We all look out for each other." He leads me to the door and we step outside. "I haven't seen her since last season. She was telling me how she broke her leg in the Dash last spring."

I remember hearing about that, but at the time it was information that went in one ear and out the other. "But she's okay to be out here?" The words come out automatically—I'm well-trained to say the right thing at the right time—but I'm surprised to feel something bordering on empathy, especially for someone I treated so cruelly in the past.

"She's not allowed to do any jumps, and her air is killer." A sad look crosses his face, and it strikes me that he's sacrificing a day of real boarding to help me.

"This must be torture for you."

"What?"

"Babysitting me instead of really riding."

He sets my board on the ground, then crouches to strap in his foot. "A day on the slopes is always better than any other day."

I step into the bindings and reach to fasten them at the same time he moves to help me. Neither of us are wearing gloves and when we bump hands, he loops a finger through mine. We both stare at our hands like we're wondering what happens next. He brushes his thumb over my other fingers, then finishes securing my foot and stands.

"Want to do the same run or something different?"

I glance at the mountain behind him. The downside of coming to a new place is I don't know the runs. At Eldora, I know all the blues and greens and could tell you exactly which run I'd like to try—Snail or Bunnyfair are both super easy, and International is so long you can make it last half an hour—but here, it's like playing Russian Roulette. "Are you opposed to greens?"

He thinks for a moment. "I know where we can go. It's the same chairlift but there's a green that cuts across the back of the mountain so it's nice and slow." His eyelids lower when he says nice and slow and now I'm thinking of other things I'd like to do nice and slow. "That okay?" he asks.

I nod, unable to speak past the breath caught in my throat. I shuffle-hop past him toward the lift and try to clear my head. This boy can hypnotize me with a look and a few words, and I need to stay focused on boarding—not falling for him.

But a fling wouldn't be all bad.

We glide into line and this time I get on the lift without his help. Once in the air, I'm determined to keep my distance, but there's already been too much incidental touching. He shifts on the cushioned seat and our boards bump, followed by our knees.

"So what's your story?" he asks, while the heat from his leg casually crawls up mine like it's perfectly reasonable for him to be touching me.

"What do you mean?"

"What'd you do to get the Chain Gang?"

While I knew this moment would come, I still haven't figured out the best way to spin it. *So don't spin it.* I take a quick breath and spit it out. "Shoplifting."

He turns to look at me like he's appraising me. "Really." It's not a question, and he doesn't push for more.

"What about you?" He had to know I'd ask since he asked me, but for the first time today, he looks uncertain.

"It's a long story."

"So's mine. One word answer."

He breaks eye contact and stares out over the trees. "Fighting."

Last time I checked—which admittedly was never, but anyways—you don't get arrested for fighting unless it's bad. Like really bad.

Is he dangerous?

Was it was stupid to come here where there's no one else I know? Aside from a couple half-conversations we don't know each other at all. But nothing about the way he's behaved makes me nervous, and the only safety I'm worried about is my chastity. Figuratively, of course.

I bump my shoulder against his. "If it makes you feel better, I was suspended for fighting last year."

He bursts out laughing and slaps a glove over his mouth. "Sorry. I didn't expect you to say that."

"True story. But I didn't get arrested." I don't want to ask specifics but he shouldn't have brought this up if he didn't want to talk about it.

"Another time," he says, his voice so low I almost don't hear him. We ride the rest of the way in silence and by the time we reach the top I'm nearly crawling out of my skin. Why did I have to push him? The mood from earlier is broken and now it'll be uncomfortable and oh shit it's time to get off the lift.

"Remember, push off once then let the board do the work."

"You didn't say anything about pushing off last time!"

"That's because I was helping you. This time you're doing it solo."

As much as I appreciate his unfounded confidence in my abilities, I want more than anything to loop my arm through his and have him help me. It reminds me of the first time Dad took me on the chairlift when I was a kid. I was so scared I was in tears but he made me do it on my own. And I survived.

So I can do this, too.

There's not as much preparation to disembark as there is with skis. You just lift the foot attached to the board and make sure it hits the ground flat. My board hits the snow and I stand, and the chair pushes the back of my legs, guiding me down the ramp. I set my back foot on the board but it gets tangled with the bindings. I break out into a sweat, but I grit my teeth and somehow stay upright. We coast side-by-side to the huge trail map at the backside of the landing area.

"Way to go!" He holds up his hand for a high-five and it feels a little awkward but I slap it anyways. He points at a trail that winds around the back of the other runs and eventually comes out near another lift. "I was thinking this one."

"Nice and slow," I repeat, and dammit if my tongue doesn't moisten my lips completely on its own.

He grins without looking at me and my heart does a little pitter-patter. We move closer to the top of the run and flop unceremoniously onto our butts.

"I'm gonna need extra cushioning if I do this again."

"Those aren't boarding pants?"

I run a finger over the seam. "Not specifically. They're ski pants and they're waterproof. I figured that's good enough."

"If you decide you like this, you'll want to find something better." He fastens his bindings and moves to help me but I brush his hand away. I want to do this on my own. "People are always selling used gear so you shouldn't have to drop a ton of cash."

"Oh. Thanks." Never in my life has someone suggested I buy something used, especially clothes, and the response that flies to my lips—*I can afford to buy whatever the hell I want*—is so not appropriate right now. I'm not sure how he came to the conclusion that money's a problem for me but—

"I figured that if you were busted shoplifting, maybe money's tight."

Because that would make sense. "It...it's complicated."

"You don't have to talk about it."

I finish strapping in and rock my body forward to stand. "You ready?"

"You want to lead?" He pops up next to me and brushes snow off his butt. "There's nothing too tricky on this run, it's just not super wide."

"Um, sure?" My confidence yo-yos with each passing minute. The high from getting off the chairlift unscathed wanes and I stare at the run in front of us with uncertainty.

He rests his hand on my lower back and I lean into his touch without meaning to. "Take your time and stop when you need to."

"Preferably not with my face," I mutter.

With a couple hops, my board starts sliding. My arms go out to the sides to help me balance and I slowly point my board downhill, but my speed picks up too fast. I twist so my board's parallel to the hill and I'm riding on my edge.

"You're gonna clear-cut all the snow off the hill," he shouts from behind me.

I slow to a stop. "What the hell does that mean?"

He points at the trees on either side of us. "Like clear-cutting a forest. You're scraping away all the snow."

He's right. There's a noticeable path twenty feet up the hill behind me.

"Take your time with the back and forth. It's okay if you have to stop a lot." With a giant hop, he moves in front of me and looks at me over his shoulder. "Do what I do." He twists and gravity pulls his board across the snow. When he reaches the edge of the tree line, he twists again and stops, then waves for me to follow. "Now you."

He makes it look so easy. All this time I've been making fun of boarders, it's actually more difficult than I thought. I lift my front foot to turn my board and start moving. Instinct tells me to slow down, but he's only another ten feet away. *I can do this.* I keep my arms out, even when I start going faster than I want, then twist my body to turn the board and stop hard, sending a small spray of snow at Xavier.

He props his goggles on his helmet and gives me an appraising look. "Is that how it is?"

I give him a shit-eating grin. "Like I had any control over that."

He narrows his eyes at me, but they sparkle in the sunshine. "I'm keeping my eye on you."

Please do.

He puts his goggles back on, then crosses the hill and waits for me again. We do this for what feels like hours, until we reach the end of the run. When I come to a stop next to him he pulls me into his arms. I wasn't expecting it and our helmets slam together.

"Woah, sorry," I say.

"You did great!" he says.

I look back at the hill. "Really?"

He gives me a squeeze then lets go. "You barely fell and you're still smiling. Totally legit."

I try to fight the smile that's plastered on my face but it's useless. I did have fun.

"Ready for more or need a break?"

"One more then rest?"

"Sure thing." We unhook our back feet and do the shuffle-hop that's really more like riding a skateboard, then we're back in the air.

The silence isn't necessarily uncomfortable, but I keep feeling like I should tell him more about the shoplifting. But that will lead to everything else and for once I don't feel like bragging about my life. Not like Mom and Dad are anything to brag about.

"You okay?" His voice is soft and I look into his eyes. "You got quiet."

I start to reach for his hand but catch myself and tap his leg instead. "Thanks for doing this. I have to tell you, I never in a million years thought I'd go snowboarding."

"Why? I mean, besides the edges." He smiles, and my insides warm.

"I don't know. My parents ski and it was never really an option to try anything else." The weight of everything I leave unsaid hangs between us—or maybe I'm the only one who notices it. I don't want to mention our family vacations to Europe or the top-of-the-line equipment I get every other year, or the unspoken agreement that the perks only last as long as I stay in line. It's a good thing I got my season pass to Eldora before my arrest.

"They pretty hard on you?"

I shrug. I really don't want to go down this path. "Yes and no. I have a lot of freedom—at least I did until I got arrested. That didn't go over so well."

He laughs softly. "Yeah, I get that."

It's on the tip of my tongue to ask about his arrest, but part of me doesn't want to know. What if it's something really bad? A month ago I'd have sold my 4Runner before talking to someone who'd been arrested, but now the only people who talk to me are my fellow arrestees and I'm realizing there are varying degrees of breaking the law. But he may have done something unforgiveable, and then where will that leave us?

Exiting the chairlift goes about the same as the last time—minor squealing from me but I don't fall—and we take the same run, except this time I lead. At one point I stop near a break in the trees where you can see the valley below, and Xavier stops close behind me.

"This is my favorite part about this run," he says.

"I didn't think this was a run you normally take. I thought you were just slumming with the newbie." I laugh, but my words fall flat. He may not know the economic status of my family, but he doesn't seem to be from money and throwing around the term slumming probably doesn't sit well.

But when I twist around to look at him, he doesn't look pissed. In fact, he's not looking at me at all. His gaze is trained on the forest below. "I usually take this at least once, just for this view."

"You should have told me to stop here last time."

He blinks several times, then looks me in the eyes. "You were pretty focused when we passed this spot. But I looked. I always do."

There's a faraway look in his eyes that makes me want to pull his face close to mine, but I hold back. Until I know his story—scratch that. Even when I find out his story, nothing can happen. I'm debating if I should suggest we keep riding or hang out a little longer when his phone rings.

He fishes it out of his pocket and frowns when he sees the display. "Cómo," he says. His frown deepens as he listens. "Espéra allá. Me voy." He ends the call but the frown remains.

"Everything okay?"

"It's my little sister. She—uh..." he scrubs his glove over his face. "I need to go pick her up."

"Is she okay?"

"Not really. It's a long story." He takes a breath as he looks out over the forest. "I'm sorry."

I'm not sure if he's apologizing for having to leave or not telling me more. My curiosity urges me to needle him, to push him until I have more details, but I swallow my questions. "It's totally cool. But," he looks concerned until I smile. "I can't promise I'll go any faster."

He grins, and I'm relieved to see the scowl disappear. The tattoos and piercings already make him look intimidating, but when his face darkens it makes me wonder again why he was arrested and if I should be concerned about hanging out with him. "Thanks for understanding."

I honestly can't think of a time when someone said that to me, and I have to admit, it gives me warm fuzzies to know I made him feel a tiny bit better. Maybe not enough to make him forget whatever's going on with his sister, but enough to put a smile on his face.

I adjust my goggles and point the front of my board downhill. So far I've stopped every time I've criss-crossed the slope, but it's time to attempt turning without stopping. I kick out my heel to slow down as I approach the other side, then shift my weight and start sliding in the other direction. "Yes!" I pump my fist in the air, but catch my edge and my entire body slams to the ground.

Xavier's at my side before I can assess the damage. He touches my hip, my shoulder, then settles on my face. "You don't have to rush for me." His eyes are steady on mine and I probably shouldn't read into that statement, but it's impossible when his full lips are right there and the concern he'd shown for his sister is back on his face.

"I'm okay," I mouth, but no sound comes out. Because I can't breathe. Like no air will come into my lungs. I try to sit up, panic filling my chest. I touch my throat and he holds me down with a hand on my shoulder.

I'm going to die. This is how I'm going to die. Suffocating on a mountain with a stupid snowboard strapped to my feet and this beautiful boy in front of me who I can't stop wishing would kiss me.

"You knocked the wind out of yourself. It feels like you're dying, but it'll come back in a minute."

"Just a minute?" I mouth, blinking back tears.

"I promise."

Edge Rule #6: What doesn't kill you makes you stronger.

I close my eyes and try to concentrate on breathing. Anything but him watching me while I struggle for breath. Mom sometimes drags me to yoga and while I never had patience for the breathing exercises, the instructor's words come to me now. *Deep breath in, hold for one... two... three... deep breath out.* I inhale deeply but it's like the air just stops at my throat.

My eyes snap open and if I had breath to catch, it would. Xavier's face is even closer. His eyebrows are creased and he's biting his lower lip. I open my mouth to speak and as suddenly as my breath left me, it comes back. I gasp, then cough, and he helps me sit up. My chest feels like an elephant sat on it, but at least I'm breathing.

"I'm guessing that's never happened to you before?" he asks.

I shake my head. "I'm all for new experiences, but that sucked."

He smiles. "You okay to get up?"

"Give me another minute." I break eye contact so I'm not looking at him while my lungs remember how to function. It's not that I'm embarrassed, but I loathe feeling vulnerable and being unable to breathe is the ultimate in vulnerable.

He rests his hand on my back and starts humming. I don't recognize the tune, but it's soothing.

"Is that supposed to make me relax?" I smile at him so he knows I'm teasing, but he seems surprised.

"Oh, I didn't realize—it's something my Mom used to sing when I was upset."

There's so much in that statement showing how very different we are, and for a second I'm jealous that he has a mother who cares enough to sing to him. "It's sweet."

His gaze lowers and a flush creeps up his cheeks. "You seem to be breathing okay now."

I poke him in the chest. "Thanks for waiting. Help me up?"

He takes my hands and pulls me upright, and we both hesitate. My entire body feels electrified and he must feel it too because he leans ever so slightly toward me, but before anything happens a group of skiers fly by, one close enough to make me flinch, and the moment ends.

I clear my throat. "Wish me luck." Then I push off and inch my way down the hill.

I make it to the lodge with only a couple more falls. While my balance is stellar from skiing, turning still eludes me. He waits while I turn in my equipment and put on my snow boots, then we head to the parking lot.

"Where are you parked?" he asks. I point in the direction of my 4Runner and he hooks his thumb at the opposite side of the parking lot. "I'm this way."

My smile fades. We had so many almost moments while we were on the mountain that I was sure he'd kiss me before we left. Sure it could happen right here but—

"Come with me to drop off my gear, then I'll walk you to your car."

"Sure."

When we get to his disaster of a car, I must not do as good of a job hiding my distaste as I thought.

"You don't like Subie?" he asks, pouting a little.

"You named your car?"

"You didn't?"

He runs a hand over the front of the hood like it's a fricking Rolls, not a hunk of metal covered in smiling woodland creatures.

"What's with the foxes?" I point at the passenger door. I can't imagine riding in a car that's literally held together with duct tape.

He laughs. "It's a joke with my sister. Some dickhead hit her and shredded the door, and this was her solution."

"Wait, your sister was hit or the car was hit?"

"Both. She borrows it sometimes. She got her license this year but hasn't saved enough to get her own ride."

I do quick math. If she just turned sixteen, he's at least seventeen, which puts him the same age as me. Not that it makes a huge difference, but I like to know these things.

"And the foxes because..."

He opens the hatchback and slides his gear inside. "It reminds me of the forest. Plus it's a Forester. So foxes, woods, you know."

I roll my eyes. "I cannot believe I missed that."

He slams the trunk and pokes my arm. "That's because you were too busy turning up your nose at how she looks. There's a lot of depth to this baby." He holds my gaze for a beat, then grabs my hand and tugs me toward my car.

On the walk across the parking lot, my emotions flit from excitement that I'm holding hands with a smoking hot guy to terror that someone will see me, then shame that I'm thinking that. But it's hard to turn off years of training. By the time we reach my car I can't decide if I should tear out of here and never speak to him again or press him up against the driver door and have my way with him.

I press the remote start button for my car and turn to face him. "Thanks for today."

"Be sure to stretch tonight. You're gonna be sore." He presses his hand against my belly. "Especially here."

The butterflies are working so hard I can't imagine ever feeling anything but bliss. His hand slides to my waist and my lips part so he knows it's okay to kiss me. His head comes closer, but instead of making my toes curl, his lips brush my cheek and he takes a step back.

"I really do need to go."

"Your sister," I say like an idiot, and he nods. *Grab him and kiss him yourself!* But that's not my style. He wants it, I can tell, but maybe he's got too much on his mind right now. "See you Tuesday?"

He nods again. "Hasta luego."

I paid enough attention in Spanish to know that means *until later*, so I smile and give a little wave. I climb in the car and drive home, feeling more unsettled than I did when Mom told me Dad left. As much as that sucked, divorce is as common as lipo and a tummy tuck for your fortieth birthday, and I'd always figured it was just a matter of time before our family became part of the statistic.

But everything about today goes against how I was raised. Snowboarding, hiding the truth about who I really am—not to mention falling for a boy who could get me disowned. Nothing good can come from this.

I just wish my heart would listen.

twelve

Sore doesn't begin to describe it. I expected my legs to be tired—what I didn't anticipate is being unable to sit up in bed because every muscle from my neck to my belly button hurts. After three unsuccessful attempts, I text Mom.

Help.

She's at my door in under a minute. "What's wrong?"

"I can't move."

She rushes to the side of the bed and presses her hand to my forehead. "Are you sick?"

I shake my head, wincing at the shooting pains in my neck. Who knew you used your neck to snowboard? "My muscles. They don't work."

She pulls her hand back and studies me. I didn't tell her I went snowboarding because that would lead to questions like, "Who are you going with?" and, oh yes, "Have you lost your mind?" To which I could only answer yes.

"I fell skiing." It's a lame excuse and one she probably won't believe, but it's all I can give her.

"You. Fell skiing." It's not a question.

"Yeah. I caught an edge and face-planted." That's putting it mildly. I feel like someone punched me in the face and ripped my stomach muscles out through my throat.

"That had to be embarrassing." Not "Wow, that must have hurt," or, "No wonder you're sore." But why am I surprised?

It's not like she's the type of mother to sing me a song to make me feel better. I don't think Miranda Vines even knows any children's songs.

"Yeah. Could you bring me ibuprofen and help me sit up?"

She raises an eyebrow. "It's that bad?"

I nod, trying not to wince.

"Do you need to stay home?"

I'd love nothing more than to hide beneath the covers for the foreseeable future, but if I could show my face after my arrest, I can show up like this. "Nah, I should be okay after a shower."

She palms my cheek and studies me for a moment. Some days I feel like I know her better than any other person on the planet, and others, like now, she seems like a stranger. Whatever she's thinking is staying locked in her head. "Be right back." The bed shifts as she stands, making my abs scream.

She returns with a glass of water and ibuprofen, and watches as I swallow, the tiny pills feeling like boulders scraping down my throat.

I'm never boarding again.

"I started the shower for you. Coffee's ready downstairs." And with that, she leaves.

I arrive at school looking less than perfect and barely able to hold my cup of coffee. Even my fingers hurt. I fumble with my locker combination, then drop my pen in Homeroom and have to ask the guy in front of me—who I've never spoken with—to pick it up for me. I give him a grateful smile and he shrinks away like I'm going to bite off his head.

But that's just the beginning. Kenzie continues to ignore me in History, but it's more of a hyper-aware ignoring, like she's fully aware of everything I do and is tucking away bits of information to use against me later. Every time I shift positions, my face scrunches like someone kicked me in the kneecap and I'm sure she's come up with a dozen reasons why I'm in so much pain. Kenzie has always lacked creativity, but all it takes is a whisper and raised eyebrow for half the school to believe

I'm either doing manual labor because my family's broke or screwing the entire basketball team—all at the same time.

Halfway through class, I cough and the sudden burst of air hurts so badly that I gasp loud enough that Crusty Ray asks if I'm okay. Mike twists in her seat and gives me a weird look. I brush away her concern with a shake of my head, but she's not that easily dissuaded. When class is dismissed, she waits for me in the hall. I'd try to outpace her, but who am I kidding? At this rate I'll be lucky to hobble to class on time.

We turn the corner and slam into a wall of awkwardness. Evan, Mike's tall, dark, and handsome ex, jumps back, his eyes darting between us, confusion clear on his face.

"Hey," we both say, neither looking directly at him.

He mumbles under his breath and moves around us.

"Tell me again why you broke up with him?"

"I don't believe I ever told you in the first place." Her tone is sharp, and she takes a deep breath. "Sorry. So what's wrong with you?" she asks, glancing at my malfunctioning body.

"What have you heard?"

"Nothing, but I wouldn't believe what's said around here anyways." Mike learned first-hand from me that half the BS floating through these halls is just that—BS. She lowers her voice. "Bri, what's going on?"

I shake my head, and press my lips together. How many times will I do that before I remember that sudden movements are not a good thing? "I wiped out skiing yesterday." The lie I told Mom is the closest I'm getting to the truth. It's stupid to hide that I was snowboarding, but I've spent my life declaring that skiing is the superior, more elegant sport and that boarders are a lower species, and I'm not ready to eat my words. At least not publicly.

"You?" Her eyebrows shoot straight up and she fights a smile.

"Go ahead and laugh." I giggle despite the pain. "It was pretty epic."

When we arrive at Ethics, she stops me with a hand on my arm. "I'm not going to pry, but whatever's going on, I hope you're okay." I start to walk to my desk but she's not done. "And Bri? This less-than-perfect, almost self-deprecating thing suits you."

Her compliment surprises me. Is that what's happening to me? Perfection has always been my goal, but it's like the first crack in my armor started a snowball effect that's turned me into someone who no longer cares what people think and just wants to be happy. Whatever that means.

"Thanks."

I puzzle over her comment through class, and I'm still thinking about it when I head to lunch. If I truly am changing, it shouldn't bother me that Kenzie's taken over my old table and filled it with a group of sophomores who fawn over her every move. Their eyes track me like I'm somehow still a threat, and a tall, too-skinny brunette glares at me as I make my way to an empty table in the back of the cafeteria. If Kenzie's the new me, this girl must be the new Kenzie.

"Good luck with that," I mutter, and she purses her lips at me. I feel like a total loser eating alone, but at least here I can keep an eye on my enemies.

A familiar laugh a few tables from Kenzie's makes me look up. Austin is doubled over, his hand resting on the back of the chair next to him. Which happens to be holding Mia. Who's also laughing. When they first started dating I wanted nothing more than to rip the perfect smile off her face, but I have to admit she makes him happy in a way I never could.

Or wanted to.

Evan, who seemed stuck in a mopey funk after Mike dumped him, seems to have forgotten his earlier awkwardness. Now his attention is on Mia's equally pretty friend sitting next to him.

I take out my phone and pretend to answer texts, but no one's contacted me since Xavier last night. His message was brief—*thanks for a fun day*—and my reply was equally short.

Until I know what's going on with him I'm sticking to playing hard to get. At least that part of the old me still exists.

By the time I get home, I feel like I slid down the entire mountain chest-first naked and I want nothing more than to crawl into a hot bath, then bed. But a white sign in the front yard stops me cold.

For Sale.

*****

The next day, I pull into the parking lot for community service, still in shock that we're actually selling the house. Mom's only comment was "you knew this was coming," but I can't help feeling hurt that she didn't say anything Monday morning. Every few months she acts sort of motherly and yesterday morning would've been the perfect time to bring up the fact that, oh hey, I've already hired a realtor and the house is on the market.

My muscles aren't quite as sore today, thank god, because the last thing I want is to be hobbling around in front of Xavier. I debated texting him to tell him how miserable I was but A) I didn't want to come off as whiny, and B) part of playing hard to get means not texting a boy every day, at least not until you're sure how they feel about you.

Even though it's before the shift, I text Dad. *2 more = 6.*

Drea waves at me as she gets on the bus. It's Tuesday, which means Heidi is here, and while Drea warned me that they buddy up, part of me hopes she'll ditch Heidi. But when I get on the bus, they're already sitting together.

Drea mouths "sorry" and seconds later my phone buzzes.

Maybe you'll get paired up with X.

Maybe... I reply. He seems to roll in at the last minute, so it's not until Bruno boards the bus and gives us the "you know the drill" routine that I start to worry. For as much as I know nothing can happen with Xavier, the thought of seeing him is the only thing that's gotten me through the past two days. I do a quick head count—the Jocks, Crue and Laina, and Sarah— which means I'll be with Sarah.

I text Drea. Does he ever not show?

Not since I've been coming.

I catch her eye over the back of my seat. She gives me a little frown, but that'll have to be enough for now.

"Looks like it's you and me," Sarah says from across the aisle. She doesn't sound exactly thrilled, but I smile anyways.

"I'm a little gimpy today so I hope you're okay going slow."

"Aww, baby, you can come with us," one of the Jocks says.

"Nah, I'm good," I say with a roll of my eyes.

Sarah gives me a look like she wants to say more, then nods.

That settled, I lean back in the seat and stare out the window, doing my best to avoid the Jocks.

Bruno parks us along yet another stretch of highway. Who knew Colorado's highways had so much litter? Or maybe they always seem clean because of criminals like us. We grab our green pinnies and step into the brisk November air. Most of the snow from Friday has melted, but drifts cover the ground beneath the trees where the sun doesn't reach.

"How cold does it have to get before they let us do something inside?" I ask Sarah as she blows on her hands. She's wearing fingerless gloves that look like they've seen better days, but they're more practical than the wool mittens I grabbed before leaving home.

"Don't let Bruno hear you complaining," she says.

I grab my stick and garbage bag and watch Bruno from the corner of my eye. I wait until we wander away before speaking. "He seems like a giant teddy bear."

"He is, but he also doesn't tolerate any bullshit. Including bitching about where he takes us."

"Wait, he decides where we go?" I figured he was just our babysitter.

"Nah, the courts or the city or someone decides that. But he takes it real personal." She points a finger at me. "So watch what you say around him."

"Got it. Thanks."

She's not as chatty as Drea, but I'm not in a talkative mood. Disappointment at not seeing Xavier hits me hard. It's not like we would've automatically been paired up just because we spent a day together, but no matter how hard I try, I can't deny the connection between us.

We eventually meander toward Heidi and Drea, and spend the last half hour tackling a couple of garbage bags that must have burst when someone threw them from a moving car.

"Who does this?" Drea asks. "I mean, seriously. What is wrong with people?"

"You need to ask?" Sarah says.

Drea pulls rubber gloves over her cotton ones and bends to pick up the trash by hand.

"Ew, seriously?" I pretend to vomit, but stop when the back of her shirt lifts, revealing dark bruises across her lower back. "Woah, Drea. What happened?"

She turns her head to see what I'm looking at, and quickly stands. "Oh, nothing. An overly aggressive volleyball game in PE."

Sarah bites the side of her lip. "No class is worth doing that to your body."

Drea shrugs and Heidi hands her a pokey stick. "It looks worse than it feels. I forgot it was even there." She tugs her jacket down so it's covering her backside, and something about the way she avoids my gaze makes me think she's hiding something. "Come on, help me with this."

We use our sticks to pick up the rest of the trash and Drea doesn't say anything else about the bruises. I'm no volleyball expert, but I don't know how you could get a bruise like that in PE. It's a straight line across her back, like she hit the edge of something.

Or someone pushed her.

When we get on the bus, I'm surprised when Drea sits next to me.

"What about Heidi?"

"She's cool. Plus she barely talks. She said she could use the quiet time."

"Quiet on this bus?"

Drea laughs, and I almost forget what I saw.

I lean close and whisper, "Seriously, are you okay? That bruise looks nasty."

Her gaze wavers for a millisecond and if I wasn't so good at reading people, I would have missed it. "Really, it's not a big deal. But I appreciate your concern."

The bus shifts as Bruno climbs on. The engine rumbles to life and he calls back to us. "Let's hear it!"

"An unopened package of socks," Drea calls.

"Did you set those aside?" he asks.

"Of course."

"A nerf gun with bullets!" Jock number two yells, fist pumped in the air. "Maybe I'll actually win since Xavier isn't here."

I turn at his name, and it doesn't go unnoticed.

Toby leans across the aisle toward us. Drea presses into my shoulder to get away from him but he either doesn't notice or doesn't care. "Miss your loverboy, ladies?"

"Excuse me?" Drea snaps. "How many times do I have to tell you morons I have a boyfriend?"

He rolls his eyes, then narrows his gaze at me. "She doesn't."

I try to shrink away but we're trapped in the seat.

"I see the way you look at him when you think no one's watching." Heat flames my cheeks, but he's not done. "I told you the first day, you're one of us. Messing with a loser like him will either get you killed or in jail."

I'm so startled by his comment that the scathing words I was ready to hurl dissolve on my tongue. "What are you babbling about?" Were my instincts right? Is he actually dangerous? I never felt in danger when we were boarding, but I'm proof that people can have more than one version of themselves.

Toby leans closer and Bruno shouts, "In your seat, Toby!"

Toby retreats, but his gaze never leaves mine. "Didn't he tell you why he's here?"

"Yes, he did." Never mind that he didn't elaborate.

"If he told you the whole story, you wouldn't be defending him."

"Am I defending him?"

He laughs, but it comes out a sneer. "Maybe not with your words, but your body language says you don't want to hear the truth."

I cross my arms over my chest and level my nastiest glare at him. "I don't know who you think you are or what you think you know about me, but—"

"Just ask him about the Nortenos."

Drea's head whips from Toby to me, her eyes wide, and my jaw drops. The Nortenos are a gang in Boulder, notorious for everything from drugs to robbery and I don't want to know what else.

"So he didn't tell you."

I snap my mouth closed and try to pierce him with my glare. "You worry about yourself and erase me from your head. Don't speak to me. Don't look at me. I don't exist to you."

People usually run away when I unleash my full rage, but Toby just laughs, making me even more angry. Drea rests a hand on my arm. "Ignore him. All he wants is to piss you off."

"Do you think it's true?" I whisper.

She shrugs. "I don't know. I hadn't heard that before but at this point, nothing surprises me." She looks at me. "What kind of vibe did you get from him when you were snowboarding?"

I immediately blush, and she laughs.

"Oh, lord."

"Let's just say I didn't get a gang vibe."

Her eyes widen. "Did you kiss?"

I shake my head. "But there were several times I thought we might."

She wiggles in her seat. "Man, I can't imagine kissing someone that hot."

I elbow her. "What about your boyfriend? From what you've said, he sounds amazing." She hasn't actually said anything to make me think that, but it's the type of thing girls like to hear.

But I don't get the giggle I expect. "Oh, Colton's cute. He's just not dark and mysterious."

Or questionably dangerous. "At least you know where you stand, right?"

She presses her lips together. "Depends on the day."

I cock my head. "Are things not okay?" If someone says they have a boyfriend or girlfriend, I usually assume things are good unless they say otherwise. Drea's never said anything to make me wonder, but now I'm wondering.

"No, they are." She shifts in her seat and I remember the bruise on her back. "He's just... I don't know, moody sometimes. Makes it hard to know which version of him I'm gonna get, you know?" The pleading in her eyes for me to please say, "Yes, I totally know what you mean," is so desperate I can feel it in my gut.

"Yeah, totally," I lie. My relationship with Austin was never perfect, but that was usually because I kept changing what I wanted. He was always reliable.

My words must be enough because she relaxes against the seat. "Have you asked him why he got arrested?" The change of topic makes me even more curious what she's not saying about her boyfriend, but I don't press her.

"He just said it was for fighting."

"Which could be gang related."

"Or not."

When we arrive at the parking lot, we say our goodbyes and she makes me promise to update her if I learn anything new. I drive home, unable to get Toby's taunts out of my mind. Could Xavier really be in a gang? His unwillingness to talk could mean anything—embarrassment, shame—but what if it's some kind of oath where he's not allowed to talk about it? It was bad enough when it was just first impression stuff that I knew would make my parents lose their minds, but with each layer I peel away, I become more and more convinced that I need to erase Xavier from my mind and pretend my growing feelings for him don't exist.

thirteen

Between community service and recovering from boarding and wondering about Xavier, I somehow missed that it's Thanksgiving. There's no Chain Gang because of the holiday, but Drea texted that some people would be at a soup kitchen outside Boulder for lunch. Serving, not eating—because I asked. Mom made reservations for dinner at our usual fancy place in downtown Denver, which means I have no excuse not to go.

My brain refuses to accept that I need to forget about Xavier. I haven't texted him to ask why he wasn't there Tuesday, but it's not because I'm playing hard to get. It's because I no longer want him to catch me. If he does, I don't think I'll be able to say no and I'm terrified of how deep I could fall into his world. It's not like me to be afraid of anything, but my feelings for him scare me.

And if I'm honest, he scares me.

Stone Soup is in an old brick church on the north side of Boulder. It's just minutes from the shops and restaurants on the Pearl Street Mall—and where I was arrested—but it's like another world. I'm not so self-absorbed that I didn't know there were homeless and needy people in our community, but I didn't expect them to look so... normal. Sure, there are a couple guys who look like they haven't seen the inside of a shower in months, but for the most part they look like people you'd see at the movies or in the grocery store.

When a family of four—mom, dad, and two kids under the age of five—come through the line, it strikes me just how fortunate I am. Sure, my parents suck and they don't pay attention to me, but I've never gone a single day wondering where my next meal is coming from or where I'll sleep tonight. Even having to sell the house just means we're moving to something smaller, not to a shelter or a car or box in the street.

Speaking of Dad, I text him during a pause in the line. *Special occasion. 3 hours. That makes 9.*

Drea texted right after I arrived to apologize for not coming, saying something came up last minute, and I actually believe her. The only people I know from community service are Laina and Crue, and they're so wrapped up in each other I don't think they're aware of anyone else. She ladles green beans onto people's plates and he sets a piece of bread on the edge of the tray before they hand it to the next volunteer.

I roll my eyes at them for the hundredth time.

"You too fancy for the likes of us?" A scratchy voice startles me. A weathered man with scraggly hair and more wrinkles than a plastic surgeon's Before picture scowls at me from across the table. His mismatched clothes hang from his gaunt frame and they look like they've never been washed.

"What? No." I look around, but the other volunteers are smiling and talking with the people in front of them. No one's paying attention to me.

"I seen you roll your eyes. You think you spend a coupla hours doin' this and poof! You're a good person?" He leans toward me and shoves a dirt-streaked finger at my face. "I know your type, girly. Sittin' in your ivory tower lookin' down on the rest of us."

I shake my head. Tears burn my eyes but I clench my jaw and sharpen my gaze. "You don't know anything about me. So back off."

He takes the tiniest step back, then plants his hands on the table and leans forward again. "I'm watchin' you, girly."

"Hank, leave her alone!" The director of the soup kitchen, a portly man with a bushy gray beard and clean white apron points at us. "She's just helping. Take your food and move along."

The man narrows his eyes at me and I scoop mashed potatoes onto his plate. I've wished every other person a Happy Thanksgiving but I keep my lips pressed firmly together.

"What about the gravy?"

I spoon gravy onto his potatoes and don't break eye contact, refusing to let him intimidate me. Adrenaline makes me stand straight and I push my shoulders back to show that I'm in control. But as soon as he shuffles toward an empty seat at a nearby table, my entire body slumps.

The director moves next to me and rests his hand on my shoulder. "Don't let him get to you. Most people are pleasant enough, but Hank, well, he's pissed off at the world and thinks it's his life's mission to make others as miserable as he is." He gives me a comforting smile. "Can't imagine going through life that way, can you?"

I shake my head, but his words hit me harder than Hank's.

Lashing out at other people used to make me feel better about myself, but is Hank a preview of how my life will turn out? I'm not saying I'll end up homeless, but I've already chased away all my friends and I'm barely seventeen. What kind of person does that? I don't want to spend the next sixty years being the nasty hag no one talks to because she hates the world. I want to have friends I can trust and someone who loves me. I'm still not convinced about the having-kids thing, but I've got time for that.

What I don't have time for is being angry at the world. Yeah, my life sucks right now, but it sucks for most of the people in here and they're still smiling over their soup-kitchen turkey dinner like it's their best meal of the year. And maybe for them, it is.

I can't do anything about my family falling apart, and my only recourse with my arrest is community service, but I can change my attitude and try to make amends with the people I've hurt.

And it starts today.

*****

Mom and I sit across from each other at Evening Star, where we've had Thanksgiving dinner for as long as I can remember. It's what I describe as fancy American and while they typically serve birds like duck and quail, for Thanksgiving they serve the best roasted turkey in downtown Boulder. If the maître d' notices Dad's absence, he's smart enough not to mention it.

Besides, it's possible he already knows. A story as juicy as ours is bound to spread fast, and all the bar and restaurant owners know each other. I'm shocked it hasn't hit the halls at school.

We order our meals—standard turkey dinner for me; no skin, no butter, no flavor for Mom—but when they arrive, they're identical. I clench my hands in my lap, bracing for the lashing the server's about to get. Miranda Vines does not tolerate mistakes and she especially doesn't tolerate fat.

But she just smiles and thanks the girl who isn't much older than I am.

"Your order's wrong," I say, pointing at the hunk of meat still sheathed in its skin. It's not clear to the naked eye, but if I had to guess, I'd say there's butter on her mashed potatoes.

She rests one elbow on the table and takes a sip of her Sauvignon Blanc. "Do you know how exhausting it is being a bitch all the time?"

"Well, you make it look effortless." I press my lips together but the words don't climb back into my mouth.

Her eyes widen, then narrow. She takes another drink, this one a little longer, and I kinda wish I had my own glass to get me through this conversation. "You can't earn respect by forcing it from people. Believe me, I've tried. And look where it's gotten me. Having dinner with my convict daughter while my husband plays house with some woman half my age."

Anger burns in my gut. My narrowed gaze must not be the reaction she was hoping for because she lets out a long sigh.

"I'm trying to be heartfelt."

"The fact that you have to announce it says volumes." I know I shouldn't antagonize her but maybe she shouldn't call me a convict.

Her jaw ticks and I take a sip of water.

"I'm not a convict."

She waves my words away like I'm a fly buzzing her ear. "Fine. My trouble-maker daughter. But that's not my point. The point is I've spent my entire life playing to a certain set of rules and now the rules have changed. Being faithful to your father no matter how overbearing he became was supposed to guarantee me a lifetime of security."

"I thought you said we'd be okay?"

"We will, but this isn't what I signed up for." She drags her fork through her potatoes, wrinkling her nose at the butter that oozes onto the plate. "Your father changed the rules without telling me and all he gets is a slap on the wrist. I'm left picking up the pieces."

"Like the house?"

"And the brewery."

"What's happening to Mischief?" If they have to sell, will they get enough money to pay for the lifestyles we're all accustomed to?

"I'm part owner. And I'm forcing him to buy me out. But after that," she shrugs. "I don't know." She sets her fork down and takes a gulp of wine. At this rate I'll have to drive home. "I do have a bit of good news."

Anything. I nod for her to continue. If I've learned one thing in this family, it's to save my words until they count.

"I found us an acceptable condo a couple miles from the house. The neighborhood isn't as established as ours, but it has three bedrooms, two baths, and is a fairly new construction. Only one garage though."

The thought of having to brush snow off my SUV in the middle of a Colorado winter threatens to spoil my mood, but if the kids at the soup kitchen this morning don't even have a driveway, I can deal with downsizing. "What doesn't kill you makes you stronger, right?"

She smiles—a real smile that reaches her eyes—and she seems a little surprised. She must have expected an argument from me. "I know this hasn't been easy for you either."

I smile back.

She lifts her glass and holds it toward me. "To new beginnings."

I clink my glass of sparkling water against hers and take a sip. Fizzy bubbles tickle my nose. "You're a lot more optimistic about this than I thought you'd be."

"What choice do I have?" she asks.

I think of the horrible man from earlier today. While he didn't choose the course his life has taken, his past behavior probably led him there.

She sighs. "Maybe being a hard-ass isn't worth the effort."

A laugh escapes me. Without knowing it, we've been coming to the same conclusions. I take another sip of water. "I'll drink to that."

*****

By Saturday, I'm ready to crawl out of my skin. I still haven't heard from Xavier—not that it matters, really—and I've thought about asking Drea to hang out but I'm not sure if we've surpassed the I'm-hanging-out-with-you-because-you're-the-best-option-at-community-service level to actually being friends. Besides, she's probably busy with Colton and her family.

As a last resort, I slump next to Mom at the kitchen table. "Want to go skiing?" I ask.

She looks up from the article she's reading on her tablet and blinks several times. "I'm sorry. Did you just ask to hang out with me?"

I run my finger over the cool marble. "Maybe."

"This is the second time you've asked." She sets down her tablet and gives me a look that tells me that whatever she's about to say, I'm not getting out of it easily. "Are you ready to tell me what's going on?"

"Now?"

She looks around the empty room. Sunlight streams through the window over the sink, reflecting off the spotless counters. You'd never know we actually eat in here. "Do you have something better to do?"

I let out a sigh, then take another breath. "I don't even know where to begin."

fourteen

The story spills out of me, starting with Cally's arrival last winter, Mike leaving the Bunnies, and Austin and I breaking up, but I leave out losing Homecoming Queen and keying Austin's car. Looking back, I can see that things were falling apart for Mom and Dad at the same time, which might be why neither of us noticed the other's life spiraling out of control. I also stop short of telling her about Xavier, but I do mention Drea and confess that most of the other Chain Gang kids aren't so bad.

She promises to try to be there for me more, and I promise to trust her.

And I'll try.

We go skiing, but it isn't the same. The smooth back and forth rhythm across the slopes that used to bring me so much satisfaction is—I hate to say it—a little boring. The chairlift doesn't carry a hint of foreboding, there's no challenge in swooshing down the freshly groomed trails, and frankly, I'm a little annoyed at having to carry my poles.

Later, back at home, I break my rule and text Xavier. *You've ruined me.*

I plead the fifth.

I wiggle in my seat. I didn't think he'd write back so quickly. *Went skiing today...*

And you missed me?

My heart skips. I have missed him, but I'm not telling him that. *...and it was boring.*

You can't see me, but I'm smiling.

Me too. Understatement. I believe the word to describe my smile is beaming. *But I'm a little ticked off.*

Because I've ruined you.

Yep.

So you're saying you want to go again?

Am I? I suppose I am. And if he's asking me then... *I don't think you've left me any choice.*

Still no Eldora?

Is that okay?

My season pass is getting dusty.

Sorry..... maybe after this. I need more practice without witnesses. I realize too late that I basically asked him to go a third time. My hands sweat as I wait for his reply.

You realize people can see you at Echo right?

I laugh. *Yessss.*

Then that's cool.

Sweet. Thanks. I do a little dance on my bed. Yes, I'm not supposed to like him and nothing will ever come from this, but there's nothing wrong with hanging out, right? And we'll be snowboarding. It's not like we're going to dinner or a party or watching movies on my couch—although all of that sounds absolutely wonderful. We'll be wearing a hundred layers and falling on our asses while I try not to break myself.

I'll see you Tuesday.

A hundred questions rush to my fingertips—various forms of "Will you really be there?" and "Why weren't you there last week?"—but I don't ask. We still barely know each other and he might not be willing to share. *See you then.*

It's not until later, when I'm falling asleep, that it occurs to me that he might have brought up the season pass because day passes to ski resorts, especially on the weekends, are expensive. I don't know his situation, but a lot of kids my age can't afford to go wherever they want regardless of the price. Should I offer to pay for him? That might get weird, but the sinking feeling in my gut tells me I need to do something.

*****

"Where's Bruno?" I ask the man standing next to the Chain Gang bus. The other kids linger nearby, staring at the man who's the complete opposite of Bruno. He's short and wiry, with a receding hairline and weathered skin that looks like he's spent most of his time outside. But while he may be half the size of Bruno, energy courses through him like a current, warning people to keep their distance.

"I dunno," he snarls. "I didn't ask for his life story, just did what I was told." He narrows his eyes and scowls at all of us in one glare. "You all could learn a thing or two about that." He steps away from the open door and points at the bus. "Get a move on."

I hurry up the steps, take my regular seat, and text Dad. *2 more = 11.*

Just once I'd love a response, but Frank Vines doesn't do courtesy unless it helps him close a deal.

Drea's not here yet but Heidi takes their usual seat at the back. The jocks sit across from me, Sarah's behind them, and Laina and Crue take the other back seat. The man scurries up the steps, shuts the door, and starts the engine—and I panic. Xavier's not here yet. He said he'd be here and I was really looking forward to seeing him, but if New Bruno leaves now he won't make it. I open my mouth to tell New Bruno to wait when the door opens and Xavier's black hair appears.

"You're late," the man growls.

Xavier looks at his bare wrist. "This says I'm on time."

The door shuts and the bus lurches forward while Xavier's still standing at the front. His gaze lands on me and he smiles, sending my heart into overdrive. I smile back, expecting him to slide into the seat behind me, but he pauses next to mine.

"This seat taken?"

I shake my head and he sits next to me. Our thighs bump while he stretches his legs beneath the seat in front of us, and I silently wish for his knee to stay pressed against mine.

"Thought you weren't going to make it."

He rolls his eyes at the front of the bus. "That guy knows he can't leave until the scheduled time."

New Bruno seems to think he can do whatever he wants. "How was your Thanksgiving?"

He looks surprised for a second, like he didn't expect a personal question. "It was nice. My mom always makes too much food. We'll be eating turkey for weeks."

Another tradition I've never experienced. When you eat dinner at a restaurant, there's not much in the way of leftovers.

"How about you?" he asks.

I hesitate. I could lie and keep up the appearance that my life is perfect, but since this thing between us isn't going anywhere, what's the difference if he knows?

He crosses his arms over his chest, his jaw tight. "You don't have to tell me."

I touch his arm, and startle at the contact even though I'm the one who initiated it. His arms are completely solid under his jacket. "No, it's not that." I look at my hand, which is still resting on his arm, and set it in my lap. "My parents split up a few weeks ago so it was just me and my mom. We went to the same restaurant as always and it was fine, but it wasn't the same."

The hardness in his face disappears. "I'm sorry. I didn't know."

I sigh. "No one does."

"Not even your friends?"

How much am I willing to tell him? "I'm kind of—cómo se dice?" I steal his phrase from the other day. "Between friends right now."

A mix of emotions flash across his face. Curiosity, surprise, and something else that makes my stomach flip. "You speak Spanish?"

"If hola and buenas dias count, then sure, I speak Spanish."

He winks. "It's a start." Then his smile fades. "So what's with your friends?"

"Short version? I drove everyone away and now no one talks to me." I hold my breath while he digests this. If I were him I'd want nothing to do with the spoiled brat sitting next to me, but he doesn't switch seats, so maybe I'm okay.

After several excruciating moments, he rubs his hand on his jaw and locks his gaze on mine. "Maybe you need new friends."

My fingers twitch, wanting to touch that same spot on his jaw. The intensity between us amplifies and I swear the whole bus has to feel what I'm feeling right now. "Is that all?" I ask, my voice softer, hoarser, than before.

He leans toward me and my entire body reacts. My hand inches toward his leg and my shoulders turn so I'm facing him. My gaze bounces from his eyes to his mouth, and he bites the corner of his lip, making my heart pound even harder. His hand touches my knee—no different from when we were snowboarding but so different because now there's just a thin layer of denim between us. He leans closer and my eyes drift shut. I part my lips, ready, but there's no soft press of his lips. Instead, his cheek grazes mine and he nuzzles the sensitive skin near my ear.

"Querida, not here." His warm lips brush my jawbone and I feel like I might burst into flames. He cups my other cheek and meets my eyes.

"O-okay. Right." I smile as his thumb traces the edge of my lip. "Then you're gonna have to stop doing that."

He drops his hand but the intensity in his eyes makes it hard to breathe. *How long until I can get this boy alone?*

By the time New Bruno parks along the side of yet another littered highway, I'm ready to sprint outside. The cool air and long stretch of highway are exactly what I need to clear my head.

"Wanna be my buddy?"

I turn to find Xavier smiling down at me, a goofy grin on his face. I don't need to check how the others have paired up to answer him. "Yes."

We set off in the opposite direction of the Jocks and keep walking until we're a football-field length away from the others. If it weren't for the green pinnies, plastic gloves, and garbage bags, I could almost pretend it's a date. The question about him being in a gang niggles at the back of my mind. If I ask him, then it's only fair that I tell him my story and I'm not ready for him to know that side of me. Shame isn't an emotion I'm familiar with. Maybe it's better if we don't talk about the past and only worry about the future.

But there's no future with him, my stupid inner voice reminds me.

Xavier picks up a Barbie car—a silver Corvette with hot pink seats—and turns it over, inspecting it. Black scribbles mar the sides and the front is dented like it was in an actual car accident. "This is my winner."

"That?"

"Yep."

"How do you always win? The Jocks were bitching about you the other day."

"Those whiny babies?" He shakes his head. "I look beneath the surface. This car may not look great but it was well-loved. It's the things that are beautiful on the outside that are usually messed up on the inside." He doesn't look at me while he says it, but it feels like he's talking about me. Or maybe I'm just projecting my insecurities. "Those guys can only see what's right in front of them."

Screw it. It's not my style to back away from something just because it scares me. Sure, I may not like the answer but it's better to know now, before anything happens between us. "They said something else about you, too."

He pauses with his stick halfway through a Styrofoam cup. "And it bothers you?"

I shrug, a casual lift of my shoulder that hides the uncertainty I'm feeling.

He drops the stick and garbage bag and takes a step toward me. "Let me guess. They told you I'm in a gang." That's not exactly a denial. His eyes search mine and I fight the urge to look away. *Better to know now.*

"Something like that."

"Do you believe them?"

My head shakes from side to side before I can get the words out. "Nothing about you says gang member." My fingers reach for the tattoo that peeks from the collar of his shirt. His warm skin is a shock and he inhales sharply. I hook a cold finger inside the edge without thinking, just wanting to feel more of him, and his hand covers mine, holding it in place.

"But?"

"No but. Fighting doesn't equal gang. I know that."

He slips his fingers through mine and lowers our hands so they're pressed over his heart. His pulse hammers against his chest. Does he want me to know that I'm affecting him the same way he's affecting me? "I'm not in a gang. Never was."

I try not to look relieved, but I am. Who knows why the Jocks said it, but the little I've learned about him says he's a good person. "Me neither." I smile, hoping to lighten the mood, because if this intensity continues we're going to end up fifty feet away in the trees.

"This isn't social hour," a harsh voice shouts from near the road.

We jump apart, looking completely guilty as New Bruno stalks toward us.

"You're here because you screwed up, so how about you show some remorse and work instead of flirting with each other."

"Sorry," we both say.

"If your bags aren't full by the end of the shift, I'm not signing your hours."

My head snaps up. "You can't do that."

He sneers, revealing discolored teeth and a black soul. "I can and I will." He gives me a once over that makes my skin crawl and Xavier steps between us. New Bruno scoffs, a disgusting sound from the back of his throat. "Don't get all macho on me, hombre. I know why you're here and it means jack shit to me."

Xavier stands several inches taller and uses his full height to stare down at New Bruno, but I'm no shrinking wallflower. My shoulders push back and I give him my coldest glare. Everything around us falls silent—the only sounds are the passing cars and birds chirping in the nearby trees—until New Bruno finally breaks the stand-off. "Don't forget who's in charge here," he says before turning and walking away.

We both unleash a flurry of anger.

"Can we report him?"

"Who the hell does he think he is?"

"Can he really dock our hours?"

"What a slimy piece of shit."

That last one was me.

Xavier reaches for my hand but quickly drops it. "I don't think he can, but it's not worth finding out. Guys like that get off on making other people suffer."

I bite my tongue. What can I say to that? That I'm the same way? Or at least I was until a month ago when people stopped caring what I did.

"Don't let him get to you," he says, and I choose to let him think that's what's bothering me.

"I don't think New Bruno's gonna do show and tell."

"New Bruno?"

I spear a paper bag from a fast-food chain. "You don't give people nicknames?"

He shakes his head and laughs.

"He didn't introduce himself and I had to call him something in my head."

He seems to consider that. "So what did you call me?"

Hottie McHotterson.

His hip grazes mine. "You're blushing."

"It's not a big deal."

His smile broadens. "Now I have to know."

I duck my head so he can't see my eyes. "Mystery Boy."

"Hmm. I like it." He moves toward a plastic bag and I fall in step beside him. "So you like mysterious?"

"Predictable is boring."

He gives me a devilish look and I have to remind myself that nothing can happen with him. Even if everything about him makes me want to throw away the rules, consequences be damned. "You still want to board this weekend?" he asks.

"If you're free."

He holds my gaze so long that I swear he can read my mind. "I am."

Time ticks away and we still haven't filled our bags. For the first time in my life I'm worried there isn't enough litter. "You're sure he can't penalize us?"

"We'll figure something out."

But the grass around us has been picked clean. I'm starting to think we'll have to borrow trash from the other kids when Xavier points at a lump of plastic half buried in leaves.

"It's not a dead body, is it?"

He raises an eyebrow at me. "This isn't where they dump bodies." My jaw drops and he laughs. "I'm kidding, querida. But you should have seen your face."

But I'm not thinking about the joke. *Querida.* I don't know what it means but it sounds like a promise. A dark, sexy, promise of what's to come.

New Bruno doesn't ask us about our favorite find and he barely looks at our bags. Xavier sits next to me again and as his leg settles against mine, it occurs to me that I never texted Drea. "I meant to ask Drea why she wasn't here."

"Text her now."

Missed you today.

She writes back almost immediately. *Had a fight with Colton.*

What does that have to do with skipping community service? But I don't write that. *Everything okay?*

It will be. I should be there Thursday.

Good.

Who'd you buddy with?

<3

Oh reallllllllly?

I peek at him to make sure he's not looking at my phone. *I'll tell you about it later.*

Can't wait.

I tuck my phone into my coat pocket and he slides his arm around my waist.

"She okay?"

My heart gallops at his sudden nearness and my concern for Drea. "I don't know. She said she had a fight with her boyfriend, but why would that stop her from coming?"

His arm stiffens around me, pressing into my lower back. The same place Drea had that bruise. "How much do you know about her boyfriend?" he asks.

I replay everything she's said about him, but nothing stands out as a warning. "I'm thinking not enough."

fifteen

Drea didn't show Thursday either, but this time she texted me ahead of time. Her excuse was different, but after the way Xavier reacted when I mentioned her fighting with her boyfriend, now I'm wondering what she's not telling me. I've texted her a couple times to see how she's doing but her answers are vague.

Xavier wasn't there either, and he didn't text.

I'm still thinking about Drea when I arrive at Echo Mountain Saturday morning. Xavier didn't bring up his season pass again, but I feel bad making him pay when I'm the one hiding from my friends. Or former friends. So I've come up with a plan: get there first, buy both our lift tickets, then tell him I had a two-for-one coupon and got his for free. Boys can be weird about girls buying them things, especially if he's thinking this is a date, so now I just seem thrifty.

Ha.

We agreed to meet at ten, so I'm through the line and pacing out front a few minutes before. The lot's pretty full so my first sight of him is walking across the parking lot, his jacket half zipped and his board balanced on his shoulder. My stomach does the little quiver that seems to be standard when I first lay eyes on him, and his face lights up when he sees me.

"You been here long?" He leans toward me like he's going to kiss my cheek, but hesitates before getting too close.

"Just a few minutes." I hold up the passes. "I had a two-for-one thing so I went ahead and got our tickets."

"Can I pay you for half?"

I hand him his ticket and smile. "Buy me lunch instead?"

He grabs my hand holding the ticket, but instead of taking it, he pulls me into a hug. "Thank you." This time he does kiss my cheek, then steps back. "You ready to shred this mountain?"

I snort, and quickly cover my mouth. I cannot believe I just made that noise in front of him.

But he doesn't seem to care. He grabs my hand and leads me to the rental counter, where he once again sweet talks the guy into giving me nicer equipment. It's not until we're on the lift that the nerves kick in.

"I feel like I forgot everything you taught me. Also," I pat my belly. "You need to show me a way to do this without destroying my abs."

"Were you sore?"

"Understatement."

He brushes his hand over my belly and even though he's wearing thick gloves and I'm buried under three layers, my body reacts like he's touching my bare skin. "You should have told me."

"I'm fine now." I bite my lip, not sure if I should ask what's been on my mind. My curiosity wins out. "Where were you Thursday?"

His face darkens. "I had to help my sister again." He rests his forearms against the bar holding us into the chairlift and stares out at the trees.

"Is everything okay?"

"I keep thinking it is, then she goes and does something stupid again."

I run my hands over the railing. The scrape of my gloves on metal fills the silence. "You don't have to talk about this if you don't want to."

His forehead drops to his hands and for a moment I'm not sure what to do. Keep talking? Wait him out? This is uncharted territory for me. I reach for his shoulder but pull back when he straightens.

"I don't wanna dump all this on you."

I point at the ground twenty feet below. "I'm not going anywhere." Only after I say the words do I realize the extra weight they carry. If he trusts me now, will I still run? And does this mean I'll need to be honest too? I'm not sure if I'm ready to let him see the whole me.

"She used to be a good kid. But ever since our dad left she's changed. My mom got promoted and started working extra hours so it's been on me to keep her out of trouble, but it's like nothing I say gets through to her."

"That's a lot of pressure on you. Does your mom know?"

He shakes his head. "A little. She figured out most of it when I got arrested. After that, Lily promised to stay straight, but now she's doing the same shit all over again."

With each word he says, more questions spring to my lips. What she's doing? And how is he keeping it from his mom? But the biggest question bursts out of me before I can stop it. "What did your arrest have to do with Lily?"

He rolls his neck. "She was dating this guy who's a couple years older than her. I vaguely remembered his name from school a few years back but he dropped out, and from what I heard, he was in a gang."

"Is that where those tools got that story from?"

"Probably. It was bad enough she was getting mixed up with them, but then she started hiding things from me. We're only a year apart so we've always been close, and I couldn't get through to her. One night she came home so high she could barely walk straight, and that's when I saw bruises on her."

My hand covers my mouth. I want to close my eyes and shut out his words, but it's like watching a train derailing. It's going to be awful and tragic and there's nothing I can do to stop it. And in this case, the damage is already done.

"She tried to play it off like it was no big deal. When she sobered up, I wouldn't leave her room until she told me everything. This asshole was treating her like a piece of property, but because he said the right things and had enough drugs, she convinced herself it was love." He scoffs. "Barely sixteen and she thought she was in love."

"So what did you do?" I feel like I already know the answer but I need to say something.

"Nothing at first. Made her check in with me when she was out, that kind of thing, but nothing changed. A few days later she came home with a busted lip and a bruise on her cheek and it's like something flipped inside me. I waited 'til she went to the bathroom, then took her phone and texted him, pretending to be her." He bites his lip and swallows hard. "He said all this crap, apologizing for what he did. I was pretending to be her so I said it was okay and asked to meet him. I wasn't stupid enough to try to go to his place, so I suggested a park near our house. I didn't think he'd agree, but he did."

"Xavier..." My voice is barely a whisper.

He looks at me as if he forgot I was here. He reaches for my hand. It's clumsy with our gloves, but I rest my hand in his and wait for him to continue.

"I took her phone so she couldn't warn him, then headed to the park. Even then, I wasn't sure what I was gonna do, I just knew I had to do something. When I got there, I realized I didn't even know what he looked like, so I scrolled through her phone to see if she had pictures." He covers his mouth and I squeeze his hand. "You don't have siblings, right?"

I shake my head. The Seconds hardly count.

"Let me tell you, you don't ever wanna see the pictures I saw. My baby sister with this... guy, doing things I haven't even done yet. And in some of them—" he takes a deep breath.

"You don't have to tell me this."

"I want you to understand why I did what I did."

I already understand whatever he did, and that's without knowing the full story. "Okay."

"There were a couple pictures of her naked and her boyfriend wasn't the only guy in the picture."

My stomach twists. "Oh my god."

"It seemed like they just were watching, but it was my baby sister." His voice cracks and tears burn my eyes. His love for her and imagining what he saw breaks my heart. "I finally found a picture of just him, and I burned that into my mind. It was getting dark out, but when a car pulled in, I could tell it was him."

Part of me doesn't want to hear the rest of the story. Knowing he got arrested for fighting is enough to fill in the pieces.

"I went up to his car and pounded on the window. That's when I realized I probably should have brought some kind of weapon, but I still didn't know exactly what I was gonna do. I didn't have a plan. He rolls down the window and starts yelling at me, telling me to back off before he beats my ass, that sort of thing. But there was no way I was backing down. Not after what he did to Lily."

His grip tightens on my hand, like he's reliving that night.

"I told him who I was and that he and Lily were over, and he started laughing. He laughed at me. So I punched him through the window. After that, it was all a blur. He got out of the car and landed one punch before I slammed his head against the car. He dropped to the ground but I couldn't stop. It's like I went out of my body and watched myself beat this guy until he was a bloody mess."

"Holy shit." I want to shut out the image he's painting, but I can't blame him. I've never had the kind of connection he has with his sister, but I'd like to think I'd do the same thing for someone I loved.

"The scariest part is I could have killed him. It was dark. No one else was there. But I climbed back in my head and stopped myself. Then I called an ambulance and drove to the police station."

My jaw drops. "You turned yourself in?"

He holds out his hands. "What else was I supposed to do? That wasn't me. I'd been in fights before, sure, but it was all stupid middle-school crap. This was life and death. By turning myself in, I got to tell the whole story, including what he'd done to my sister. The prosecutor wanted to let me off but the judge insisted on community service."

"What happened to him?" He still hasn't mentioned how the gang fits into this and I'm terrified to find out.

"I broke a bunch of bones in his face, so he was in the hospital for a while. Then he was arrested for drugs, child pornography, and a bunch of other things I had no idea about."

"You're like a super hero."

He looks at me, his jaw hard. "He's in a gang. He's no one important, but now they know who I am and he's promised to pay me back."

My breath catches. Hearing him say the words is so much worse than just suspecting. "Can't the police do anything?" Is he scared? How do you go through your day knowing a gang is after you?

"Not really. They said they'd keep an eye on him once he got out of jail, but he's not their biggest problem."

"And Lily?"

"There was a lot of crying. Mom never found out the full story and Lily promised to get out of that world, but now she's slipping back in. Different guy, but the same signs are there."

I'm so lost in his story that I jump when he lifts the guard rail. We're thirty feet from the top of the chairlift and I've completely forgotten to be nervous.

"Remember. One push with your free foot, then ride the board down." His voice is thick with emotion. He hooks his arm through mine and I'm grateful for the help.

Our boards hit the snow and I do as he says. It's easier with him keeping me upright, and we glide to the side, out of the way of the people in the next chair.

I stop him before he sits. "Xavier, I don't know what to say. Thank you for trusting me."

He flips his goggles on top of his helmet. His eyes shine and he smiles down at me. "I wanted you to know the truth. It sucks having the arrest on my record, but it's not who I am."

"You were helping your sister."

He nods, and touches my chin. "Thanks for understanding."

My heart feels so full for this boy who put himself at risk to help someone else that I need to do something. Now. Without thinking about where we are or who can see us, I push up on my toes and press my lips against his. Or at least I try. My goggles hit his nose and our helmets clink, stopping the kiss before it starts. He lifts my goggles off my face and rests them on the top of my helmet, but that's not good enough. I unclasp the strap beneath my chin, yank my helmet off, and toss it at my feet. "That's better." The breeze lifts my hair, swirling it in my face. He brushes it back, his dark eyes locked on mine, then our mouths crash together.

We don't waste time with soft or gentle. His lips are cool against mine, but his tongue is hot and fills me with a desire that warms me from head to toe. He pulls me tight against his body—or as tight as we can get with two snowboards strapped to our feet—and my hands roam his back. I want to unzip his jacket and really feel him, but reality pokes through the fog in my brain, and laughter and whispers reach my ears. I break the kiss, keeping my face pressed against his. "I kind of forgot where we were."

He laughs, a deep rumble in his chest. "Not me." He presses a more chaste kiss to my lips. "Don't care."

My arms drop to my sides and I step back, but I can't take my eyes off him. Who knew getting arrested would lead to this beautiful boy with gorgeous eyes, full lips, and a heart that's bigger than anyone I've ever met?

He reaches for my arm. "Tell me what you're thinking."

"Snowboarding is overrated." He laughs, and his gaze flicks over me, keeping the heat in my belly simmering. "But we *are* here..." My helmet rolled away while we were kissing and I have to hop several feet to grab it. I brush the snow from it and glance at the lift and freeze.

A boy from school is staring at me, his mouth open.

And not just any boy.

Luke.

One of Blake's best friends.

Someone who knows firsthand how awful I can be and could ruin this—whatever this is—with Xavier before it even gets started.

I'm still standing with my helmet in my hand when Xavier touches my back. "You coming?"

Luke's eyes dart from me to Xavier to us. I silently plead for him to keep his mouth shut and be on his way, but an easy smile spreads over his face and he shuffle-hops toward us.

"Hey, man," he says, holding his fist out to Xavier.

"Luke, what's up?"

They bump fists as my world crashes around me, then Luke nods at me like it's the most natural thing in the world. "Brianna."

"L-Luke." My voice comes out shaky but my face doesn't reveal the panic I'm feeling. *Please don't say anything please don't say anything please don't say anything.*

"You slumming?" he asks, and Xavier's head whips toward me.

My mouth falls open, but I quickly snap it shut. "Turning over a new leaf."

He seems to consider this for a moment, and smiles. "Cool." Then he shuffle-hops away, leaving me to deal with the consequences.

"What was that about?"

I look up at Xavier.

Confusion is clear on his face, mixed with frustration and a hint of anger. "I think it's about time I got the truth."

Edge Rule #7: The scariest part of falling is just before you land.

sixteen

"You're right." I move toward him but the tenderness from before is replaced with irritation. I reach for his chest and rest my hand over his heart. "If I promise to tell you my deepest darkest secrets, can it wait until we're back on the chairlift?"

His eyes never leave mine but I can't tell what he's thinking. Then he lifts the corner of his mouth. "Sure."

We make our way closer to the edge and strap ourselves into our boards. My senses are still humming from our kiss, but dread is slowly taking over. I knew this moment would eventually come, but I was hoping it'd be later, when I was more confident about where we stand. This is still new enough that it'd take very little for him to decide he's done with me.

And my truth is not very little.

"Show me how you've been getting up," he says, interrupting my thoughts. He's sitting next to me, knees bent, the edge of his board in the snow.

I mimic his position, then swing my arms forward to jerk myself upright.

He shakes his head. "Try to use your legs more." He plants his hands behind his body and pushes up, balancing his weight on the edge of the board until his body is over the board, then he magically stands.

"Oh, is that all?" The sarcasm drips from my voice and he smirks.

"Just try."

I sit back down, then push off like he did and while I end up on my feet, it certainly isn't as effortless as he made it look.

"See. You're a natural."

I roll my eyes. "You must have abs of steel."

He runs a hand over his belly and shrugs.

And just like that I'm imagining him with far less clothing. I shake the thought from my head. "Are you leading or am I?"

"That depends."

"On what?"

"On if you're planning to stall."

It's spooky how well he knows me, even though there's still so much he has to learn. I punch him lightly in the chest. "I'll go first."

I set off down the hill, stopping when we reach the edge. He's right behind me, but instead of stopping, he turns and cuts back across the hill and waits for me on the opposite side. *Okay, I can do this.* I head straight for him, shifting my board every couple feet to slow down, and when I'm almost to him, I shift my weight and cut back across the hill. This time I keep the fist pumping inside my head, and before long I fall into a rhythm that leads me to the bottom of the hill.

Xavier is right behind me and before I can catch my breath, he wraps his arms around me and lifts me in a bear hug. I can't stop the laughter that bubbles up. "You did it!" he shouts. He gives me another squeeze before setting me back on the ground. His smile is so pure it's like all the stuff he told me earlier has been erased from his mind. I'm not used to living for the moment—I'm always thinking about what other people think or how I look or what they think about how I look—and never just let go.

Maybe he can teach me that, too.

But that will have to wait. Right now he's unstrapping his back foot and watching me. I'd love to sneak in another kiss before we get on the lift, but I get the feeling he's holding out until I tell him what he wants to hear. And aside from faking cramps and running inside, there's no getting out of this.

He rests his hand on my lower back while we wait our turn, and once we're in the air, he presses his knee against mine. "I don't know what it is that you're so afraid to tell me, but you can trust me." He touches my hand. "Like I trusted you."

I lean my head forward but my hair is tucked in my helmet and doesn't shield my face like I want it to. He can't be expecting a full list of every awful thing I've ever done, so maybe the highlights will be enough. "I'm not really sure where to start."

"How about the shoplifting?"

"When I got busted or the first time I stole something?"

He shifts on the narrow seat so his body is facing me. "You've been holding back."

"It all seems so stupid after what you told me."

"It's not. And quit stalling."

I take a deep breath and close my eyes. "The first time I took something it was an accident. I'd tried on this bracelet I had no intention of buying, and didn't realize I was still wearing it until I got home."

"You didn't return it?"

"Would you have?"

He hesitates. "This isn't my story."

So that's a yes. Let me just dig my hole even deeper. "I guess I was embarrassed. My family... we're not exactly hurting for money and I was afraid the store would make a big deal out of it. The next time I was in there I bought a couple things to make up for it."

His jaw twitches and I want to jump off the chairlift. It's only a twenty-foot drop. If I land on my board just right I could glide away and never see this look on his face again. But I promised him the truth and I'll give it to him. At least a portion of it.

"I'm not really sure how it snowballed, but I started taking things whenever I was out. Never stuff I'd wear—which I realize is beyond stupid—but I kept telling myself that if it wasn't benefitting me, it wasn't really that bad." I meet his gaze then quickly look away, my cheeks burning. "The first time I got caught, I thought the world had ended. I managed to talk my way out of it with an apology and offering to buy the necklace plus a bunch of other stuff. That worked once more, but, as they say, the third time was the charm."

"They pressed charges?"

"Oh, yes. There was no getting out of that one. I spent a couple hours in jail before my dad bailed me out, and I kind of wished I could stay there." For a second I'm back on the Swiss slopes, but instead of Pierre, Xavier is next to me. And instead of skiing, I'm snowboarding. I wonder what Dad would think of that.

"And that's how you ended up on the Chain Gang."

I nod. "Trash duty was not my first choice, but I have to say, it's been better than I expected." I wink at him. "Except for the whole picking up trash part."

He smiles, and guilt hammers away at me. Yeah, I told him about my arrest, but he shared so much more. After a minute, he leans into me so our shoulders are touching. "I don't feel like you're telling me the whole story."

I close my eyes. What does it say about me that I'm okay sharing about breaking the law and getting arrested, but not the details of how I've lived my life?

"Brianna, it's not gonna make me like you any less."

"You say that now."

"Try me."

Our eyes meet, then I drop my gaze to the snow below. A path cuts through the deep powder—two pairs of skis and a couple snowboards. It'd be so easy to run away. "I'm not, how shall I put this, the nicest person in the world." I peek at him out of the corner of my eye. His head is facing forward but he's watching me like he's afraid any sudden movements might spook me. "Status has always been important in my family. My parents belong to all the right clubs, drive the right cars, know the right people. I just assumed that when I got to middle school, I'd be the most popular girl in school."

"Nothing wrong with having a goal."

I can't tell if he's teasing. "It was more than just a goal. It became my mission. I recruited two other girls as my best friends—Mikayla and Kenzie—and we terrorized our way to popularity. We threw the best parties, wore the best clothes, and hung out with the right boys." I cringe at that last part. He may not know my concerns about how he'd never fit into my world, but he'll figure it out soon enough. The question will be whether he still thinks I'm worth seeing when he knows the truth.

"Anyone who got in our way regretted it. By the time high school started, I was the queen of the school."

"I didn't realize I was with royalty." His voice is low, like he's uncertain he should say anything.

I face him. "I've done things I'm not proud of. It started falling apart last spring when a new girl moved to our school. I invited her into our group but she wanted nothing to do with me, then she stole my best friend and let's just say I didn't react the best. Remember how I said I was suspended for fighting?"

His eyebrow quirks.

"Junior year was supposed to be the best year yet, but Kenzie ousted me as the head of our group. Then I lost Homecoming Queen, and my parents." I shake my head. "Getting busted was just the icing on the cake."

He runs his hands over the guard rail. "It sounds like you've had a pretty shitty year."

"Yeah, but I feel like I deserve it."

"Because you were popular?"

Past tense. "It's more than that. I've been really mean to people." *Slow down Bri. No need to convince him what a bitch you are.* I choose to skip over my history with Blake. "Terrible things fly out of my mouth. You saw what happened with that guy Jordan. It's like lashing out at people is the only way I know how to react when I feel cornered or upset."

"That doesn't make you a bad person."

"It doesn't make me a good one."

"So stealing was like an outlet for you. A way to burn off energy."

"Something like that." Does he hate me already? From what he's told me, the only reason he'd steal is for survival, not to satiate some rich-girl urge for excitement. "I got a rush leaving the store knowing I'd pulled one over on someone."

"Have you—" he pauses.

"What?"

"Have you stolen anything since you were arrested?"

"It's never even crossed my mind. Of course, my dad announced that he was leaving us that same day and now we have to sell the house, plus I was grounded, so aside from boarding, I haven't really been out."

He gives me a sly look. "Do I need to keep an eye on you in the pro shop?"

I swat his arm. "Funny."

He holds up his hands and shrugs. "I'm not sure what level of criminal I'm dealing with here. If it's just for the rush, who knows what you'll do to get it."

My mind leaps from shoplifting to other, more exciting ways to feel that overwhelming sense of toeing the line between being in control and completely losing it. "I have a couple ideas." Lucky for me we're reaching the top of the chairlift, ending my confessional.

He raises the guardrail. "Do any of them involve snowboarding?"

The corner of my mouth lifts. "A few."

He mutters something in Spanish and my pulse races. "You got this on your own?" he asks. The ramp is ten feet away and it's time to shift back into trying-not-to-kill-myself mode.

"We'll find out." My board touches the snow and I stand, feeling unsteady. It's like telling him my secrets zapped my energy. I follow him to a clear area and drop to my butt to strap into my board, when he leans over and kisses my cheek.

"Thanks for telling me your secrets."

I thrill at his words, at his trust, but deep down I know there's so much more I hope he never finds out. "It feels stupid compared to what you went through."

"I wouldn't wish that on anyone. At least with you, no one got hurt."

Not physically.

My smile is tight. "You ready?"

He takes off first, cutting across the snow on his front edge, looking so natural that I can't imagine him anywhere else. I try to copy his movements, pushing my balance forward so I'm on my front edge, but I lean too far and slam face-first into the snow.

"Shit!" I scream into the snow, not caring who can hear me. Snow's packed along the inside edge of my helmet and when I push up onto my knees, it falls inside my jacket. "Ugh!" I shout again. I fling my goggles to the ground and yank off my helmet, then brush snow off my face. Snow is now melting against my chest, so I unzip my jacket and shake out my sweater, but it's already wet.

Laughter behind me makes me pause.

"Listen, I'm not in the mood right now," I growl, and immediately regret it. He doesn't deserve to meet Old Brianna.

Xavier grabs my goggles and nods at my helmet, then plops down next to me and shoots me a mischievous grin. "What happened here?"

"Face-plant."

He scoots closer and touches my cheek with his glove. "Looks like it hurt."

It's a good thing I have abnormally strong control over my facial features because my insides are melting. "A little."

He lifts his feet so his board is resting on mine, trapping me, and our legs are touching. But instead of wanting to run, I want to pull him even closer. He slips his hand behind my neck and I fall into him. His arms wrap around me, holding me against his chest while his mouth covers mine. I push his goggles off his face and brush my lips over his impossibly dark lashes.

"Girls would kill for these," I say.

He snorts. "I'm sorry?"

"Your eyelashes. They're insane."

He flutters his lashes, his laughter rumbling beneath me. "Benefits of my fine Mexican heritage."

"You're Mexican?" It sounds stupid as soon as I say it.

"What did you think I was?"

I plant my hands on either side of his head and look him directly in the eye. "I hadn't really thought about it. I guessed you were Hispanic since you obviously speak Spanish."

"My parents came over when they were our age. Lily and I are both Americans, just like you." His smile fades as he stares back at me, and suddenly our proximity feels invasive.

I roll to one side, but his board is still pinning mine and I end up twisting my knee. Pain shoots through my leg but I don't react. "I didn't mean anything like that."

He lifts his board so I can move and I shift so I'm sitting next to him.

"I hope you don't think that matters to me."

He looks anywhere but at me—his board, his lap, the trees around us—and takes a deep breath. The silence between us becomes an ocean of doubt. I've never had a filter and I've never cared, but the one time I honestly didn't intend anything hurtful, I've somehow upset him.

"Xavier, please look at me."

He does, and my heart pounds. "Sometimes I think that's all people see when they look at me. My mom tells me to be proud of who I am, but then guys like those douches on the Chain Gang assume shit about me because of what I look like and I guess I have a hard time remembering that not everyone is like that."

"Well, I'm not." Never mind that I totally judged him on his appearance the first time I saw him—but it wasn't because of his race. His tattoos and piercings, sure, but those are things he chooses to project to the world. Not the color of his skin. "So," I say, running a gloved finger over his chest. "Are we gonna board, or what?"

A smile spreads over his face and fills me with lightness. "I want to take you out, like on a real date."

I press my hand flat against his chest, relieved I've passed whatever test he put me through. "Oh, yeah?"

He nods, and gives me a quick kiss. "Yeah."

"I'd like that." He kisses me again, but I pull away before it can get too heated. "I figure since I've got this board strapped to my feet, I may as well use it." I roll away and pop to my feet like I know what I'm doing, then we spend the next several hours working on my technique.

By the time we turn in my equipment my legs are shaking and my butt is sore, but I'm happy. I'm actually happy. When Xavier kisses me at my car, my legs almost buckle beneath me. It's the first time we've kissed without a helmet or goggles or gloves and the feel of his skin under my fingers is intoxicating. My knuckles graze the tiny hoops in each ear, then trail down his neck to the tattoo that peeks from the collar of his shirt. I break the kiss to brush my lips over his throat, ending at the black ink. I've never kissed a boy with tattoos—at least not like this—and I want to see more. I tug at the soft material, exposing his collarbone and an intricate design that spreads over his chest. Heat flares in my belly as he dips his head to capture my lips with his once again.

Too soon he pulls away, tucking his cheek against mine. "How's Friday?" he asks, his breath warm on my ear.

"Too far away." My eyes are closed but I feel his smile against my cheek.

"There's still the Chain Gang."

I look up at him and flutter my eyelashes. "I'm the luckiest girl in the whole wide world."

This time he laughs, and he tickles under my arm, making me squeal. "I'll talk to you soon, querida." He kisses my cheek, next to my eye, then my forehead. "Text me when you get home, okay?"

My heart's pounding. "Okay." For as much as I've always prided myself on getting whatever I want, I've never had a boy ask me that. Maybe they assumed I could take care of myself and would get home safely, or maybe they didn't care, but he's looking at me like I'm the only thing in his world. I kiss him once more, get in my car, and shut the door. He presses his hand against the window, then steps back so I can leave.

Driving home, I feel like I'm floating above the car, lost in the memory of his kisses and the way he looked at me when I left. Is this what it's like to have someone trust you? Because while I've confided in friends before, it was always in the back of my mind that they could use what I've told them against me. But I don't get that feeling with Xavier. He's as loyal as they come and I believe everything he says—and he's trusting that I'm being honest with him, too.

And I'm terrified that I'm going to destroy that trust.

I may not be able to change what I've done in the past, but I can try to fix it. Or make amends. Or something. Mike will eventually come around—at least I'm pretty sure she doesn't hate me—but Blake and Cally will be more challenging. For good reason. Cally got my full wrath not long after she moved here and Blake... well, Blake has every reason to despise me. They may not be willing to give me a chance, but I have to try.

And it's not just because I'm scared of what they'll say to Xavier. I really am tired of everyone hating me. I used to think having control over people gave me power, but really, they're the ones with the power. They're living their lives and the only time they think of me is when we cross paths at school. I'm not sure how I screwed this up so badly, but I'm ready for a change.

seventeen

I get my first chance sooner than I expect. Cally and Blake are cuddling and being nauseatingly adorable at his locker before Homeroom, but instead of ignoring them or rolling my eyes like I normally would, I smile. And the word "hey" somehow comes out of my mouth.

They pause mid-giggle, mouths open, and stare at me.

"Are you lost?" Cally asks, her tone sharp.

"Or high?" Blake asks.

I shrug. "Just saying hello." They keep staring, and I take a step forward before I lose my nerve. "Hey, I was hoping I could—"

"Stroke your ego by insulting us?" Blake's normally relaxed face hardens and his blue eyes pierce through me. "Hard pass."

My heart races. Is this how I make people feel? "Never mind," I whisper before melting into the sea of bodies heading to class. The faces around me blur and I force a deep breath. Years of damage won't be undone that easily, but I have to start somewhere.

In History I smile at Mike, but Kenzie can bite me. There's no way in hell I'm being nice to her. But I don't need to worry because she's so wrapped up in whatever New Snow Bunny business she's manufacturing that she barely gives me a dirty look. Part of me is curious about the hot pink notebook she's scribbling in—it's definitely not History notes—but I refuse to give her any more of my attention.

When the bell rings, Mike waits at the door, then falls in step with me to Ethics. "How are things?" she asks. "With your parents. And..." she trails off.

I haven't told anyone I'm doing community service so she shouldn't know, but maybe word has gotten out. "Mom listed the house last week and I've barely talked to my dad. So aside from the fact that he's no longer sleeping under the same roof, things with him are about the same as usual." It's the most I've said about them splitting up and it feels good to get it off my chest. But I check myself before saying too much. I trust Mike not to gossip about me—she never told anyone when she caught me crying in the hall earlier this year—but we're so far past confiding in each other that I'm not sure we'll ever find our way back.

But it'd be nice to tell someone about Xavier and how nervous I am that all the nasty things I've done will ruin things between us.

"That sucks," she says.

"Dad promised to take me to Europe if I finish community ser—" *Shit.* I stop mid-sentence but her mouth's already hanging open.

"You're doing community service?"

I jerk my head so my hair falls in my face. "Something l ike that."

"What do you have to do?"

"You don't want to know." I toss my hair back over my shoulder, a hint of my domineering self resurfacing. "I'd appreciate it if you don't tell anyone."

She smiles, but it's not the catty smile I taught her. It's sweet, almost sympathetic. "Who would I tell?"

"I don't know. Your BFF. Her boyfriend." I hesitate to mention Mike's boyfriend because, A) I don't know his name, and B) I've never met him and it feels wrong to drag him into this conversation.

"No offense, but they don't exactly care what's going on with you."

My toe catches on the smooth linoleum and I stumble. Mike grabs my arm and we stop facing each other, her hand still on my arm. Heat rushes to my cheeks.

"I don't mean to be harsh," she says, "but you made it pretty clear you want nothing to do with them. You can't expect them to suddenly care just because you've had a change of heart." She holds my gaze, her eyes soft. She's not trying to be hurtful, she's just telling the truth. "Is that what's going on?"

I don't know how to answer her. How do I explain that Xavier has me second-guessing everything I thought I stood for? Although of all my former friends, Mike's the most likely to understand. "I don't know."

The bell rings and kids scatter to their classes. We're still a couple classrooms away so we take off running, and for a moment we're twelve again, late for class because we were spying on older boys. But the spell breaks when we step into Ethics and Miss Simpson gives us both a disapproving look. The word SACRIFICE is written on the whiteboard, and she doesn't waste time launching into her lecture.

I'm still thinking about the lesson when I arrive at community service the next day. About how people have different levels of sacrifice that they consider worthwhile. Like I think I'm noble for serving meals to homeless people on Thanksgiving, but Xavier thinks nothing of sacrificing his future to protect his sister's honor.

Yeah, he's wormed his way so deeply into my thoughts that he's intruding on homework. And I might be a little excited to see him. We've texted since snowboarding, but even his sexy Spanish comments—thank goodness for Google Translate—don't compare to being close enough to touch him.

Drea's smoking when I walk up to the bus. I'm surprised at how relieved I am to see her, and that she seems to be in one piece. Xavier's reaction and story about his sister had me thinking Colton had beat her senseless. Which is silly, because she looks like she always does.

"Hey, stranger," I say, leaning against the wall next to her. "I was beginning to think you'd bailed on us."

She smiles around her cigarette. "You can't keep me away from this hellhole." Her eyes flick past my shoulder and her smile broadens. "Incoming."

Seconds later, strong arms wrap around my waist and Xavier nuzzles his face against my neck. I slip my fingers through his and turn my face to kiss his cheek.

"Love on the Chain Gang," Drea says. "Never ceases to amaze me."

Xavier moves to my side, one arm holding me against him. He's wearing a heavy barn jacket but it's considerably thinner than his snowboarding gear and his body feels good against mine.

"I guess I don't need to ask how snowboarding went."

For once, no smart-ass comment flies out of my mouth. Maybe I really am turning over a new leaf.

"She's getting good," Xavier says.

"Good might be an exaggeration. But I'm breaking my face less and less."

Drea's smile falters for a heartbeat, so quickly I almost miss it.

Xavier tenses next to me. He saw it too.

I squeeze his side to let him know I noticed it, but keep my gaze on Drea. "You doing okay? We missed you."

She takes a final drag of her cigarette before putting it out on the brick wall and tossing the butt in a nearby garbage can. "I missed you, too. Come on, the Goodship Lollipop awaits." We follow her onto the bus. Heidi's waiting for her in the back row and Xavier slides into my regular seat next to me.

"Something's going on," he whispers.

"What should I do?"

"Do you two talk much outside of this?"

I shake my head. "We text a little, but nothing crazy."

"But you like her? And you want to help?"

I nod.

"Maybe ask her to hang out. If it's what I think it is, she's not gonna trust you that easy."

My head falls against his shoulder. Gaining someone's trust is new territory for me. She doesn't know my history, but I feel like there's a giant FRAUD sign blinking over my head, warning people that I'm not to be trusted.

Bruno climbs onto the bus and flashes us a smile. "You kids miss me?"

"Yes!" we shout in unison.

He chuckles to himself and starts the bus. "You know the drill. Remain seated until we stop. No smoking on the bus. No funny business."

"I didn't realize how tolerable he makes this," I say.

"Bruno's good people. He's seen some shit in his day, but he's mostly a teddy bear now."

"Listen up, I got an announcement," Bruno yells into the rearview mirror. The chatter around us quiets. "Thursday's the last two-hour shift. Next week is the final tour of the Goodship Lollipop. Gettin' too dark to have you on the side of the highway. There'll still be weekend slots with more hours, but you'll have to check with the county for other options."

Everyone starts talking at once. My stomach drops. "This is ending?" I ask. How am I supposed to finish my hours in time?

As much as I dreaded trash duty at first, it's become the best part of my week. Which is completely pathetic and so bizarre I'm questioning my sanity, but there you have it.

I text Dad, but leave out Bruno's news. *2 hours = 17.*

Trees and buildings fly past the window as we move down the highway, and I can feel Switzerland slipping through my fingers.

"Check with the court for other options," Xavier says. "At least it'll be inside."

But will it be with you?

"Hey, listen!" Bruno says. "If you can't get enough of me, I'll be helping at the men's shelter in downtown Denver. But ladies, you'll have to wait until spring to see this mug again." He winks in the mirror, pressing pause on my anxiety, then it's back in full force. "I'm also leading a crew at a park this weekend. Last big cleanup of the season. Three hours, meet at the same place at ten AM. Let me know today if you plan on being there."

I pull out my phone and enter the date in my calendar. Those three hours will make up for the next week, but I'm still over thirty hours from finishing. "Can you go this weekend?"

"Probably." He smiles. "That'll be it for me."

"What it?"

"My hours. I only need seven more so with this week and Saturday, I'm done."

My heart sinks even further. "You're done?" I force a smile. "That's great!"

"How many more do you have?"

"Too many." And if I can't find a new service right away, I can kiss Switzerland goodbye.

The rest of the afternoon goes quickly, but I can't stop thinking about Bruno's announcement. Even kisses from Xavier next to my car don't stop the knot of worry that's looping through my mind. *What am I going to do?*

On Thursday, Xavier sits with me again but I'm already promised to Drea. "Hos before bros," I tell him, and he kisses my cheek.

"No worries," he says. "Sarah's been giving me crap for abandoning her."

Is she jealous? I figured they were just friends, but maybe she likes him too. I peek at her over the back of our seat, but she's staring out the window with her headphones on.

He lifts my hand and brushes his lips over my knuckles, erasing my worries. "Plus we have tomorrow."

I smile. "And Saturday."

"And more boarding?" he asks, eyebrows raised. He's still holding my hand and I relax into him, ready to promise him whatever he wants as long as he keeps looking at me like I'm the most fascinating person in the world.

"I think you've converted me."

He smiles, and we stay like that until Bruno parks on the side of yet another highway, then he heads in one direction with Sarah and I lead Drea to a promising row of bushes. Promising because plastic bags and bits of paper are caught in the branches and it'll take the full two hours to untangle it all.

"Did you know trash duty was ending?" I ask her.

"I wondered, but I figured it'd get cut short because of snow. It's weird we've barely had any."

I stab a cardboard coffee cup but it gets caught on a branch. "As long as the slopes have snow, I don't care about the rest of Boulder." I give the cup another yank and a branch smacks me in the face.

"Consider that a sacrifice to the coffee gods," Drea says. "So do you know what you're going to do?"

"No idea. But Bruno mentioned the men's shelter and that got me thinking."

She smirks. "I don't think women are allowed. Especially not underage."

Grabbing the coffee cup, I roll my eyes at her. "A women's shelter. Serving food on Thanksgiving made me realize that a lot of the people who need help are just like us. I'd love to be able to help them in some way. Plus, it's gotta be better than this, right?" I look up at her from my crouched position and my breath catches. Her face has gone pale and the easy smile from before is a distant memory. "What?" I straighten and grab her arm, and she flinches. "Drea, what'd I say?"

She shakes me off and moves toward a fast food bag. "Nothing. It's not you."

I repeat my words in my head. Something triggered her. "Then what is it?"

She smiles at me but her eyes are brimming with tears. "We all have our bullshit, right? I guess mine's just bothering me more today than usual."

It's on the tip of my tongue to ask if it's her boyfriend but I don't know if we're good enough friends for that. But if it is him and no one else is asking, what's going to happen to her? "Do you want to meet for coffee sometime?" I wave the discarded cup at her and I'm rewarded with a pitiful laugh.

"Next week's a short week, right?"

I nod.

"Sure."

After that she shifts the conversation back to me—something I'm realizing she's better at than I gave her credit for—and by the end of our shift she knows every detail of how Xavier kisses and what I'm expecting from our date. She gives him a knowing wink when we get back on the bus.

"What was that about?" he murmurs in my ear, sending a chill down my back.

"I'm worried about her," I whisper back. "But we're hanging out next week so hopefully I'll find out what's going on."

"Do you think she'll tell you?"

"I don't know." I rub my cheek against his. "But I have to do something."

eighteen

The majority of my wardrobe is flung across my bed, including a couple scarves that got caught in the canopy. Drea's texted me a couple times to wish me good luck on my date, but she was no help with my outfit. For a hot second I consider texting Mike, but that will require explaining Xavier and how we met, and as much as I can't stop thinking about him, I still haven't figured out how he fits in my day-to-day life. This date will be the first time he's seen the real me, at least the me I try to project: no gross trash-collecting clothes or bulky snowboarding gear.

I settle on skinny jeans, a sheer top over a cami, and heels that'll make me tall enough to look him straight in the eye. My hair is down with just enough curl to look natural, and I went heavy on the eye makeup, leaving the rest of my face neutral. You should always pick one feature to emphasize, and my eyes are my favorite—plus there's no sense wearing a ton of lipstick with what I have planned for him later.

The alarm on my phone dings, warning me that he'll be here in ten minutes. When he offered to pick me up I considered telling him I'd meet him at the restaurant, but he wants the place to be a surprise and there really wasn't a good reason to tell him no unless I dropped the truth-bomb that my mom would freak if she saw his car—let alone him—in her driveway.

I grab my purse and a distressed canvas jacket and hurry down the stairs before she sees me. When headlights appear in the driveway, I open the front door and shout up the stairs. "I'm going out. Don't wait up!" Then I step outside and hesitate on the sidewalk.

Xavier's standing in front of Subie, a bouquet of yellow flowers in one hand and the other hand pressed to his heart. We stare at each other like neither of us is sure what to say. My heart's pounding so loud it practically echoes off the brick path. I walk toward him and he holds out the flowers while pulling me to his chest.

"Hi." I lean into him, kissing the edge of his jaw and breathing in the scent of his body wash.

"Hey." He pulls back to look at me, his dark eyes shining in the light from the porch. "You look amazing." He's wearing dark jeans, a navy button-down shirt, and a look that says if we don't get in the car now, we might never make it to dinner.

"So do you." I turn to get in the car but he catches my hand.

"Do I need to meet your mom or anything?"

The house looms behind me. The longer we stand here, the more likely Mom will look outside and see us. See him. "Nah, she's finishing up some work. We're good."

He moves around me to the passenger side and tugs on the duct-taped door. "I know this isn't as fancy as your 4Runner, but I love her and she's never let me down."

I smile up at him as I get in. "If you love her, then I do too." *Just keep that up and you'll be fine*, I tell myself. The interior is clean and well taken care of—nothing like I expected—and when he closes my door it's like I'm tucked into a cocoon. *Just pretend the door is fine.* Besides it's dark out so it's barely noticeable.

Xavier gets in and when he starts the car, salsa music blares from the speakers. He quickly turns it down, and the fast-paced notes filling the air match my racing heart. Instead of backing out of the driveway, he shifts to face me. "Do you like Mexican?"

I give him a slow once over, finishing with my sauciest look of approval. "Obviously."

He smiles, his long lashes lowering, and I swear he's blushing. "For dinner."

"Sure, that sounds great." Boulder is foodie heaven and I've been to a couple of the Mexican restaurants downtown, but I'm hardly a connoisseur.

"Perfect. There's a place not far from downtown that has the best enchiladas in the state. My mom says they're just like she used to get back home."

So not downtown, but I get a little thrill at seeing a glimpse inside his world. Old Brianna would turn up her nose at anything less than a high-end restaurant, but I'm realizing that it's what's beneath the surface that counts. "Where in Mexico is she from?"

"A fishing town on the Pacific called Zihuatanejo. She grew up on the ocean and has a hard time being away from the water, but aside from that she loves it here." His whole body relaxes when he talks about her and I find myself wondering about this woman who sacrificed everything she knew for a life here.

"Have you ever been there?"

"Just once, when I was a kid. It's gorgeous—palm trees and sandy beaches and cobblestone roads—all the stuff you see in pictures. Her family lives in the foothills of the mountains."

"Why would she ever leave someplace like that?"

He shrugs, like I should already know the answer. "It's hard to get by if you're not in the upper class. When she met my dad he already had his visa to come here, so they got married fast and she came with him. They put together a good enough life here, but I think she'd love to move back someday."

For as much as I've traveled, I've lived in the same town— the same house—my entire life. "I can't imagine just picking up and moving to another country. That had to be hard."

"Dad's got some cousins here so we're not completely without family, but we haven't seen them as much since he left."

I reach for his hand in the dark. "I'm sorry."

"It is what it is." He squeezes my hand. "But it's why I try so hard to keep Lily out of trouble. We're all we've got."

A pang of jealousy catches me by surprise. To have someone be that dedicated to you, to be willing to do anything for your happiness, is something I've never known. "She's lucky to have you for a brother."

He laughs, but shakes his head. "Try telling her that."

We fall into a comfortable silence. When he pulls into a parking lot next to a two-story house, I look around, confused. "I thought we were going to a restaurant."

He nods at the house. "This is it. They started off serving food in the front of the house like a lot of places do back in Zihua, and eventually turned the entire first floor into a restaurant."

"I can't believe I've never heard of this place."

"It's not online, so they aren't on the review sites or anything like that. Javi says he does this 'cause he loves cooking."

Imagine doing something simply for the joy of doing it, not for money or recognition or because you want people to admire you—all the traits I've learned from my father.

"Wait there." He gets out of the car and runs around to my side to open the door for me.

"You didn't have to do that," I say, getting out and brushing another kiss on his cheek, unable to stop touching him.

He dips his head and I swear he's blushing again. "Actually, I did. Until I fix the door, it can only be opened from the outside." He takes my hand and leads me across the full parking lot, which looks like it used to be grass until they added gravel, up the steps to the porch.

"So you know the owner?"

"He's from the next state over in Mexico. Our families go way back."

I break out in a sweat, but my smile conceals my nervousness. This isn't just dinner, this is meeting people that are practically family. "Cool."

We step inside and are hit with the intoxicating aromas of spices and roasted chicken. Tables are tucked into every available space, covered in worn cotton cloths and flanked with mismatched chairs. Several customers glance at us before returning to their meals. The walls display art that I'm guessing comes from Mexico, vibrant colors depicting farms and sunsets and white lilies. Looking around, the lilies are everywhere. Crawling up the backs of chairs, wrapped around the host stand near the front door, and printed on the back of the menu.

"What's with the lilies?" Only when I say it out loud do I make the connection. "Your sister."

A guy our age with hair as black as Xavier's but shorter and spikier greets us. "Xavi, man. Good to see you!" He pronounces his shortened name like it starts with an H. Like Havi. He slaps Xavier on the back and they do that guy handshake hug thing before they both look at me.

"Fer, this is Brianna. Brianna, this is my brother from another mother, Fernando."

I start to smile when Fer lets out a low whistle. "Damn, bro. You're stepping up." Normally I'd be all over the attention, but when several heads turn our way, their curious stares aren't what I'd call friendly. As I stare back, I'm struck by the fact that I've never felt so white in my life.

Xavier pushes Fer in the shoulder. "You got my table?"

"Your table?" I murmur.

Fer does an exaggerated bow. "This way, sir. Y mamacita."

Xavier swats him again and slips his arm through mine. "Calla lilies are really popular near where my mom and Javi grew up. A lot of the decorations and stuff in here are from there. And yes, my sister was named after them."

We sit at a table tucked in the far corner, away from the judgmental looks from the other customers. "Does everyone here know each other?"

He glances around. A couple people wave at him, and he nods back. "Not everyone. But I usually know one or two people when I'm here."

A curtain on the far wall opens and a girl who's the opposite of me in every way saunters toward us. Long dark curly hair, curves in all the places I don't have them, and a smile that lights up when she sees Xavier. "Xavi," she purrs when she gets to the table. He half stands and they touch cheeks, each kissing the other.

"Gladys, this is Brianna."

She holds her hand out to me and I take it uncertainly. Am I supposed to kiss her cheek too?

"Mucho gusto," she says, then turns her focus back to Xavier. "Papa said you were coming. I haven't seen you in forever." She drags out the word forever into a whine that sets my teeth on edge.

"I've been busy." His tone is friendly enough, but his shoulders tense and his hands clench together on the table.

She sticks out her lower lip, then cocks her hip and smiles. "You know what you want to drink?"

"I'll just have water," I say.

"Jarita for me."

"Naranja?" she asks. He nods, and I bite back irritation at not knowing what she said.

Once she's gone, I force a smile. "She seems nice."

He sighs. "She's a pain in my ass. For years our parents thought it'd be perfect if we got married and Gladys bought into it. But she's like a sister to me." He shudders, and the knot in my stomach loosens.

"I'm glad to hear it."

He leans forward and hooks a finger through mine, resting our hands in the middle of the table. "Was this a bad idea? I wanted you to have the best Mexican food in town, but I didn't think about having them on our date." He jerks his head toward the kitchen, where Gladys is talking to Fer, her hands waving as fast as her lips are moving.

"No, I'm glad you brought me here. It's like seeing a new part of the town I've lived in my entire life." I mean it as a compliment, but my words hang between us, a giant flag reminding us how very different our worlds are. I open my menu and read it like I'm studying for a test. "So what's good here?"

"Everything."

I raise an eyebrow at him. "Not helpful."

"The seafood is amazing. So are the enchiladas, the sopas... oh, and the molé is the best you'll ever have." He points at an item on the menu. It's in Spanish but I know pollo is chicken. I must give him a blank look because he keeps talking. "Molé is a spicy chocolate sauce that'll make you cry it's so good."

"Chocolate on chicken?"

"Trust me."

I close my menu. "Done."

He stacks our menus and smiles softly. "I gotta say, it's nice seeing you without a helmet or a garbage bag."

"Likewise. Although you do look pretty fierce in your snowboarding gear." He looks fierce in everything, including the plain shirt and jeans he's wearing tonight.

His eyes crinkle as he smiles, but he pulls away and leans back in his chair.

"Here you go." Gladys sets our drinks in front of us. "You ready to order?" She looks expectantly at me, her hand resting on her hip.

"I'll have the molé," I say, hoping I pronounced it right.

"Gambas con ajillo for me."

She presses her hand to her chest, and I swear she's unbuttoned a button since she took our drink order. "You're not having the molé? But that's your favorite."

Does everything she says come out as a whine? No wonder he's not interested in her. I'd claw my ears off having to listen to that all night.

He smiles at me. "I'm sure Brianna will let me have a bite. I want her to try your dad's shrimp."

She makes a tsk-ing sound. "Okay, but I'm not responsible if he gets mad." He hands her the menus and she saunters away, her hips swinging so hard that every man in the room turns to stare.

Except Xavier.

"She can be a bit... dramatic."

"Hmm." A thousand insults flip through my mind but no matter how annoying she is, she's his friend. Or at least the family's friend. "So what are you going to do with all your free time when you finish community service?"

His gaze flicks over my shoulder before settling back on me. "I might try to pick up a few shifts here. Get some money to fix my car. Lily promised to help pay for it, but that's about as likely to happen as my dad coming back." His face grows hard as he speaks.

"I'm sorry."

He drags his hand over his face. "No, I'm sorry. I shouldn't have brought that up, especially with you..." he trails off.

Because my dad left, too. I'm officially a statistic. But at least I know where my dad is. "I didn't tell you the worst part." He cocks his head and I take a breath. I wasn't planning on talking about this but he's shared so much and invited me into his world, I need to give a little back. "My dad didn't just leave. He announced he's got another family. Like a girlfriend and a daughter." Bile rises in my throat admitting his betrayal out loud.

Xavier reaches for my hand. "That's messed up. And you and your mom had no idea?"

I shake my head, my eyes burning with tears. I dab the corner of my eye with my sleeve, making my fury burn hotter. My father doesn't deserve my tears. "She's seven, so it's been going on practically half my life."

He squeezes my hand. "I don't know what to say."

"You don't have to say anything. I just wanted you to know."

He seems to consider this. "Have you met her? The daughter."

I shake my head again. "It's crazy that I have this half-sister out there who I never knew existed. I'm curious what she's like, if she's anything like me, but then I feel guilty for even thinking about her and push the whole thing out of my head."

"Sometimes that's the easiest way to deal with things." His thumb moves over the back of my hand, rubbing small circles against my skin.

If I focus on Xavier, on the sensation of him touching me, I can forget about my father and his other life and how he's destroyed everything I know. "Can we talk about something else? Like what else do you do for fun when you're not snowboarding?"

He tells me about his friends and how they play soccer any chance they get, and has me laughing so hard that by the time Gladys arrives with our food, I've forgotten about my father and The Seconds. She sets his plate of grilled shrimp and rice in front of him, then sets a plate with a huge piece of chicken and rice covered with a thick brown sauce in front of me.

"Oh my god, this looks amazing."

She smiles, the first genuine smile she's given me. "Papa will be happy you like it." She turns her attention back to Xavier. "Xavi, let me know if you need anything else." The suggestion in her voice leaves nothing to the imagination, but he brushes her off.

"We're good. Thanks, Gladys."

Once she's gone back to her brothel or kitchen or whatever, I pick up my knife and fork and stare at my plate. "When you said chocolate sauce I wasn't picturing this." I cut a piece of chicken, drench it in the sauce, then take a bite. The molé has a sweet, smokey, spicy flavor that wraps around the chicken and overwhelms my taste buds. "How do they get so many flavors in there?"

A smile spreads over his face. "Javi is magic." He rolls his sleeves to his elbows, revealing more of his tattoo, and it's a good thing I'm sitting down because I nearly fall over. No wonder Gladys loses her shit whenever she's near him. I'm surprised she hasn't poisoned my food.

"You should have ordered your own, 'cause I'm not sharing." His eyes go wide and I burst out laughing. "Okay, maybe a bite or two." I look at his plate. A pile of grilled jumbo shrimp sits in a pool of buttery garlic and little red flakes. "You said their seafood is good but I didn't realize that's what you ordered."

"Zihua is a fishing village so they know the best way to cook it. Javi has to pay a little more to get it fresh in the middle of Colorado, but it's so worth it." He cuts a piece and dredges it through the sauce, then holds his fork out for me.

I pause, not sure if I should take the fork or open my mouth. His eyes dip from mine to my mouth, and he bites the edge of his lip. Mouth it is. I part my lips and lean forward, and he meets me halfway. I take the bite and can't help but close my eyes and let out a soft moan. Butter and garlic and a different kind of spice fill my mouth, contrasting with the molé. "How? How can that be so good?"

"I told you. Magic."

As I'm cutting another piece of chicken, an older man in a white button-down shirt, gray pants, and white apron approaches the table. He sets a bowl with a folded napkin inside on the edge of the table and smiles at us.

"Javi!" Xavier says, jumping up from the table. They do the same handshake bro-hug thing he did with Fer, but they also kiss each other on the cheek. They turn to me, smiles on both their faces.

"And who is this lovely lady?" His accent is stronger than his kids'.

"I'm Brianna." I start to stand and he waves me back into my seat.

"No, no. You sit and eat. How do you like the molé?"

"It's amazing."

"She threatened not to share," Xavier says.

"You should have ordered your own," he says, winking at me. I laugh. "That's what I told him."

He faces Xavier. "How is your mother? And Lily? We haven't seen her in here for too long."

Xavier's jaw tightens for a second. "They're good. I'll give them your love." If Javi doesn't know about Lily, it doesn't look like he's going to find out now.

"Xavi, you sit with this young lady and maybe I'll find an extra piece of molé for you." He rests his hand on Xavier's shoulder and gives him a smile that's so loving it confirms these families are more than just friends from back home. They're family.

"Thanks, Javi."

He gives me a warm smile. "It's a pleasure to meet you. I hope we'll see more of you around here."

"I hope so, too." The words come out automatically, but I mean them. Aside from Gladys and her overactive hips, this place is so warm and welcoming that I never want to leave. Javi heads back to the kitchen, stopping at each table to chat with customers. "He's so nice."

"He took it really hard when my dad left. They'd been best friends forever and he stepped in, helping around the house, that sort of thing."

"Is that why they call you Xavi?"

He laughs softly. "Yeah. When I was a kid I made sure everyone knew it was Xavi with an X, not a J. But they've always pronounced it like his." He picks up the bowl Javi brought and unfolds the napkin. Steam billows out. "You ever have fresh tortillas?"

I rest my forearms against the edge of the table. "At this point, let's just assume that all of this is new for me."

He removes a yellow tortilla the size of his hand, but instead of scooping his food into it like a taco, he rips it in half, then again. Holding the piece of tortilla between his thumb and fingers, he uses it to grab a piece of shrimp and some rice and shoves the whole thing in his mouth. He chews slowly, his eyes closing as he swallows, and I decide Xavier enjoying his food the most sensual thing I've ever seen. He opens his eyes and hands me a piece. "You try."

I take the tortilla and stare at my hunk of chicken. "Am I allowed to cut it first?" He nods, and after a minute I've decimated the chicken into bite-sized pieces. "Here goes nothing." I pick up a piece of chicken with my tortilla hand.

"Be sure to get the sauce." He's watching me intently, but I don't feel scrutinized. It's like when he's teaching me to snowboard. There's no judgment—he's eager for me to do well.

I drag the chicken through the sauce and pop it in my mouth, and it tastes even better. The tortilla has a subtle corn flavor that mingles with the chocolate and I think I've died and gone to heaven. After I swallow, I give him a serious look. "How do you not weigh three hundred pounds? This is so good."

He pats his belly and my gaze lingers on his stomach. "I work out. And I don't eat this every day. We usually only get fresh tortillas for our big meal on Sunday."

"I would be a blimp."

"I'm really glad you like it."

We dig into our food and eat so many tortillas that Gladys has to bring another bowl, which he assures me is normal. When we finish, I'm so full I feel like he'll need to roll me outside. Xavier leads me to the host stand where Fer is waiting with a smart-ass smile.

"What're you kids up to now?" he asks.

Xavier and I glance at each other. "I'm still thinking about that molé," I say, dodging the question. We didn't talk about what comes after dinner. I hope he wants to stay out—or find a secluded place to park.

He must see something in my expression because his gaze grows heated, his eyes settling on my lips, and he takes a shallow breath. "I dunno man," he says without looking at Fer. "But it doesn't include you."

Fer clutches his chest like he's been shot. "That hurts."

Xavier hands him the check and a couple bills, then they do the back-slappy hug thing before Fer turns to me. He holds out his arm like he's going to hug me, so I step in and he kisses my cheek. His lips don't actually touch me—just a light brush of his cheek against mine—so I do the same.

"Pleasure to meet you," he says. "Now you kids have fun."

Xavier shoves his shoulder before opening the door for me. The cold air is like a slap in the face and I pull the top of my jacket tight against my neck. "So...." I say.

"Do you want to go downtown?" he asks.

"That sounds great." But before I can take a step, he slides his hand behind my neck, burying his fingers in my hair, and kisses me. His lips move softly against mine and I lean into him, breathing him in. My hands wander over his back, settling on his hips, and I gently pull him closer. His lips part and I follow his lead, and when our tongues touch I nearly lose my mind. He tastes like garlic and the sweetness from his soda and while I've never imagined wanting that combination, I can't get enough. He backs me up until I'm pressed against the side of the building, and a loud pounding on the window makes us jump apart.

"Órale, hombre!" Fer's standing in the window with a huge smile and both thumbs up.

I duck my head so my hair falls in my face, but Xavier grabs my hand and leads me to the parking lot. "Sorry about Fer," he says as he yanks my door open. "But I've been wanting to do that for the past hour."

Instead of getting in the car, I reach up and kiss him. "Me too."

He rests one hand on the top of the car and the other on the open door, and leans into me. "You okay with going downtown?" His voice is husky and from the look on his face he'd be okay going someplace much more private. But as much as I'm drawn to him, the annoying little voice in my head insists that I don't jump in with both feet. At least not yet.

"Yeah. We could get coffee or ice cream or something."

His eyebrows quirk at the "or something," and I touch his chest. We stay like that for several moments, staring at each other like we're the only people in the world, and the voice in my head grows quiet. So what if his bank account is a fraction of the other boys I've dated and he doesn't fit the squeaky clean image they try so hard to maintain. He's the sweetest, most thoughtful, and loyal boy I've ever met. Or that I've let get close enough to find out.

And that has to mean something.

nineteen

Sometimes I wish life didn't keep leading back to the Pearl Street Mall, with its constant reminders of my arrest and how badly I screwed up.

Xavier parks a block over and we stroll the pedestrian mall hand in hand. The sidewalks are filled with other people, young and old, doing the same thing, and I'm content to blend in with the crowd. Before, I'd encourage Austin to make a grand gesture so others would look at us—jump on one of the bronze statues or pick me up and spin me around like we're in a fricking movie—but I no longer feel the need to announce my happiness. Having Xavier's hand in mine, his arm pressed against me, is enough.

A blond girl about seven or eight years old skips ahead of us as her mom window shops, and I stumble.

Xavier tightens his grip on my hand. "You okay?"

I stare at the girl, who's oblivious to the people around her as she dances around a bench. Her blond hair is the same length as mine—not that that means anything—and her blue eyes sparkle in the light shining from the storefronts. "Yeah. I must have tripped or something."

He steps between me and the girl, and I look up at him. "Your face is pale. What happened?"

The mother fetches the girl and they enter a toy store.

"Brianna."

I like that he uses my full name. I've never minded the shortened Bri, but my name sounds different in his mouth. The R rolls a little and the As have a softer sound, like ahh, instead of the nasally way everyone else says it.

He touches my cheek. "Talk to me."

The girl and her mother are gone, but I close my eyes against the memory. "It's stupid. There was a little girl and she looked enough like me that I wondered if she could be my sister. Which made me wonder if her mom is my dad's new girlfriend or whatever he's calling her. And then I went down a wormhole wondering if I've been in the same place as them before."

He looks over his shoulder, and he's frowning when he faces me again.

"They're gone now," I say.

"That must really suck. The not knowing."

I shrug. "It's so new I don't really know what to think. Part of me wants to meet her, but it's not like we'll ever be close like you and Lily, so what's the point?"

"Meet her and see what happens."

"Just call my dad and tell him I want to come over?"

He rubs his hand up and down my arm. "If you want to meet her, you might have to be the one to make the effort. He might think you want nothing to do with them."

"You're probably right." This whole time I've put the responsibility on Dad—I mean, he is the one who caused all this—and assumed that since he left, any future contact would be initiated by him. I'm still pissed he just walked out of our lives, but knowing I have a sister out there—correction. Not out there. In the same fricking town—makes me willing to look past all that.

We stop in front of a coffee shop but my usual latte sounds boring after that flavor-fest of a meal. "Are you okay with ice cream?" It's so cold out I can see my breath, but I don't care.

He takes my hand. "Sure."

Just then, something inside the coffee shop catches my eye. The tables are packed with the after-dinner crowd so I'm not sure how I even saw her, but Miss Simpson is sitting at a table in the center of the room, sipping from a ceramic cup. Teachers are obviously allowed to have a life outside of school, but that's not what makes me pause.

She's on a date.

The guy's face is blocked by someone putting on their coat, but from the way her eyes light up when she smiles, she seems really into him. She laughs and reaches across the table for his hand just as Coat Guy moves and my eyes widen.

She's on a date with the owner of Calliope Brewery, one of Mischief's competitors. He's a good looking guy and part of me is like Go Miss Simpson, but that's not what's got me itching to pull out my phone and snap a pic and announce her date on social media.

The guy is Cally's dad.

Gossip was my lifeblood for so long that I can't stop the excitement that pulses through me. The ways I can use this to my advantage are endless, starting with simply embarrassing Cally and ending with spreading rumors that she's only passed Miss Simpson's classes because her dad is sleeping with the teacher. Never mind that it probably isn't true. Having people hang on my every word, their eyes widening as I feed them more lies, is addictive. And I've gone without a fix for too long.

My hand, the one Xavier's not holding, caresses my phone in my pocket. It'd be so easy. Even without a picture, I could have the entire school talking about this before the end of our date.

But with a picture...

It's like I'm caught on the edge of good and evil, balancing what I know is right with what will make me feel powerful, even if it's short-lived.

Before I can second-guess myself, I swipe the screen to open the camera. Xavier's not looking, and it only takes a second to aim my phone at the window, capture their date for all the school to see, and tuck my phone back into my pocket.

His thumb trails over the back of my hand, snapping me out of my gossip-fueled euphoria. The adrenaline that had my senses humming half a second ago ends abruptly.

I don't want to be that person anymore.

But it's too late.

"What is it?" Xavier asks.

How would he react if he knew what I just did? Or that he's making me want to change? "I saw one of my teachers. Weirded me out, you know?" I force an innocent smile, one that masks the nasty thoughts that raced through my mind.

"You sure that's it? You seemed, I don't know, like you were someplace else." His brows lower like he's trying to figure me out, but I'm a pro at hiding my thoughts.

"Nope. I don't want to be anywhere but here, with you." This time my smile is real, and the softness in his smile makes my pulse race—for good reasons this time.

We continue along the mall to the ice cream shop, and once we get our cones, I push the photo out of my mind. We settle into a table near the window and two bites in, I realize my mistake. Watching the concentration on his face as he eats—no, licks—an ice cream cone is a slow torture, and the heat that's building inside me is enough to melt my ice cream before I have a chance to eat it.

He catches me ogling him and pauses. A drop of mint chocolate chip clings to his upper lip and it takes all my willpower not to climb over the table and lick it off. "Why aren't you eating yours?" he asks, oblivious to the effect he's having on me.

"Just thinking." I lick around the edge of the cone—plain chocolate chip for me—and almost choke when I swallow. The same heat I felt a moment ago is plain in his eyes, and now his cone is the one that's melting.

"Maybe this wasn't the best idea." His voice is low. Under the table, his foot bumps mine and I press my leg against his. A blush creeps up my cheeks.

"That's pretty much what I was thinking."

He shakes his head, a smile playing on his lips. "Ay, querida, lo que me haces."

I don't know what the second part means, but I've figured out that querida means lover or love or something similar, and from the way he's looking at me, I'm guessing the rest of what he said is good.

My ice cream is legitimately melting, but now I'm so self-conscious about eating it that I can't move. Old Brianna would tease him, making my cone as seductive as possible, but now those games seem childish. And pointless.

Because I don't think I need to convince him of anything.

I finally smile. "Okay, I need to eat this before it melts but I can't do it with you looking at me."

He bursts out laughing and criss-crosses his finger over his chest. "Promise."

We dig in, each catching the other watching through lowered lashes. When I get to the end of my cone, I shove it in my mouth with a flourish and pump my arms over my head like I finished a race. He does the same and we're laughing so hard I don't care that my mouth is full or that people at the other tables are staring at us. Getting through that cone was rough.

"You ready?" he asks after we've calmed down. I nod, and he leads me outside and toward his car in silence. He pries the door open for me and I climb in, barely noticing the ridiculous door. What makes this boy so special that I want to change for him? Before, I wouldn't be caught within breathing distance of this car, and now I can't wait for him to be in here with me.

He gets in, starts the car, and faces me, and the desire is so strong it's like a physical pull. We crash into each other, lips on lips, hands in each other's hair, no room for breathing or thinking or anything but feeling. His mouth slides over my jaw to my neck, and settles at the sensitive spot beneath my ear. I exhale, but it comes out a soft moan, and his arms tighten around me. He pulls back to look in my eyes and time seems to stand still. We barely know each other, yet I feel like I know everything I need to. His heart, his determination to keep those he cares about safe, and the way he makes me want to be a better person.

I turn his head and my lips find the tiny hoop in his ear. The hard metal is cool against my tongue and his breath hitches as I run my lips over his skin. Then our mouths connect, and I lose myself in him.

Voices drift through the closed windows and he ends the kiss, resting his cheek against mine. We're both breathing heavily and neither of us seems willing to let go, but when I finally open my eyes, I laugh. The windows are completely fogged up.

The voices outside the car turn to laughter and I hide my face against his neck. "Guess it's pretty obvious what we're doing."

"Is it?" he asks against my hair. His voice is serious, not light or teasing.

My heart pounds with the realization of what he's asking. Or suggesting. Or am I imagining this?

"What are we doing?" he whispers, his mouth moving against my ear.

I've never been one to profess my feelings. If I'm spending time with a boy, I like him. If I don't, I don't. Telling a boy that I like him, or worse, that I love him, is something I've never done. But I've also never had a boy make me feel the way he does. I take a breath and even though he can't see my face, I close my eyes. "I like you," I whisper back.

I can feel his smile against my cheek. "I like you, too."

"I'm not—" I pause. "I'm not very good at this."

His lips find my neck and I tilt my head back. "You seem pretty good to me."

My fingers twist in his hair as he kisses my collarbone. "The talking about it part." Keeping my eyes closed makes it easier. The kisses don't hurt either. "I don't know what I'm supposed to say."

His head pulls away. He brushes the back of his fingers along my temple and I open my eyes, then quickly close them again. His face is inches from mine and the emotion in his eyes is too much. "Look at me," he whispers.

I do, and it feels like I'm exposing all my secrets. Like he can see into my soul and know the worst parts of me, every terrible thing I've said or done or thought.

He holds my gaze, then kisses me lightly. "There's no pressure, and I'm not making a declaration. I just want to know if we're on the same page."

"Does your page include more of this?" I kiss the tender skin next to his eye and his lashes close.

"Mm-hmm." He leans into my caress. "I know I don't have the right to ask, but I'm not a player and if I'm kissing one girl, I'm not kissing anyone else." He opens his eyes but his gaze drops from mine. "I just wanna make sure you're not doing this with other guys."

I can't stop the smile that spreads over my face. He's not asking me to be his girlfriend—which, honestly, I'm not sure if I'm ready for—but it's the next best thing. "You are the only boy I've kissed in months."

His shoulders relax beneath my arms and he matches my smile. "Good to know." He kisses me again, but it's soft and gentle and unhurried. When it starts to get heated, he breaks the kiss. "I should probably get you home."

Mom's always been flexible on my curfew but I'm not about to suggest we go park someplace, so I nod.

As we get closer to my street, reality crashes around me. No matter how amazing Xavier is, he can't park this car in my driveway. Not when Mom might be watching for me.

"Do you mind parking on the street? I don't want my mom to come out." I'm so focused on her not seeing his car that I don't realize how that sounded until it's too late.

The corner of his mouth lifts and he gives me a heated once over. "Oh yeah?" He does as I ask and leaves the car running.

I swat his arm. "That's not what I meant. But," I unfasten my seatbelt and shift closer to him. "Since we're here." I reach for him, my hands running through his hair, pulling him toward me. His lips meet mine and I melt into him, feeling more content in his arms, parked in this beat-up Subaru, than I have in a very long time.

After more kissing, we say goodbye until tomorrow morning and I hurry up the long driveway to the house. Maybe this can work after all.

And maybe he'll never have to know how horrible I've been.

twenty

When I pull into the community service parking lot the next morning, a bright yellow school bus idles where the Goodship Lollipop usually sits. Drea's already here—I'm impressed that she's early even on a weekend—but Subie is nowhere to be seen. I make my way over to her and she puts her cigarette out on the side of the building.

"Morning," she says, toeing the sidewalk with her purple Chuck. "How'd last night go?"

I haven't stopped thinking about Xavier since he dropped me off. Everything I learn about him makes me like him even more, and the fact that he's an amazing kisser is like icing on the proverbial cake. As for the picture, I didn't delete it, but I didn't share it either.

She laughs. "Girl, you've got it bad."

My eyes widen. "I didn't say anything!"

"You didn't have to. The look on your face says it all."

"He's dreamy." I flutter my eyelashes, making her laugh again.

"I'm happy for you." She lifts the hand still holding the cigarette, then looks at it like she's surprised it's no longer burning. For a moment she just stares at it, and I get an uneasy feeling.

"Drea, are you okay?"

She blinks before focusing on me. "Yeah, sorry. Just got a lot on my mind."

"Do you want to talk about it?" I ask, but before she can

answer, a sleek Benz parks in front of us and a man and woman get out, mid-argument.

"I'm telling you, this is the place," she says, glaring at the guy. Her auburn hair is held back with a cloth headband that matches her leggings, and her manicured hand grips a venti cup from Starbucks.

He glares back, or at least I assume he's glaring behind his expensive aviator sunglasses. "Can we not this early in the morning?" He slams the door and notices us for the first time. "This is the park clean-up group, right?"

We nod, eyebrows raised.

The woman rolls her eyes. "I just told you that."

His jaw clenches. "Fine. You were right. Happy now?"

Her scowl relaxes and she smiles as she moves around the car to stand next to him. "This will be fun."

While part of me isn't sure what the hell is going on, the other part wants to bow to her bitchitude. "Why are they here?" I whisper to Drea.

"To brighten our day?" She shakes her head as the woman hooks her arm through the man's and they walk toward the bus. "I honestly have no idea."

As we wait, other people we've never seen arrive, and soon the bus is half full. I scan the parking lot but Xavier still hasn't arrived. I could text him, but if he's driving he wouldn't be able to reply anyway. "Should we get our seats?"

"I guess."

We turn to walk toward the bus when Bruno comes out of the building.

"Oh, thank god," Drea says. "Bruno, what the fresh hell is all this?"

He chuckles, a deep sound that rumbles in his chest. "You all never been to a Saturday clean-up?" We shake our heads. "Well, this'll be a treat. Lot of people come who need community service hours for their jobs. Most of them just get in the way, but it's usually a fun morning."

I still refuse to call picking up trash fun, but a change of pace can't be a bad thing. We follow him onto the bus. The front seat has three boxes of the lovely pinnies and most of the Weekend Crew is sitting in the front half of the bus. Drea and I make our way to the back, but I pause before sitting with her.

"We don't have to sit together," she says, and I hate how transparent I am.

"I'll just save him a seat." I unzip my jacket and toss it on the seat across from us, then settle in next to her and wrap my arms around myself to keep warm. "Do you know where we're going?"

She shakes her head. "Not a clue. Gotta be big though with all these people."

I text Dad. *Weekend fun. 3 hours = 22.*

I can practically smell the crisp Swiss mountain air.

As more people fill the bus, the anxiety I feel every week when it's almost time to go and Xavier still hasn't arrived starts to creep in. *He won't miss this*, I reassure myself.

Drea nudges me. "What's got you down all of a sudden?"

With all my worries about her and her boyfriend, I'd almost forgotten what drew me to her in the first place. She really is a sweet person. "If Xavier shows, he'll finish his hours today."

"And with the Chain Gang coming to an end, you're worried about starting over with a new group."

I raise an eyebrow. "Am I that obvious?"

"Yes and no. I've been thinking the same thing. The shelter doesn't really appeal to me, and I'm not sure what else sounds good. I liked being outside, you know?"

I nod. I want to push the shelter angle with her, but she giggles near my ear.

"Your boyfriend's here."

"He's not my boyfriend." *Yet.*

"Maybe not, but you want him to be." She clutches her hands to her chest. "I love new love."

A giggle escapes me and I hesitate for a moment before pressing my forehead to her shoulder, fighting the impulse to overthink my every movement. "Please don't embarrass me." I've spent so many years trying to control what people think about me that I never let myself just live in the moment.

Drea rests her head against mine, clearly not thinking anything of my affection. "Never."

"Am I interrupting something here?" Xavier's voice makes us both jump, and we dissolve into giggles like fricking precious cinnamon rolls. He smiles at Drea, then me, and in a flash my insides turn to mush and I wish I hadn't sat with her.

"We saved you a seat." I grab my jacket and stand to put it on, and he closes the space between us.

One arm slips behind my back while the other cradles my cheek, and from the look in his eyes I think he's going to lay one on me right here. His lips press against mine, soft and warm and minty, but are gone far too quickly. "Thanks," he says.

Drea's got a smirk on her face that makes me blush.

"Not a word," I say as I sit back down.

"Oh, I've got far more than just one word." She shifts in her seat so her back is to the side of the bus. "Morning, Xavier. Have a good night?"

He gives me a questioning look and I shrug. "It was pretty good, yeah." The corner of his mouth quirks, his eyes roaming my body, and I play with the zipper on my jacket. I'm not inexperienced when it comes to guys but one look from him makes me feel things that I've only dreamed about.

"Morning, everyone!" Bruno's deep voice booms from the front of the bus. "Thanks for coming out. We've got a good crowd here today so that park will be clean in no time."

The adults cheer, and Drea and I burst out laughing.

Bruno holds up a clipboard. "Just a couple things to go over. Be sure to sign in before you get off the bus. Pinnies are in the boxes on the front seat. I know they're god-awful but they help me keep track of you and they help you stay visible. Other than that, please remain seated until we stop and no smoking on the bus." He doesn't say anything about funny business, and I can't help it, I peek at Xavier out of the corner of my eye.

He must have noticed it too because he's watching me with a devilish grin. I swat his arm across the aisle and he catches my hand, bringing it to his lips.

"Girl, you are in trouble," Drea whispers.

"I know," I whisper back. He holds onto my hand, and they dangle in the open space between our seats for everyone to see. But my concern about us is starting to fade. So what if we look like we come from opposite worlds? I may have more money, but he's by far a better person, and that has to balance things out.

The clipboard works its way to the back of the bus, and Xavier releases my hand to sign in. When he hands it to me, I glance at the top of the sheet and it's like everything freezes. Blood roars in my ears, drowning out the chatter around us. My hand grips the clipboard so hard I start shaking and my vision blurs with tears.

No.

We can't be going there.

The words at the top of the page swim but I already know what they say. I scribble my name and address on the line below Xavier's and it registers that I should memorize his address and look up where he lives, but the thought flits in and out of my brain. I'm too focused on the name of the park.

I hand the clipboard to Drea, who doesn't seem to notice that I'm freaking out.

"Damn, you didn't tell me you're a rich girl." Her voice is teasing, but her smile falls when she looks at me. "I'm just kidding. I don't care where you live."

I shake my head, and she touches my arm.

"Seriously. Couldn't give two shits."

"I—I know." My eyes follow the clipboard as she hands it to the person in front of us.

She watches me for another beat before settling against the side of the bus and staring out the window.

But I can't relax. I've avoided this park for over four years, ever since the horrible moment that changed my life. I've refused to let myself think about it, even in the darkest parts of the night when I can't stop the memories from overwhelming me, and now we're going there.

For three hours.

With the two people I never want to find out about that day.

twenty-one

By the time we arrive, I'm shaking. Drea, Xavier, and I are the last ones off the bus, and I grip the back of each seat to steady myself as we near the exit.

Xavier touches my back when we step into the bright sunshine. "What's wrong?"

"Forgot to eat breakfast and now I'm a little shaky." It's a weak lie but the only thing I can think of. After so many years, I cannot believe I'm here.

"I don't think I've ever forgotten a meal," Drea says. "Xavier, you must have really showed her a good time last night."

My mouth falls open and Xavier smiles, but neither of us say anything.

She smirks. "That's what I thought."

Xavier wraps his arm around my back, pulling me close to his side. "Do you want me to find you something to eat? There's probably a vending machine or something around here."

I shake my head. "I'll be okay." I do not deserve someone so sweet.

We wait near the bus while Bruno explains to the Weekend Crew how to pick up trash with a stick, then he heads our way. "You three are the only ones from the weekday group, so how about you stick together?" We nod and he points to the equipment. "You know the drill. You've got more freedom today so be back in three hours and please return with trash in your bags." He gives a knowing look to me and Xavier. "And no funny business."

I smile and press my hand to my chest, pretending to be shocked. Which isn't much of a stretch right now. "Bruno, I thought you knew me better than that."

He roars with laughter. "Girly, I know you're a teenager and you got eyes for this one. That's all I need to know."

Drea bursts out laughing and I can't help but join her. "I promise to make good use of my time," I say.

Bruno walks away and Xavier nuzzles my neck. "This should be fun."

I may be a Broadway-level performer, but pretending to have fun here might be my biggest challenge yet. We walk along a paved path that winds through trees stretching high into the sky. Most of the Weekend Crew is already combing the underbrush for trash, so we walk until their voices fade away.

And keep walking.

The trail grows steeper and the ground at the edge drops off. A brick wall wide enough to walk on separates us from the steep drop-off and Xavier jumps on it.

Drea and I both shout.

"Wait!"

"Get down!"

He peers into the ravine before turning around, arms spread out wide. "What? The view's amazing." He kicks at the wall. "This thing isn't going anywhere." He gestures for me to join him. "Come up here with me."

"Be careful," Drea says.

But I can't move. This isn't the exact spot where it happened—it was another quarter mile up the trail—but everything's rushing back to me. Cody's scream, Blake jumping over the edge after him, the ambulance that carried them away.

The horrible things I said at the hospital.

Xavier steps off the wall but I still can't breathe. "Hey, what's wrong?" He lifts his hand to my face and I lean into his caress, wanting to feel anything but the guilt that's overpowering my senses.

"A little boy died here," Drea says, snapping me out of my daze. She's staring farther up the trail, closer to where Cody fell.

Shock slams into me. *How can she know?*

"He was friends with my cousin. He was walking on this wall and fell."

Xavier goes still. "Cody McMillan?"

We're both startled, but he's looking at Drea and doesn't see my reaction. "How do you know that?" she asks.

"I've known his brother, Blake, half my life."

My breath stops.

"Wow," she says. "That's terrible. Siblings aren't supposed to die." She stares into the trees and the memory of Blake's horrified shouts mix with the image of Xavier defending his sister's honor and I don't know how much longer I can pretend to be okay.

Xavier takes my hand and squeezes. "Blake was with him when it happened. Tried to save him but it was too late." He looks into my eyes. "I can't even imagine what that must have been like."

Awful. It was awful. The only reason Cody fell is because I made Blake walk slower so I could kiss him. The moment I pressed my lips to his, Cody screamed and our lives changed forever. Xavier's still watching me and I realize I haven't spoken since he stepped off the wall. "It's horrible."

"It gets worse," he says. "This girl was with them when it happened and she blamed it all on Blake. Even though it was an accident."

And just like that, my world implodes. Being snowboarding friends is one thing, but if Blake and Xavier know each other well enough that Xavier knows about Cody, then it's only a matter of time before he pieces everything together and wants nothing to do with me.

"What?" Drea shouts. "What kind of person does that?"

This girl.

He rubs his thumb over the back of my hand and I feel like I'm going to be sick. They can't know this. How does he know? "Blake just calls her the Snow Bitch. I guess they were friends, but after that day she turned into an evil monster."

"So his brother dies and this crazy chick blames him and—" she stops. "I don't get people."

"Me neither," Xavier says. He tucks my hand against his chest, lost in thought, and despite his grip on me, it feels like everything is slipping away. Soon he'll connect the dots and he'll be gone from my life.

Drea's pacing along the low wall, shaking her head. "How do you—" she pauses to look at us, then stares out at the trees in the ravine.

She'll be gone too.

When I first met Drea and Xavier, I figured talking to them would help pass the time while I was stuck in community service, but they've quickly become the most important people in my life. And seeing the looks on their faces as they think about what I did—not knowing it was me—makes me regret every horrible thing I've ever said or done. I can't take it back, but I can vow to never be like that again. To try to be a good person.

But starting over is impossible. Everyone at school already hates me and I don't think I'm lucky enough to find two more people like Drea and Xavier.

"We should probably keep moving." Xavier lowers my hand and continues farther up the trail, closer to where Cody fell. When we reach the spot where Blake and I'd been standing, my knees give out. Xavier catches me before I fall, his arms hooked around my waist.

Drea rushes to my side. "Are you sure you're okay?"

I nod, but everything is blurry. *This is why I haven't come back here.* I blink away tears and stand upright. "I guess I'm hungrier than I thought."

Xavier dips his head so he's looking in my eyes. "Should we just hang out here?"

"No!" I lower my voice. "No, let's keep moving. I'll be okay." The last thing I want is to sit at the scene of the crime for the next hour.

They exchange puzzled looks but start walking. We don't find any trash until we're well past the spot where Blake jumped over the edge to save his brother. Where he lifted an unconscious Cody over the edge of the wall, both their bodies bloody. Where I stood, panicked and unable to do anything but cry, while Cody took his last breaths. After we called for help, there was nothing to do but wait and replay the day over and over. People gathered around us, trying to help the broken boy on the ground, but all I could think was that if Cody had stayed home, if it had been just me and Blake like I wanted, he wouldn't have gotten hurt.

Unfortunately it didn't come out that way in the hospital.

While we paced the hall waiting for his parents, I tried to comfort Blake, but he kept brushing me off. Looking back, I get it, but at the time I didn't know how to compartmentalize my emotions and I erupted. I told him that if his family had money, Cody would have been with his nanny instead of us and this never would have happened. The look on his face shamed me to my core, but it was too late. I couldn't suck the words back in, and we never spoke again. We started eighth grade hating each other, and shortly after that I declared myself head of the Snow Bunnies, Austin and his friends the Moguls, and Blake and his friends the Ski Bums.

Standing here now, at the epicenter of where my life first shattered, I can't help but wonder if it's too late to go back.

The next couple hours feel like they last forever. The only highlight is that Xavier can't seem to stop touching me, dropping little kisses and caresses whenever Drea isn't looking. And sometimes when she is. But each time his lips brush mine, my stomach twists tighter because each minute that ticks away brings us closer to the moment he discovers I'm Blake's Snow Bitch.

When we get back on the bus, I sink against Xavier's side, soaking in as much of him as I can. He wraps his arm around my shoulders, pulling me closer.

"You gonna tell me what's wrong?" he whispers into my hair.

I shake my head, blinking back fresh tears. "It's just been a long day."

He grips my shoulder and it feels like he's holding me together. I'm not sure how my life got turned so upside-down. It's like I'm having an out-of-body experience where I'm looking down at myself and wondering how everything led to this moment. To me and this boy who I never should have met, sitting on a bus at the park where I destroyed everything.

Back at the parking lot I say goodbye to Drea and she reminds me about coffee on Tuesday. My casual smile takes all my energy. The more time I spend with her, the sooner she'll find out the truth, but I don't cancel like I want to.

Edge Rule #8: Protect yourself so you don't get hurt.

Xavier leads me to my car and turns me so my back is against the driver door. He grips my shoulders lightly, concern heavy in his eyes. "Will you please tell me what's going on?"

I try to avoid his eyes but he cradles my cheek so I can't turn my head. Those damn tears burn again but this time I can't hide them.

"You're scaring me."

"It's just been a long day." I turn my head to kiss his palm, and he exhales.

"You sure that's it?" His brows furrow and I can't escape those dark eyes that seem to look into my soul. Except if he could see that far, he'd be running away as fast as he could.

"Yeah." I lean in and kiss the edge of his tattoo. "I promise."

He pulls me against his chest and we hold each other as the parking lot empties. So many things bubble to my lips—confessions, excuses, lies—but I don't say any of them.

"The Chain Gang isn't going to be the same without you."

"Hey." He pulls back to look at me. "This isn't goodbye."

Then why does it feel like it?

twenty-two

I pulled myself together enough to kiss Xavier goodbye. We promised to text this week and at the very least, go snowboarding next Saturday. It sucks that I may not see him for a whole week, but the odds of him figuring out that I'm the Snow Bitch before then are low, so at least I'll get to see him one more time. I just have to get through the week.

The photo of Miss Simpson and Cally's dad is still on my phone, but I've almost deleted it several times. The rush I felt when I took it has long passed, and now it just makes me feel dirty. To think I used to get off on this crap. If I'm trying to make amends with Cally and Blake, outing her dad will make that impossible.

After the lamest Saturday night in my existence—do other people do homework before Sunday night?—Dad called before I went to bed, demanding I come over for lunch. This means I won't get on the slopes at all this weekend, but the idea of meeting my half-sister pushes away any irritation. Now I'm sitting on my bed trying to put together an appropriate outfit to meet The Seconds.

The only thing keeping me calm is knowing that this other woman—Dad's girlfriend person—is probably even more nervous. It's a little surreal to think all my questions might be answered today. Even the ones I'd rather leave unknown.

Mom's at the kitchen island reading her tablet when I come downstairs. "Where are you off to?"

"Meeting friends for lunch," I lie. The lunch part may be true, but this will not be friendly.

"I'm glad. You've spent so much time in your room lately I've started to worry about you."

"Well, there was the whole grounding thing..." And my pathetic lack of a social life.

She waves her hand, dismissing my words without looking at me. "Right. Please be home for dinner. I'd like to catch up."

Isn't that what we're doing right now? For once I manage to catch my words before they fly out of my mouth. "Sure." I grab my keys from the counter and enter the address Dad gave me in my navigation system. His new neighborhood is older and the houses aren't as big as ours, but it's still nice. When I pull into the driveway of a brick two-story home with mature trees and a porch swing, everything stops.

My breath.

My pulse.

The only thing that speeds up are my thoughts, which are screaming to back out of the driveway and pretend I don't know this house exists. A curtain in the front window moves and I take a deep breath. It's too late to back out now. I turn off the car and head to the front door, drawing from the hurt and anger that's built up over the past months and bracing myself for whatever lies inside.

What I'm not expecting is the burst of energy that greets me.

"Hi!" A girl half my height with long blond hair, blue eyes, and fairy wings twirls inside the open doorway. "I'm Piper Douglas! You're Brianna Vines! Mom and Dad are in the kitchen!" Every sentence is punctuated with a punch in the air like she's holding a magic wand, and the last one feels like it shoots straight through me.

Mom and Dad.

But she doesn't have our last name.

"Hi." My voice lacks her enthusiasm, but I can't help but smile. She's my mini-me. My zest for life may have faltered over the years, but I used to spend hours dancing around the house and I remember how excited I'd get whenever someone would come to visit.

She clearly already knows about me, and from the smile on her face, has been looking forward to this moment. "Come on!" She holds out her hand, which I take, and leads me through the tastefully decorated, yet comfortable, living room and into the kitchen. My focus bounces from the white cabinets and marble counters that are eerily similar to ours, to Dad and—my mouth goes dry.

Before he left, I knew how to handle Dad in any situation. As long as I held my head high and kept my gaze steady, I could get through anything. But that was Before. Now there's a strange woman standing in my mother's place, clutching Dad's arm like a lifeline, and my years of training unravel around me.

What do I call this woman who could pass for my mother a decade earlier? Her blond hair is styled differently and her clothes aren't tailored, but she's beautiful. Despite her tight smile there's a calming aura around her. And there's a rock on a very important finger on her left hand.

Fiancée. She's his fiancée.

Piper bounces to her side and I realize this woman is as nervous as I am.

Dad clears his throat. "Brianna, this is—"

The Seconds. In the flesh.

"—Susan. And you met Piper."

Piper beams up at me, oblivious to the tension in the room. "He's your dad too, right?" I stumble back, but Piper keeps going. "I've never had a sister before! Do you want to play in my room?" She flits around the kitchen, waving her imaginary wand.

"Piper, we're going to visit a bit before lunch. Why don't you go wash up?" Susan's voice is soft yet commanding, and there's not a hint of the frustration or annoyance that I grew up with. Piper doesn't wince or roll her eyes—she simply twirls out of the room, leaving us alone. Susan steps forward and extends her hand. "It's lovely to meet you after all this time." She and Dad exchange a brief look but her smile doesn't falter. "I'm sorry it's under these circumstances."

I shake her hand—it's cool yet firm—and she doesn't shrink away from me or try to exert dominance. She simply welcomes me to her home. I get that detached feeling again, like I'm watching us from across the room. Watching Dad watch us. He shifts from one foot to the other, no doubt waiting for me to cause a scene, but while I have every right to hate this woman, something about her makes me want to curl up on the couch with one of the knit blankets. After several moments I find my voice. "Thanks for inviting me." I may not have had much choice in the matter but I know my manners, especially when Frank Vines is standing next to me.

"Would you like anything to drink? There's fresh water in the teapot, or I could make coffee."

"Water's fine."

She moves through the kitchen with an ease I don't feel, grabbing a glass from the cabinet and filling it with filtered water from the door in the fridge. When she sets it on the counter in front of me, the clink of glass on marble echoes through the otherwise silent room. I don't think Dad has moved since I got here. Susan gestures to a round table under the window overlooking the backyard, and I carry my glass to one of the wooden chairs.

Dad finally relaxes when he sits, but he lets Susan lead the conversation. She asks about school and my interests, and on the outside it's a perfectly normal afternoon, except this is my father's mistress! Or other woman! Or whatever you want to call her.

She lifts her coffee to take a drink and the diamond catches the sunlight.

"So when are you getting married?" I blurt, interrupting her.

"Oh!" She sets her cup down and her hand flutters to her chest, then, as if realizing that's the hand with the diamond, rests it in her lap.

Dad's eyes grow wide and he looks back and forth between us.

"We haven't announced it yet."

I'm starting to like her, despite my determination not to, but I can't stop the anger that surges through me and threatens to erupt all over the room. I glare at Dad. "Worried what people will think?" My voice is harsh, any sympathy I may have felt for them quickly evaporating.

"Brianna," he warns.

Susan's shocked expression is replaced with shame. She stares at her hands, no doubt at the ring that sparked my wrath.

"Perhaps you should have taken it off before I got here."

Her mouth falls open and she looks up at me, eyes brimming with tears.

I shake my head to clear it. He had to have warned her about me. But if I'm honest with myself, I'm not mad at her. Now that I can see what kind of person she is, all my anger is directed toward my father. "I'm sorry. As much as I should be, I'm not pissed at you. I'm mad at him."

Dad scowls at me, his gaze so menacing most people would shrink away. But I am my father's daughter. I match his gaze with equal fury.

"You've handled this very poorly." I lean closer. "I realize there's no good way to announce you have a secret family, but—" I stop. "You know what? Never mind. You have fun playing house with The Seconds. Maybe you can actually be a father this time around." The chair screeches as I push away from the table and I stalk out of the kitchen.

"Brianna!" Dad's voice echoes off the walls but I don't stop.

I'm almost to the front door when a small voice stops me. "You're leaving?" Piper's standing on the steps, her fairy wings replaced with a purple helmet, her lower lip sticking out the same way mine used to when I was little. She takes a step toward me, her hand on the railing. "I was gonna show you my room."

I glance toward the kitchen, but neither Susan nor my father is coming after me. Anger simmers in my chest, leaving no room for other emotions, but Piper takes another step toward me and holds out her hand. "Okay, but just for a minute." I slip my hand into hers and she grips mine in that unhesitating way only kids can. She leads me up the stairs to a small landing with four doors. Two are closed, one is the bathroom, and the fourth—where she brings me—is bursting with color. Pink and purple walls surround a canopy bed with more pink and purple pillows. The sheer fabric on the top is a light lavender, unlike my plain white, but it suits the room.

"I have a bed like this."

She stops in the center of her room and her eyes widen. "You do?"

"Yep." I smile, reaching up to run the fabric through my fingers. "But mine's white, like clouds."

"I really like pink and purple."

"I can tell."

She sinks to the gray carpet and stares up at me, the helmet both out of place and making perfect sense in this girly room.

I sit facing her, folding my legs so our knees are inches apart. "Do you like to ski?"

She giggles. "Skiing is boring! I snowboard." She points at a board sticking out of the open closet. It's a deeper purple than the décor in the room.

"I bet that looks cool on the snow."

She nods, her helmet bobbing. "It does. I can't do tricks yet but Mom says I can learn when I'm ten."

Based on her enthusiasm, I think they're going to have a hard time getting her to wait three more years. She jumps up to grab her board, then sits with it cradled in her lap. "Do you snowboard?"

I glance at the door before leaning close and lowering my voice. "Can you keep a secret?"

She nods again, a smile breaking over her face.

"I'm learning now. Dad thinks I only ski." My brain stumbles over the collective Dad and I'm hit again with the reality that this girl sitting in front of me is my sister.

"He tried to get me to ski but there's no way." The excitement in her eyes at the thought of being on the slopes reminds me of someone else: Cally.

That's it. She may be my flesh and blood but she's totally a mini-Cally.

"Have you been to Switzerland? Mom and I haven't. Dad says he's gonna take us for spring break and I can't wait!"

The amount of information thrown at me in two seconds makes my head spin. I'm glad he's never taken them to Switzerland. That was always our trip and knowing he went there with them would just add to the betrayal. "Yeah, I've been there. You'll love it."

"Can you come too? I can help you snowboard. It'll be so fun!"

I don't tell her about Dad's promise, but suddenly the thought of having to babysit her doesn't sound so bad. "Maybe. It's up to Dad."

She gives me a knowing look. "I'll work on him."

I burst out laughing. She's definitely my sister.

"So where do you live? Do you have a boyfriend or girlfriend? What do you want to be when you grow up?"

I lean back on my hands, still laughing. "One at a time! My house isn't too far from here, but we're moving soon and I don't know where. There's a boy I like, but he's not my boyfriend yet. And I have no idea." Spitting it all out at once makes it sound almost real.

She leans closer. "What's he like?"

My lip catches between my teeth. It's one thing to tell her about snowboarding, but I'm not ready to share all my secrets. "He's really cute. And he snowboards."

"Do you have a picture?"

My hand instinctively goes for my phone, even though we've never taken a selfie. "I don't. But I'll try to get one next time I see him."

She nods, eyes wide. "You should. Then come back and show me." Her smile is so trusting and innocent that I almost lie to keep it there. But based on how things went downstairs, I don't know if I'll be welcome anytime soon.

"I'll try."

Seeming satisfied, she jumps to her feet, dumping her snowboard on the floor between us. "Let's play Barbies!"

Was I ever this exuberant? "I can't today. I have to get going."

She stops in the middle of the room and it's like being in the eye of a hurricane. It's calm now, but you know the swirl of energy will be back any second. "But Mom said you're staying for lunch."

"I know but—"

She thumps onto her knees next to me, grabs my hand, and pets it. "Did Daddy say something to make you sad?"

So she's not completely oblivious to the tyrant. "A little."

"He's probably sorry. Don't go yet." Her blue eyes shine like she's on the verge of crying and my cold, brittle heart starts to melt.

"You get your way a lot around here, don't you?"

She blinks and the tears are gone, replaced by a mischievous smile. "Uh-huh."

Damn, they've got their work cut out for them with her.

She springs to her feet, still holding my hand, and tugs me to the door. "Come on. Lunch is probably ready." At the last minute she tosses her helmet onto the bed. "I'm not supposed to eat with it on."

We march downstairs and I can't help but flinch when we round the corner to the living room, but Dad and Susan are still in the kitchen. She's making sandwiches at the island while Dad arranges veggies on a platter. This domestic side of him is new to me. We've always had a housekeeper who handled menial tasks, or Mom did it, but apparently he's learned a thing or two from Susan.

My back is straight and my shoulders pushed back when I enter the room.

Susan looks up and smiles. "Oh good, you're still here."

She still wants me here after what I said? "Piper was very convincing."

As if on cue, Piper twirls around us, laughing and waving her arms, and I get the feeling she's orchestrated most of this.

Susan rubs Piper's head as she spins by. "Yes, she usually is."

We share a smile and guilt pricks me. I shouldn't feel bad for getting angry. My feelings are legit and lashing out is how I handle them. But Susan is so warm and seems like she already understands everything I'm thinking, that I wish I could take back my words.

When Dad carries the veggies to the dining room, Piper in tow, I step closer to Susan. "I'm sorry about earlier. I shouldn't have said that."

Her face crumples. "If we start playing the 'I shouldn't have' game, I'm definitely the loser here. Or winner. However you want to look at it."

The urge to hug her or comfort her is overwhelming, but I settle for resting my hand on the counter near hers. "I don't know how I'm supposed to act or what I'm supposed to say. This whole situation—"

"Is beyond messed up," she finishes for me. A smile lifts the corner of her mouth. "I can never make up for what I've done to your family. But you're Piper's sister, and that's important. Whatever feels comfortable for you is enough for me."

I'm touched by her words. Since Dad's announcement about The Seconds, I've imagined a jewel-draped temptress living in a penthouse apartment, laughing at Mom and me. But Susan is nice. Normal. Someone I can see myself wanting to know better. "Thank you."

She brushes crumbs from the counter into the sink and hands me the plate of sandwiches. "Can you bring these to the table?" She grabs a pitcher of lemonade from the fridge and follows me to the dining room, where Dad and Piper are already sitting.

"I'm glad you decided to stay," Dad says, and I almost drop the plate. He's never been grateful or thankful for anything in his life. Or at least he's never said it to me. But sitting at this table, flanked by The Seconds, he seems content. Not stiff or angry, like he'd rather be anyplace else.

A chill sweeps through me. All those years of excruciating dinners, he probably *was* wishing he could be someplace else.

Here.

And now I'm here with them. Which means Mom is completely alone.

I drape my napkin over my lap while I compose myself. I can excuse away being here, but betraying Mom feels worse than I imagined.

"There's turkey and ham," Susan says, pointing at the plate I carried in. "Let me know if there's anything else you need."

Sure, if you could flip my life upside down and shake it like a snow globe so everything would go back to normal, that'd be great. But I don't say that.

Her smile wavers and Dad reaches for her hand. They watch me, waiting for a response.

"This is great, thanks."

The rest of the meal goes smoothly, thanks to Piper and her never-ending energy. At one point Dad gets a bunch of texts but he simply glances at them before resting his phone face-down on the table. When it's time to leave, Susan gives me a hug. It's awkward, but I get the feeling there will be more in the future. Piper doesn't hold back. She flings herself at my waist, squeezing so tight my sandwich almost comes up. "I'm so glad you're my sister."

Unexpected tears burn my eyes as I hug her back. "I am, too."

Dad walks me to my car. He clears his throat and looks down at his feet for several moments, then clears it again. "I know this hasn't been easy. Thank you for coming. For Piper and Susan."

"But not you?" I can't help it.

He meets my eyes. "I deserve that, I know. Yes, for me too."

I didn't expect him to admit it. Maybe this new life really is better for him.

"Switzerland is still on the table." Always negotiating a deal.

"I'm on track to finish on time, but the Chain—the trash thing is ending so I have to find something else." Calling it the Chain Gang might ruin this borderline touchy-feely moment.

His brow furrows, the Dad I know returning. "It won't be a problem, will it?"

"Nope. I've got it under control." Which is a lie, but he doesn't need to know that.

"It would mean the world to Piper if you were there with us. And to Susan and me, too," he quickly adds.

A trip with him and The Seconds would be different from what I'm used to. There definitely wouldn't be any French boys, but having an adorable sister around wouldn't be so bad. "Thanks."

He waits in the driveway until I turn onto the next street and I wonder for the hundredth time who that man is and what he's done with my father.

The whole way home I'm itching to tell someone about The Seconds, but with one caveat: I'm not looking to tear them down. If I ignore the fact that they're Dad's other family, I can admit that they're really nice and I wouldn't mind seeing them again. Mike might tolerate a text from me, but I've yet to earn back my right to randomly text her. Xavier's the only one who knows about them, so I text him.

Met my dad's other family today.

Mom's not home when I get back, so I settle in with my homework until he replies.

How'd it go?

Better than expected.

That's good, right?

Yes and no. I have to choose my words carefully, find the right balance between normal feelings of hurt and betrayal and the diabolical way I usually react.

Why no?

I feel like I'm betraying my mom.

Does she know you went there?

Not yet. There's no sense trying to hide it from her. Miranda Vines has a Masters in Sleuthing. Well, most of the time.

A door closes downstairs, followed by the sound of keys being tossed on the marble counter.

Gotta go, Mom's home.

I miss you.

My heart does a little flip-flop. *You sure you can't come Tuesday?*

lol. Not a chance in hell.

I miss you too. Bye.

Adios querida.

I press my phone to my chest, imagining the look in his eyes when he says that and the way his lips part when he's about to kiss me. "Aye, dios mio," I mutter. "How did I let myself fall for him?"

"You up here?" Mom calls from the hall.

"In my room."

She appears in the doorway, all smooth linens and styled hair and the calmest expression I've seen on her face since Dad left.

"You look nice." Maybe if I butter her up she won't get as mad when she finds out where I was.

"Thank you. I had a massage, then a hair appointment. There's really nothing like a day of self-care to make you feel better." She glides across the room to my desk and sits in the chair, and she practically oozes relaxation. One leg crosses over the other and she drapes an arm over the back of the chair. "How was your afternoon?"

I don't mean to break eye contact. That's the first sign of lying or deception, and she knows it.

She straightens. "You may as well tell me."

The energy to lie seeps out of me. "I saw Dad."

Her shoulders droop a little. "Oh." Then like a switch, she's back to her strong self. "So he told you the news?"

"About Switzerland? I already knew that."

Her eyes narrow. "What about Switzerland?"

Oh crap, that wasn't her news. Apparently getting divorced means you no longer share details like traveling internationally with your daughter. I wave my hand like it's no big deal. "He offered to take me if I finish my community service hours by Christmas."

"Well that's very generous of him, considering how little he seems to care about his family."

Not his family, just this family. "That's not all." I don't want to tell her, but she's going to find out anyways so I may as well get it over with.

She quirks an eyebrow, waiting.

"I went to their house."

It takes a moment for what I'm admitting to sink in, for my betrayal to work its way through her body. She uncrosses her legs, her hand grips the back of the chair, and a mix of fury and hurt darken her face. "How lovely for you." Her voice lacks its usual bite, and I hate that I've hurt her.

"It wasn't lovely." I pick at my bedspread, avoiding her gaze. "It was lunch."

The silence stretches between us, but I'm not volunteering anything unless she asks.

Finally, she lowers her hand to her lap. "How is he?"

"He seemed, I don't know, calmer." *Don't say happier, don't say happier.*

"And what's she like? That woman?"

I bristle at her tone, but she has every right to hate Susan. I force a smile. "She's no you, that's for sure."

This seems to appease her. "And the child?"

My sister. "She reminds me of me at that age, but with way more energy."

"And you what, ate lunch and chit-chatted like old friends?"

"You know that's not how it was. Dad insisted I come. I didn't want to meet Sus—her, but I did want to meet my sister."

"Is this going to be a regular thing?"

I shake my head. "I don't know."

"Did you put her in her place for ruining our family?"

Instead of smiling at the memory of snapping at Susan, I feel ashamed. Susan feels guilty enough for what she's done. "No, Mom. I had lunch."

"You're hopeless." She turns to leave and I stop her.

"Wait, what was the news you were talking about?"

A self-satisfied grin creeps over her face. "We sold the house."

The news hits me like a bullet train to the chest. The idea of having to move versus actually having to pack up my entire life and go live someplace else are very, very different.

"I texted your father while you were playing house with them. Didn't he tell you?" Her eyes light up, like she's enjoying hurting me.

Is this where I get it from? The need to hurt others just to make myself feel good?

But she's not finished.

"I've signed the lease on a townhouse. We move in two weeks."

twenty-three

Every day I feel more and more like I'm living a lie and spending half my time trying to keep the truth from people. Walking through the halls at school with kids I've known my whole life, no one looks at me or says hello. They all have their assumptions about me—most of which I've put in their heads—but so much of it isn't true anymore. If I do manage to catch anyone's eye, they look away before I can smile. After Saturday, I realize I need to apologize to Blake, but realizing and doing are two separate things.

And it might be too late.

My mood grows darker when I arrive at community service. Xavier's never been there before me, but the anticipation of seeing him made it tolerable. Knowing he won't be here combines with the constant fear that we're barreling toward the day he finds out the truth about me, and I hate that this thing between us will end before it has a chance to really start.

Drea's waiting in her usual spot with a cigarette in her hand. "I know I'm no dreamy loverboy, but come on, at least pretend to be happy to see me."

"Am I that obvious?"

She pushes off the wall and drops the cigarette on the ground, putting it out with her shoe. "Nah, you're your usual gorgeous self. I just figured you'd be bummed he's not coming." She tosses the butt in the trash and we walk toward the bus. "Heidi's here, but maybe you can buddy up with us."

"Thanks."

She pauses on the sidewalk. "Is that all that's bothering you?" Her dark eyes search mine and a lump catches in my throat. This must be what it's like to have a real friend.

"Can it wait until coffee?"

"Sure thing."

She sits on the bus with Heidi while I take my regular seat. I stare out the window so no one else talks to me, so it startles me when someone sits next to me.

"You mind?" Sarah asks.

I shake my head.

"Xavier finished his hours this weekend?"

"Yeah. We did Bruno's park clean up, and let me tell you, the people there..." I trail off, rolling my eyes.

"That bad, huh?"

The couple in the Benz comes to mind but as I start to describe them, I realize I'm describing myself. "Can I ask you a question?"

She smiles. "Sure."

There's no doubt that Sarah will give me the truth, no holds barred, so I'm almost afraid to ask. "What did you think of me my first day?"

She exhales slowly and leans back in the seat. "You don't want to know."

There's good anticipation and bad anticipation, and this is definitely bad. But if I'm going to change, I need to know how to do it. "I do. I'm asking because I know you'll be honest."

"You asked." She cracks her neck and levels her gaze at me. "I thought you were a spoiled little rich girl who screwed up bad enough to land here, but I figured you'd find a way out of it after the first day."

I laugh softly. "Sounds about right."

She laughs too. "So if you already knew, why'd you ask?"

"I've always projected a certain image, but I'm realizing I don't want to go through life with people thinking I'm a raging bitch."

She cocks her head, considering my words. "I can respect that." Then she smiles. "You know, I lost a bet with Crue when you showed up the next shift."

"You bet on me?"

She shrugs. "You seemed like a sure thing. Now I know otherwise."

A burst of pride warms me. I didn't think I'd show up again either—especially before Switzerland was dangled in front of me—but I stuck it out. And if I can change her opinion of me, maybe there's hope at school.

There ends up being an even number of people today so Sarah and I buddy up. We keep the conversation light, but I learn that she wants to be a photographer and she's originally from New York. Back in my Snow Bunny heyday, I'd spend the whole hour talking about myself or gossiping about the other kids, but when the shift ends, I feel like I know her a little better, and I like it.

Drea and I pick a coffee shop nearby and I follow her there. The tidal wave of truth I started with Sarah surges inside me, and I'm ready to tell Drea everything. We pick a pair of overstuffed chairs near the window and settle in with our drinks—my usual vanilla latte and straight black coffee for her.

"How can you drink it black?" I ask. "Isn't it too bitter?"

"My dad drinks it this way and said if I was gonna drink coffee, I was gonna drink it the right way."

It's the first time she's ever mentioned her parents. "You never talk about them."

"My parents?" I nod, and she shrugs. "They're not around much. Travel a lot for work."

So if something is going on with Colton, they aren't around to notice.

"I guess drinking coffee like them is my way of bonding." She pushes her hair over her shoulder and eyes my cup warily. "How do you drink it with all that crap? It's too sweet for me."

I take a sip, letting the sweetness warm me from the inside. "I guess it's an acquired taste."

She holds out her cup. "To acquired tastes." We click our mugs together then lean back into our chairs.

If I'm going to make this friendship work, I can't keep lying to her, but I'm afraid if she knows too much about Old Brianna, she'll walk out of here and never talk to me again. So far she seems like she's not one to judge people, but everyone has a breaking point.

"You're quiet all of a sudden."

"There's something I've been wanting to tell you, but I'm not sure where to start."

She leans forward. "You're secretly in love with me?"

I burst out laughing, the anxiety that's gripping my chest lessening ever so slightly. "I was saving that for another day but now that you mention it..."

She raises an eyebrow and I laugh again.

"You're adorable, but not my type."

"Yeah, you're a little too girly for me, too." She sips her coffee and cradles the mug against her chest. "Whatever it is, just spit it out. I won't judge."

You say that now. I take a deep breath and close my eyes. "I've told you how I haven't always been the nicest person, right?"

"Yeah, so? We all do stupid shit."

I open my eyes. There's no judgment on her face, only curiosity. "Well, mine went beyond stupid shit. I told you why I got arrested, and that I've lost all my friends, but it's more complicated than that."

"Are you some secret warlord who tortures puppies in her spare time?"

My mouth lifts in a smile. "Some people probably think so."

The amusement on her face fades, but she doesn't say anything.

"I worked hard to make people respect me, to do whatever I say, but I've hurt a lot of people in the process. Getting arrested was like a slap in the face. I want to change, but it means apologizing to people, and some of them won't want to hear it." My thumb traces furious circles around my mug. Once I tell her what I did, there's no turning back. She'll either hear me out or never speak to me again. "And I feel like if we're going to be friends, you need to know the truth about me." About Old Brianna.

"And you swear you didn't kill anyone?" Her tone is light, but her gaze hasn't left mine.

"Not directly."

Her eyes widen and I immediately wish I could take it back.

"Not like that." I take a sip of latte and swallow too fast, burning the back of my throat. "You know the kid you were talking about at the park last weekend? The one who died?"

Her entire body stills. "Cody."

I nod.

"What do you have to do with him?" I don't think she's breathing.

I stare at my mug. "I was there when he fell." Tears burn my eyes, but I can't stop now. "I'm the evil bitch you and Xavier were talking about."

She lets out a long breath and looks around the room, and the intimate bubble that protected us from the outside world starts to crack. "How is that even possible?"

"Blake and I used to be friends. He had to watch Cody a lot so he went hiking with us that day." In a blink it's like I'm back on that trail, trying every trick my almost-eighth-grade mind knows to get Blake to hold my hand or put his arm around me. Cody's running up ahead on the wall at the edge of the trail and I choose that moment to make my move. "It's my fault he fell."

Drea sets her mug on the table and leans forward. "How? I heard he fell off that wall."

I shake my head and my hair falls forward, shielding my face.

"Is that not what happened?" Her voice comes out a whisper and I realize she's thinking I pushed him or something.

I meet her gaze. "Yes, that's what happened, but it's my fault we weren't right next to him. I decided that was the perfect time to kiss Blake and that's when Cody fell."

Her hand flutters to her throat. "Oh my god."

"Blake jumped over the edge to save him, but it was too late. He died a couple hours later."

"Brianna, you need to stop blaming yourself. It was an accident. And you were kids."

"You don't think I've told myself that? I've replayed that day thousands of times and I know that if I hadn't been so focused on my own interests, Cody would still be here today."

"Is that why Xavier said the girl was an evil bitch? It was an accident. He could have fallen if you were right next to him."

"It's not just that. The guilt nearly crushed me, and when my emotions get out of control, I lash out. When we were at the hospital, instead of apologizing for distracting Blake, I blamed him for the accident."

Her mouth falls open as she absorbs my words. "Okay, that sounds like an evil bitch."

"That day was a turning point for me. I hated how terrible I felt and decided from then on, no one would hurt me. I forced my way to the top of the social food chain and shoved Blake to the bottom."

She's quiet for several minutes and I feel like I'm on trial—a trial I rightly deserve. This is the first time I've cared enough what someone thinks of me to wish I could change the past, and now it's two someones. Drea and Xavier. They have every right to decide they never want to speak to me again.

"Why are you telling me this?"

"Because I'm trying to change. And I want us to be friends. Real friends who know each other's shit and still like each other." I drop my gaze. "Honestly, I don't know if I'd tell you this if you didn't have the connection to Cody, but you do, so I am."

Her face doesn't give away what she's thinking, and I'm convinced she's going to stand and walk out of my life when she smiles. It's a small, uncertain smile, but it's a smile. "I want us to be friends, too. It's been nice having someone who isn't mixed up in the day-to-day high school drama, you know?"

I exhale, relief coursing through me.

"It's gonna take a little time for me to come to terms with this, but you seem like a different person from what you describe, and everyone deserves a second chance, right?"

"I'm so glad to hear you say that."

"Are you going to tell Xavier?"

My chest tightens just thinking about it. "I know I should, but what if he's not as understanding?"

"I guess you have to decide how important it is to be honest. With how strongly he reacted the other day, I know I'd have a hard time telling him the truth."

"Not helping."

She shrugs. "It's your decision to make, but I think you should tell him. If you want your relationship to work, you can't go in with this huge secret. Especially knowing how he feels about it. If I ever kept something like that from Colton..." she trails off, and my senses hum.

Since the day Xavier and I wondered about her safety, there hasn't been an opportunity to ask her directly. This might be my only chance.

"How are things with him?" My tone is light, and I take a sip of my latte so I don't seem overly curious.

Her body tenses, and she shifts positions so one leg is tucked under the other. "Okay. We've been together so long that I guess I don't think about it that way, you know?"

"Actually, I don't." My smile is both innocent and self-deprecating. "I've never managed to date anyone more than a few months. It must be nice to know where you stand. To be confident that the other person loves you."

"Yeah, it is." Her words sound hesitant, like she's trying to convince herself. "I barely remember what it was like before him."

"Do you think you'll get married?"

Her eyes widen and I swear her breathing grows shallow. "I'm barely eighteen."

"I didn't mean next week. But do you talk about it?"

She shifts in her chair again. Takes a sip of coffee. Avoids my eyes.

"Sorry, I'm not trying to pry. I just want to get to know you better." As easily as manipulating people is for me, I hate doing it to Drea, who's been nothing but supportive of me. But if something really is going on with Colton, I want to help.

Her mug clinks as she sets it back on the table. "No, it's okay. We don't really talk about those kinds of things. We're the same age but I'm a year behind, so right now he's all about college and scholarships and stuff." She smiles weakly. "He's already been accepted to CU, he's just trying to get a football scholarship."

I'm impressed. I can't help it. "You didn't tell me he plays football!" Everything about Drea is the opposite of athletic, and this surprises me a little. That's not to say opposites can't attract—Xavier and I are the perfect example of that—but jocks tend to stick with jocks. "So will he play for CU?"

She nods, her eyes lighting up. "He's really dedicated to it. Scouts have come from all over the country to watch him play, but he wants to stay close to home. To me."

This time my smile is genuine. "That's so sweet."

"Yeah." Her wistful tone reflects the sad look on her face.

"Do you—do you not think so?"

"I don't know. Part of me was looking forward to having a little distance between us. We've been Dreaton for so long that I sometimes forget who I am without him." She picks up her mug and holds it against her chest like it's a shield.

I bite my lip. Inside, I thrill at the couples nickname, but now's not the time to get sidetracked. This is new territory for me and I don't want to screw it up. "Have you thought about breaking up with him?"

Her head jerks toward me and she looks around like she's checking if anyone's listening. "No! I couldn't do that." She stares into her mug for several moments and I let the silence drag out.

Getting people to talk by simply not speaking first is an art form, and for once I can use my practiced bitchitude for good.

"Besides, he wouldn't let me." Her words are so soft I almost don't hear her, but then the meaning rolls over me, turning into anger.

"What do you mean he wouldn't let you?" I'm treading a thin line here, but I feel like I'm getting through to her and can't give up now.

Edge Rule #9: You can only ride the edge for so long. At some point you have to pick a side.

Her eyes fill with tears.

Shit. I pushed her too far. "We don't have to talk about this. I didn't mean to—"

A tear slides down her cheek and something inside me breaks for her. "He's not—" she pauses, and I hold my breath. "He's not always the nicest to me."

"Like verbally, or..." I don't finish the sentence. I can feel my claws coming out.

"That, and sometimes..." she stops again. More tears spill over her lashes.

I scoot to the edge of my chair and rest my hand on her arm. She jumps at the contact, but I don't pull away. I don't think I've ever felt this protective of someone, but I silently vow to do whatever I can to help her. "Has he hurt you?"

It's like I uncorked a dam. Her shoulders shake as she sobs silently. A few people look our way but I scowl at them and they turn back to their drinks.

"I'm so sorry." I want to help but this is so outside my comfort zone I don't know where to start. "What can I do?"

She looks up at me with red-rimmed eyes. Since I've met her she's seemed like one of the strongest people I know, but now, sitting in this coffee shop, she seems broken. Defeated. "Don't tell anyone?"

"Drea."

"I'm serious. I don't know what he'd do if he found out I told anyone."

"Drea." I repeat her name, louder, trying to wake her up. "You can't stay with him."

Another sob shakes her body and I slide closer until our knees are touching. "I don't have a choice."

Fury bubbles through me and I want to break something. Or hit someone. I take a deep breath to calm my racing heart. "I promise I will help you. We'll figure this out." I squeeze her arm lightly. "Can you promise me something?"

Her head shakes from side to side. "What?"

"Please call me if you ever need help."

"O-okay." Her hand covers mine and I have the overwhelming urge to throw her in my car and hide her in my room. "I can do that."

We finish our coffees and somehow manage to steer the conversation to less tear-inducing topics. When we leave, I walk her to her car. "I kind of don't want to let you go home."

She sniffles and gives me a weak smile. "I'll be okay."

"I wish I believed that."

"Bri, thank you for listening to me. Just that helped so much."

But it's not enough! "Okay."

"See you Thursday?" she asks.

I nod and we say our goodbyes. By the time I get home I'm so frustrated at not knowing how to help her that I decide I need reinforcements.

I need your advice.

Xavier writes back almost immediately. *With what?*

Drea. What we feared is true.

The boyfriend?

Yeah.

He doesn't reply for several moments. No bouncing dots, just silence. Finally his reply comes through. *Shit.*

Yeah, I repeat.

Can you come over tomorrow?

The invitation catches me off guard. Was he already planning to ask, or does he want me to come over to talk about Drea? Which would be weird, but I'll take it. *Sure.*

I was gonna ask you but you texted first.

My pulse quickens. *I'm glad.*

Uncertainty over a boy's feelings is an unfamiliar sensation, and I don't know why I keep going back and forth with Xavier. Doubting myself is new territory, and while the rush I felt while reading his text is addictive, the letdown I fear will come when he finds out the truth makes me want to protect my heart.

He texts me his address and we say good night, and I can't shake the fear that when this blows up, it's going to hurt worse than everything else that's happened this year.

twenty-four

The navigation system in my 4Runner leads me to a white two-story house with blue shutters in a neighborhood twenty minutes from home. I park in the driveway behind Subie. A dog barks from across the street when I get out of the car, and when I pull out my phone to text Xavier that I'm here, he opens the door before I can hit send.

Has it really only been four days since I've seen him? He's wearing a dark gray waffle shirt with the sleeves pushed up, showing off his tattoo, and his eyes lock on mine, drawing me toward him. "Did you find it okay?" he asks.

"Navigation is a girl's best friend."

He smiles, and my stomach flips. "Come on in." He holds out his hand, and when I slip my fingers through his, heat races through me. It's on the tip of my tongue to ask if anyone else is home, but I don't want him to think that all I want is to get him alone.

Even if that's all I've been thinking of since last night.

"Do you like hot chocolate?" he asks as he leads me through the front door.

"Does the Pope live in the Vatican?" He raises an eyebrow at me and I laugh. "That would be a yes."

We walk past a cozy living room decked out for Christmas into a kitchen bursting with color. Yellow walls frame a terra cotta tiled floor and colorful jars line the counter. A square wooden table sits in the corner and fresh fruit hangs in a tiered basket over the sink.

I follow the scent of chocolate to a small pot simmering on the stove. "You're like, cooking hot chocolate?"

He stirs the liquid with a wooden spoon. "How else do you make it?"

"I don't know. The microwave?"

He presses a hand to his chest. "Sacrilege." He stirs it once more and sets the spoon across the top of the pan. His movements are relaxed, like he spends a lot of time in here.

"I'm impressed."

He smiles. "That's not why I'm making it, but I'm glad." He takes my hand and tugs me toward him. I slide my arms around his waist and rest my forehead against his neck, and his arms wrap around me. The sweet scent of chocolate fills the room and I inhale deeply, settling tighter into his embrace. He rests his head on mine and I'm thinking I could stay here forever when someone sighs dramatically behind us.

"Ay, hermano, get a room."

I lift my head to see a female version of Xavier. Same black hair except past her shoulders, same gorgeous skin, and same soulful dark eyes. Instead of tattoos, she's wearing heavy eyeliner and bright red lipstick. She smiles at us and raises an eyebrow when she sees me watching her.

She holds out her hand and I disentangle myself from her brother. "Mucho gusto. I'm Lily."

I take her hand, then go one step further and brush my cheek against hers the way Javi and Gladys did at the restaurant. "Brianna. Nice to meet you."

She gives him a pleased smile, which I hope means I did the right thing.

Xavier squeezes her shoulder. "Qué pasa, calabaza?"

"Nada, nada, limonada," she replies, her smile growing. She picks up the spoon and stirs the chocolate. "Is there enough for me?"

"Only if you promise to leave us alone."

She presses her hand to her chest the same way he did a minute ago. "You wound me."

"How was school?" he asks, and a ripple of tension moves through him.

She shrugs, either oblivious to his concern or so used to it she no longer reacts. "It was school. I was there. No need to worry about me today, hermano." She touches his chin and gives him a smile that probably gets her anything she wants, then sits at the wooden table. "I'll get out of your hair as soon as it's ready."

Questions pile on top of each other, but I can't ask any of them until we're alone.

"So, Brianna. How'd you two meet?"

My eyes flash to Xavier, unsure if I should tell the truth, but he handles it for me.

"Community service," he says. "We both went for the same used condom and the rest is history."

I burst out laughing, but Lily doesn't look amused.

"Don't tell that to Mom." Her gaze falls on me. "No offense, but you'll never get a foot in this house again if she thinks you'll corrupt her precious Xavi." The irony that my parents would probably think the same thing of him without even knowing how we met nearly knocks me over. Are we stupid to think this can work?

He grabs my hand and kisses my knuckles. "Don't listen to her. But maybe we tell my mom we met snowboarding." He smiles against my hand and my stomach does a lazy flip. His eyes have a way of pulling me toward him and I step closer until our hips touch.

The chair squeaks on the tile as Lily stands. "Go ahead and pour mine. I'm sure it's ready."

"You know how to do it," Xavier says, his eyes never leaving mine.

A cupboard opens and closes, then Lily's pouring the liquid chocolate from the pan to a mug. She sets it back on the stove with a clang. "You better stir that so it doesn't burn. Nice meeting you, Brianna."

"You too."

She pads out of the room and Xavier reaches for the spoon without releasing me. But instead of stirring, he holds the spoon to my mouth. "Taste it."

I open my mouth and he rests the spoon against my lips, and everything inside me flares to life. The chocolate is rich and decadent and has a spiciness that makes the flavor practically explode on my tongue. "Oh my god, that's so good."

"I'm glad you like it." He licks the edge of the spoon and that hint of his tongue puts a million dirty thoughts in my mind. He turns slightly, just enough to give the chocolate a stir, then sets the spoon back on the pan.

The moment he turns back to me, our mouths collide in a mix of sweetness and heat. We explore each other, standing in the middle of his kitchen, and when he backs me up to the counter and presses the length of his body against mine, I nearly lose my mind. My hands crawl under the edge of his shirt and trail over his skin, making him sigh against me.

"The chocolate's going to burn," he whispers against my mouth.

"Would that really be so bad?"

He laughs softly. "Yes, it would. And you only had a taste." He backs away, and I'm sure the lust in his eyes is matched in my own. He's right about wanting more than a taste. Just kissing him isn't going to be enough.

Once the hot chocolate is poured into matching ceramic mugs, he leads me to the living room. He sits on the couch and I nestle in next to him. "My mom won't be home for at least an hour so—"

I don't waste any time brushing my lips against his. But this time our kiss is softer, slower. I sink into his arms as his hand moves up my neck and into my hair, and rest my hand on his hip. As much as I'd love to push this further, his sister is in the house and I've learned from past experience that parents have a tendency to come home early when their children are counting on them being late.

We end the kiss and I rest my head against his shoulder. "It's so cozy here." Lights from the Christmas tree blink lazily, bathing the walls with flashes of green and red. Blankets and throw pillows adorn the couch and loveseat, and there are plants and photos and general evidence of a family living here that makes my house seem cold and sterile. I reach for my hot chocolate and inhale deeply before taking a sip. This is so much better than anything I've ever made.

"I like it here," he says, reaching for his mug. "When my parents split up I thought we might have to move, but Dad just left. This is the only house I've ever lived in."

Sudden tears prick my eyes. Our house is the only one I've ever known too, and now we have to leave. "My mom and I have to move in a couple weeks."

He dips his head to look in my eyes and I blink away the tears. "Aww, that sucks. I'm sorry. Do you know where you're going?"

"A townhouse. I didn't ask where, but I guess I should. And we have to start packing." The details of moving hadn't hit me until just now. It's taken years to get my room to its current state of perfection. How will I undo all that? Or recreate it someplace new?

"Let me know if I can help."

The image of Xavier in my frilly room, lying beneath the canopy on my bed, pushes away my anxiety. I set down my mug and touch his jaw.

His lips part, his eyelids heavy. "What?"

"I was just picturing you in my room and—"

Then those lips cover mine and he leans into me so I fall back on the couch.

"Your chocolate."

His mug clinks on the table and his hands move up my side. He shifts his weight so he's on an elbow and knee, hovering over me. My legs are still hanging off the couch, my body twisted, so I lift my legs and stretch them out alongside him. He lowers himself and we're chest to chest, hip to hip, and my leg hooks around his, holding him in place. It's been so long since I've been held like this, like I'm the most important thing in the world and nothing else matters.

With Austin—No. He's not ruining this.

Xavier is kissing me, devouring me, and everything about him is intoxicating. The smell and taste of the chocolate intensifies my senses and when he presses his hips against mine, it takes all my strength not to drag him to his room.

He breaks the kiss, and for a moment the only sound is our heavy breathing. "I really want to bring you upstairs but my mom would kill us."

"Us? Not just you?" I smile against his cheek.

"Double homicide for sure."

My hand moves over his side and settles low on his hip. "So finding us like this would probably be bad, too, huh?"

"Attempted murder, at least."

I move my hand to a less provocative spot on his back and sigh. He nuzzles his nose against my neck and inhales, then kisses just below my ear and pushes off of me. It's cold without his body against mine. I sit up and reach for my mug, resting it in my lap. "I do want to talk to you about Drea."

His smile fades, the mood effectively killed. "She told you he's hitting her?"

Our conversation replays in my mind. "Not in those exact words, but it was pretty clear. She was crying really hard and basically said she's afraid to leave him."

He rubs his hand over his face.

"I hate to drag you into this, especially after..." I trail off, my mind running upstairs to Lily's room. I touch his hand with mine. "But I don't know what to do."

"I don't know if there's much we can do. Try to talk to her more. Make sure she knows she can trust you." He says it so easily, like having someone trust me is the most natural thing in the world, and I'm gripped with fear that he'll find out the truth about me.

"I can do that." My voice isn't as confident as it should be, but he doesn't seem to notice.

"And promise you'll tell me if there's anything I can do."

My hand covers his and I stroke his knuckles, imagining them torn up after the fight.

He looks up. "I didn't mean that."

"I don't want you to get hurt protecting someone else."

He stares at our hands and flexes his fingers beneath mine. "I promised my mom I wouldn't do that again."

"Good."

We fall into silence, each lost in our thoughts, and I rest my head against his shoulder. We're sitting like that when the front door opens. He straightens, but keeps his arm around me as an adult version of Lily enters the room. Her sleek black hair is twisted into a low bun and she's wearing a suit that could rival anything in Mom's closet. But instead of the suspicious, one-eyebrow-raised smirk I'd get from Mom, her smile is full of warmth.

"Mom, this is Brianna. Brianna, this is my mom."

I start to stand but she rushes forward and waves for me to stay seated.

"Don't get up." She takes my hand and bends over to press her cheek to mine. Then she brushes her hand over Xavier's cheek. "Xavi told me about this new guera he's dating, but he didn't say how beautiful she is." She smiles at me again. "We can chat after I change clothes."

"Okay." People have been telling me I'm beautiful since I turned thirteen and sprouted breasts, so I'm not sure why her compliment has me so flustered. Maybe it's because she's completely unlike what I expected—polished and kind, like how I wish my mother was—not to mention as gorgeous as her kids.

Xavier kisses my shoulder. "I knew she'd like you."

"Your mom is a hottie."

He laughs softly. "My friends love coming over."

This time I laugh. "I bet."

His lips find the soft spot under my ear and I melt into him. "You're a good person," he whispers. "Of course she likes you."

The voice in my head tries to argue but I shut her up. How can I tell him the truth? Maybe he'll never find out, or if he does, we'll already be—what? In love? But it doesn't matter. The minute Mom finds out about him she'll make me end it. It won't make a difference that he's the most stand-up guy I've ever met—one look at him and it'll be non-negotiable. All she'll see is tattoos and piercings, not this sweet, wonderful boy. Maybe I should confess everything and save us the trouble of getting more wrapped up in each other.

His finger trails along my cheekbone. "Hey, where'd you go?"

I blink away my thoughts, meeting his gaze. How can I throw him away? "Sorry, just thinking about stuff at home. Your mom is nothing like mine." His brow furrows and I smile. "That's a good thing. My temper doesn't come from nowhere."

"I'll remember that."

His face is just inches from mine, so I sneak a kiss before his mom comes back. I'm expecting a quick brush of our lips, but he pulls me closer, deepening the kiss and making my head spin. My hand slides up his arm and over his shoulder, settling at the back of his neck, while his roams over my hip. I want to pull him on top of me the way we were earlier, but I also want his mom to like me. I gently pull away, dropping kisses along his neck to his collarbone until our breathing returns to normal.

By the time his mom comes down the stairs, only our knees are touching and we're sipping our now-cold chocolate. She's wearing skinny jeans and a loose top and settles into the chair next to the couch.

"It's nice to meet you, Mrs.— " And that's when I realize I don't know Xavier's last name. But she cuts me off before the moment gets awkward.

"Please, call me Anna." Her warm smile pulls me in and I understand where Xavier gets his charm. Her accent is distinct, but she speaks perfect English.

And the fact that I'm surprised proves what a prejudiced bitch I am.

Her gaze bounces between the two of us. "Xavi didn't tell me how you met."

"Snowboarding," we both say, and I can't help but laugh.

"Technically I was skiing, but he convinced me to try boarding."

She smirks. "I'm not surprised. This boy could charm the last dollar from a homeless man."

Or the pants off a teenaged girl. Almost like he read my thoughts, his hand covers mine.

"I hate to see people waste their time with all that equipment. Boarding is so much freer." This is the first time he's said that to me, and I wonder how much of it's for his mom's benefit and how much is true.

"So you don't go to school together?" When I shake my head, she continues. "Where do you live?"

My mouth opens to tell her and I'm surprised by the lump that catches in my throat and the tears that blur my vision. She looks concerned and Xavier squeezes my hand.

"She's not far from here, in Louisville, but they're moving soon."

I clear my throat. "Still in the same general area, but yeah, our house is already sold."

Anna looks around the room and her eyes water. "I couldn't imagine having to leave our home, especially so close to the holidays." Even though she's sitting ten feet away, her easy nature makes me want to tell her the whole story. About Dad and The Seconds and everything else that's screwed up in my life. But I bite my lip and force a smile.

"I'm not super thrilled about it, but at least I don't have to switch schools." Although now that I think about it, maybe that wouldn't be the worst thing in the world.

"Xavi, you have friends from that area, right?"

"Yeah." He faces me, and I can feel the blood drain from my face. This is it.

The moment he finds out the truth.

"You're at Monarch?"

My mouth goes dry, like all the moisture in my body evaporated in a poof above me, and my head feels like it's detached from my body. I nod.

"Do you know Blake and Cally? They're friends with Luke, the guy we saw when—" a blush touches his cheeks as he remembers what we were doing when we saw Luke. "When we were boarding."

I nod again, and it's like everything moves in slow motion. The curiosity in Xavier's eyes, the way Anna leans forward in her chair like she can't wait to hear what I say—it's all too much. My breathing stops and blood roars in my ears. I don't want him to know. I've tried so hard to be a better person and it's sucked not having friends and now that I've found someone who looks at me the way he's looking at me now, I don't want to ruin it.

"They go to my school," I finally say, "but we're not friends or anything."

Understatement of the year.

And I've got a picture of Cally's dad in my phone.

He nods, accepting my statement like there isn't an avalanche of truth ready to bury him.

Anna asks me about school and my interests, and I must answer well because she keeps smiling and Xavier never lets go of my hand. But all I can think is it's not a question of if this will blow up in my face, but when.

Eventually Anna stands, stretching her arms over her head. The hem of her shirt lifts over the top of her jeans, revealing a small tattoo on her side. She could not be more unlike my mother. She holds out her hand to shake mine, but this time I stand and press my cheek to hers.

"It was very nice to meet you," I say, and I mean it. It's usually hit or miss with friends' parents, but she's like something out of a fairy tale.

"I like you," she says. "You seem like a good influence for Xavi." She winks at him over my shoulder. "Not that he needs it, right?"

"Yes, 'ama." He doesn't normally have an accent, but it comes out on that one word.

Then her arms are pulling me to her and we're hugging and a tiny part of me wishes it could stay like this forever.

But too soon I have to leave. Xavier walks me to my car, where we share another toe-curling kiss. I open the door and get in, but he stands in the opening so I can't close it.

"Are we still boarding this weekend?" His lips are swollen from our kiss and his gaze bounces from my eyes to my mouth.

I touch my fingers to his lower lip, and he kisses them. "Yes. Of course."

"But can we go to Eldora? I have a season pass there and—"

"Yes, of course," I repeat, because those are the only words I'm capable of forming. I can't keep insisting we go someplace else when we both have season passes, but that means the end to my secret. Unless... "Is Saturday good?" The ski team competes Saturdays so while we'll see other kids from school, Blake and Cally won't be there.

"Sure." He leans into the car and kisses me again, and I hold on like it's the last time he'll touch me like this.

Because I'm afraid it might be.

twenty-five

My stomach's in knots when I pull into the Eldora parking lot. Xavier offered to pick me up, but I don't want to end up stranded if he finds out the truth today. Not that I think he would abandon me, but discovering the girl you like is an evil monster does weird things to people.

He's already in the common area where people dump their street shoes, and I don't know how it's possible to look delicious under forty layers, but he does. We meet near a bench but pause before touching. There's easily twenty people in various stages of putting on ski boots and bundling up against the cold, and they probably wouldn't appreciate us making out in the middle of the room. He grabs my hand and that slight press of his skin against mine makes my insides flutter. We head to the rental counter and this time I check the box for intermediate.

He quirks an eyebrow and I laugh. "There's more than one way to get better equipment. Besides, I know enough not to run into anything, right?"

He winks. "More or less."

Once we're suited up, I lead him to the lift for my favorite blue. So far we haven't seen anyone from school, but the sun's shining and the snow is perfect, so it's only a matter of time before half the student body shows up. My goggles and helmet do a decent job at concealing my identity—or at least it works for Superman— and as long as I don't talk to anyone I should be safe.

"You know," he says, twisting on the narrow bench so he's facing me. "I was beginning to think you didn't want to be seen with me."

My stomach leaps into my throat. That's partially true, but not for the reasons he thinks. At least, they aren't anymore. At first I was afraid of what people would think if they saw us together—especially if they saw me snowboarding instead of skiing—but all that seems stupid now. I reach for his hand. "How could anyone not want to be seen with you? Have you seen you?" His eyes close briefly and the corner of his mouth curls into a smile. "No, I didn't want the people I've known my entire life watching me fall all over my ass while I learn how to board."

He points at two guys splayed on the snow beneath us. "Like that?"

I nod.

"Do you remember what I was doing when we saw each other here?"

"You had just wiped out."

"Everyone falls." He nods as another boarder catches an edge and face-plants. "The trick is getting back on your feet and trying again."

"You make it sound so simple."

"It is. It might hurt like a bitch, especially if you go face first like that guy—"

"And like I did the first day."

"—but we've all been there. If anyone laughs at you for wiping out, that's on them."

I couldn't tell you how many times I've made fun of people who wipe out. When I ski, I don't fall. Period. My only priorities were to look good and stay in control. That was fun to me. I shake my head, and Xavier tilts his in confusion. "I'm really glad I met you."

He smiles, but still looks confused.

"I didn't realize how tightly I was holding onto this need to be in control. But you've showed me that it's okay to let go a little."

Melanie Hooyenga

His smile brightens and he leans forward until our helmets clink together. "I'm glad you met me, too." I turn my face to kiss him. Between our helmets and goggles, our lips barely brush, but it's enough.

When we get to the top of the lift, my nerves return in full force. My board hits the packed snow and with a single push, I put my weight on it. We coast down the ramp and off to the side, and I laugh. "I'm totally an intermediate."

Xavier gives me a soft smile.

He leads on the first run and I'm concentrating so hard on keeping my balance and not catching an edge that I don't see the pack of boarders flying down the center of the run until they're right next to me, whooping and yelling. My balance wobbles, and the next thing I know I'm flat on my back. My brain feels like it's still bouncing around inside my helmet and stars dance in the bright blue sky. Silence wraps around me and for a moment I think I've knocked my brain loose, then I hear Xavier's voice from farther down the hill.

I push myself up, focusing on the nearby tree line to stop my head from spinning. By the time Xavier reaches my side, his board tucked under his arm, the pounding in my head dulls to a steady throb and the stars have faded.

He kneels by my side and touches my face. "You okay?"

"I need another minute." He plops next to me as skiers and boarders ride by. "That's what I get for bragging."

He bumps my knee with his. "Did you already forget what we talked about?" His eyes are steady on mine and a warmth spreads inside me. But this isn't the lust-crazed heat I usually feel when I'm around him. This is so strong it makes my heart hurt.

I brush snow off my pants and pop onto my feet.

Edge Rule #10: It's not how hard you fall, it's how you pick yourself up afterwards.

I manage to stay on my feet the next couple runs, and when he suggests we head inside to warm up, I feel like I'm floating. Who would've thought I'd love snowboarding? It's still scary knowing one wrong shift of my weight could land me on my face, but I'm figuring out how to use my core in a way that's totally unlike skiing.

We lock our gear to an outdoor rack and head inside. And that's where my mood pops. Everywhere I turn, familiar faces are laughing and talking. For a second, anger and sadness twist in my gut because no one turns when we enter the room. A few glance our way, but they return to their conversations just as quickly. My reign as Queen B is definitely over.

Xavier grabs my hand and leads me to a couple open seats at the end of a long table. Last season, people would have switched seats to let me have a small table—or at least clear out a bigger space so we wouldn't be crammed together—but aside from a couple double-takes, no one seems to care that I'm here.

Except one person near the window.

I meet Mike's gaze. Her eyes flick from my very un-pink clothes to Xavier, and settle on my boots. My mouth curls into a smile before I can stop it, and she smiles back before turning to the hottie sitting next to her. Aside from one picture of them riding their bikes, she hasn't posted anything of him online.

But the same could be said for me. Xavier and I are clearly together but aside from Drea, no one knows he exists.

"Is this okay?" Xavier asks. "I can go grab drinks if you want to wait here."

Here, as in the center of the room. Where I've wanted to be my entire life, but for the first time find myself wishing we were anywhere else. And not because I don't want people to see Xavier. Any hang-ups I had about him are gone. No, I'm not ready for the scrutiny that's sure to happen when my classmates realize how much I've changed.

Xavier ducks his head to look in my eyes. "Is something wrong?"

"No." I shake my head. "No. I just saw a friend—former friend—and kind of spaced out for a minute." I smile up at him and his face relaxes. "This is great."

He kisses the tip of my nose. "Be back soon."

There isn't much room at the table, just two chairs and a space wide enough for a couple trays, so I dump my gloves on the table and sit before pulling off my helmet. If I shake my head, my hair will fall in waves down my back, but I'm not feeling the supermodel-in-a-shampoo-commercial vibe right now. Instead I set my helmet on top of my gloves and run my fingers through my hair, doing my best to not draw attention to myself.

But people still notice me. The double-takes from before become open stares, and this time Mike smiles at me. I'm tempted to go to her and meet her boyfriend, but I feel frozen in place with my fingers still tangled in my hair. Kids I've known most of my life give me questioning looks, but how do I explain everything that's led to this moment—to the changes I'm making—with just one look? I'd need to take out an ad in the school paper to fully explain myself. So I return their curious glances with smiles and try to relax while I wait for Xavier to return.

When he does, it's like everyone else blurs away. He sets a tray loaded with hot chocolate and sports drinks and a couple granola bars between us, then pulls off his helmet and sits next to me. His face is flushed from being bundled up inside and I can't stop myself from touching his cheek. He turns his head so his lips press my palm, and now I'm wishing we had a more private table for other reasons.

"Do you see anyone you know?" he asks.

Only half my school. I nod. "I've gotten a few looks, but no one seems to care."

"That's because you've finally left the dark side."

I raise an eyebrow. He can't know how true that statement is.

"You know boarding is where it's at."

"I hate to admit it, but you've convinced me. But I'm still not used to knocking the snot out of myself." I touch the back of my head. The helmet did its job, but the after-effects of the fall are still lingering.

He leans closer and weaves his fingers through my hair until he touches the tender spot. "Do you want to stop?"

I press into his touch. "I don't ever want you to stop."

He laughs softly, his eyes on mine. "I meant snowboarding."

"I know. I didn't." We lean closer until our lips meet. His are soft and warm and he tastes like chocolate. When this falls apart, he'll have ruined hot chocolate for me because I'll never be able to drink it without thinking of him.

He pulls away and leans back in his seat. "Seriously. You fell pretty hard. We can stop if you need to."

"Nah. But if I fall like that again I'll consider it."

We settle in with our drinks and are eating our granola bars when the energy in the room shifts. Heads swivel from the entrance to me, back and forth, and I'm almost afraid to look.

But I don't need to.

"I wondered if you'd ever show your face here again." Kenzie's voice is loud and clear and demands attention. The attention I used to get.

I twist in my seat to stare her down. Three girls stand behind her, each wearing an upgraded version of our outfits from last year. The colors are still bright, but instead of being a solid color, stripes race down the sides. A tiny part of me is pleased that no one's wearing my pink, but that pleasure bursts as soon as I meet Kenzie's glare.

Xavier tenses next to me, but he'll figure things out soon enough.

My shoulders straighten on their own. Anger uncoils in me like a dragon that's been asleep for far too long. I don't stand, and I give her a bored look, complete with an eye roll that'd make any aspiring bitch jealous. "You've found your very own lemmings. How sweet."

Kenzie rolls her eyes before giving Xavier a once over. "And you've scraped the bottom of the barrel."

That's a flat-out lie. I know her type and she's probably drooling on the inside. "Jealousy doesn't suit you."

"I was about to say the same thing."

"Typical, since you've never come up with an original thought of your own." I push my hair over my shoulder and rest my hand on Xavier's thigh. "Now run along with your second-hand bunnies and leave us alone." A slight tremor moves through me, but I tell myself it's because of how close Xavier is sitting, not because of the fury in Kenzie's eyes. There's nothing else she can do to hurt me.

So why am I so unsettled?

Kenzie stalks away, her girls trailing close behind, and I face Xavier. "Sorry."

"What the hell was that? WHO the hell was that?"

"Former BFF."

He looks across the room to where Kenzie and her minions have crowded in with several seniors. "You were friends with her?"

"I was the leader." The words slip out before I can stop them. "The blond by the window was my actual best friend."

He scans the room until he sees Mike, who's watching us between sips of water, and it occurs to me that they may already know each other through Cally and Blake. But he doesn't seem to recognize her. He stays silent, watching me like he wants to say something. With each passing moment I grow more and more anxious that he's making a decision about me—one that I can't talk my way out of.

"Is this why you didn't want to come here?"

"Pretty much." I take a deep breath to calm myself. "Now that she had her little power trip, it should be over." At least it better be.

"I feel like there's more you're not telling me."

Because there is. "I told you I'm not friends with them anymore."

"Yeah, but I figured you grew apart or something like that."

"Something like that," I repeat his words, my energy draining. My hand is still on his leg and I slide it over his waterproof pants. "There's more to the story, but this isn't the place."

He nuzzles his face into my neck. "We've got time."

I want to believe him. And as his lips caress my neck, I need to believe him, but the part of me that pushes people away before they get too close insists that it's a fantasy to think this could work.

We finish our snacks and I manage to convince Xavier that I'm fine, but I can't shake the unsettled feeling that wraps around my heart.

twenty-six

I've officially become the girl who hides in her room on Saturday night. Weekends used to mean partying and rolling in hours past my unenforced curfew—an amazing way to forget how miserable I was—but when every face I'd see would be anything but welcoming, being miserable in my room sounds considerably better. I didn't ask Xavier to hang out despite his hints that he was free, further evidence that something is clearly wrong with me.

A romantic comedy plays on my laptop while I scroll social media on my phone, and eventually I fall asleep to the credits.

Sunday Mom and I spend the day circling each other. Empty boxes appear in the foyer, the kitchen, and outside my bedroom, but I still can't accept that we're actually moving. It's not until she calls me downstairs for dinner and sushi from our favorite restaurant is spread out on the table that it hits me. We're really leaving. She only orders in from Coast when she's celebrating or feeling really down, and since there hasn't been much to celebrate lately, she must not be handling this as well as she's led me to believe.

She's already poured herself a glass of wine, but I fill two glasses with water, carry them to the table, and take my seat. She sits with a heavy sigh. "How's the packing going?"

"Is that what the boxes are for? I thought you were experimenting with homeless chic décor."

Her eyebrow barely lifts and she lets out another sigh. "I know this is awful. And I'm sorry I haven't been around lately.

It's just—" she waves her hand in the air—"it's all been too much, you know?" She takes a very unladylike gulp of her Sauvignon Blanc and notices me watching. "Help yourself."

I get up slowly, not wanting to look too eager, and return with a matching glass and the bottle from the fridge. I pour a modest amount and take a sip, letting the tartness of the wine wash over my tongue and down my throat. After another drink, I set down the glass and relax against my chair.

Mom starts with the seaweed salad, dividing it between our plates, and once the rolls are split we start eating. She looks up several times like she's going to say something, but then she takes another drink or bite and remains silent. I continue eating, waiting her out. If there's something she wants to say, she'll get to it eventually. It might take another glass of wine, but she'll break.

When the salad is gone and we've finished the spicy tuna, she refills her wine glass and looks up at me. From the look on her face, I'm going to need more wine, too.

"Brianna," she starts, then sets down her glass. "I haven't been fair to you."

I watch her but don't say anything.

"Blaming you for all this was—" she picks up her wine, then sets it back down and rests her hand flat on the table, like she's pulling strength from the hard surface. "That wasn't fair. Things between your father and I haven't been good for years, so while the timing of your little incident couldn't have been worse, I can't blame this on you. And I shouldn't have." Tears shine in her eyes, surprising me. Miranda Vines does not cry.

"Thanks," I say, but she holds up her hand.

"I'm not finished. I know we've never had the perfect mother-daughter relationship, but I never once asked you what was going on. I should have insisted we talk when you stole that notebook from the owner of Calliope Brewing. Getting arrested was another red flag that something's wrong, but I was so wrapped up in my own life falling apart that I never pulled my head out of my ass to be your mother."

Yes, I definitely need more wine for this. I reach for the bottle and she slides it across the table toward me. It sloshes into the glass as I pour, and I set the empty bottle onto the table with a thud.

She leans her elbows on the table and levels her gaze at me, but it lacks the usual Miranda Vines flair. She almost seems defeated. "Will you please tell me what's going on?"

"Didn't we already do this?"

"I feel like you left out a few things."

My fingers trail around the base of my glass. *Where do I even begin?* "My life has pretty much fallen apart."

She lifts her glass. "Cheers to that." I air clink my glass in her direction and we both take a drink. "Maybe start with why you were stealing. That's the part I can't understand."

"I don't know. The first time was an accident, and after that," I shrug. "It was a rush. And I didn't have anything else exciting in my life. Mike and I stopped talking last spring, Austin and I broke up for good over the summer, and Kenzie..."

"But Mike was here not too long ago."

"Yeah, out of pity. We kind of talk in class, but we're definitely not friends anymore." I poke at the unagi roll with my chopstick. "Homecoming court was my last grasp at keeping up the façade that everything was normal. So when I lost and Kenzie pulled a power trip and declared a coup, I didn't have the energy to fake it anymore.

"You didn't tell me you lost."

"I didn't tell you I won."

"Touché."

"Anyway, things kind of spiraled after that. I don't know why I kept taking things. It's not even stuff I like. It's cheap jewelry that I'd never be caught dead wearing, so it didn't seem like it mattered."

She pops a roll in her mouth and chews, watching me.

"That night," I shake my head, remembering how the store owner freaked when she caught me, treating me like a common criminal. "I couldn't talk my way out of it. You know the rest." But she doesn't. She doesn't know that the Chain Gang led me to the only friends I have.

But my mother isn't an idiot.

"So who have you been skiing with?"

"Someone I met from the Chain—community service."

This time her eyebrow raises to its full height. "Another convict?" Her voice is shrill, the easiness from the past few minutes evaporating as quickly as her wine.

"He's not a convict." Shit. I didn't mean to tell her—

"A boy?"

"He's just a friend. And there's a girl I'm friends with, too. They're nice."

She takes a gulp of wine and sets the glass down so hard a little spills over the top. "You can't find anyone at school to be friends with? You have to associate with hoodlums doing court-appointed community service?"

I slam my hands on the table. "Careful, Mom. I'm one of those hoodlums."

"My daughter is not a hoodlum." Anger replaces her tears, but I'm just as pissed.

"Apparently I am. I got arrested. I'm doing community service. And everyone at school hates me. I'd say things are pretty hoodlum-y."

She glares at me, and silence wraps around us. The clock in the foyer ticks away the seconds, neither of us willing to break. Finally, her shoulders droop and she reaches for her wine. "I was trying to have a nice evening."

"Maybe you should have tried a little harder." I push away from the table, bringing my wine glass with me. My head swirls from standing too quickly and I grip the edge of the table. In that split second, Mom's anger cracks and the tears return.

"Please don't leave like this."

"Isn't this how we do things?"

"I can't have you hate me, too."

My anger deflates and I slump into my chair. "I don't hate you, Mom."

"But you don't like me very much."

Now tears burn my eyes. "You don't make it very easy. Everything that comes out of your mouth is judgmental and critical." Like mother, like daughter. No wonder I don't have any friends.

"I'm trying to be better."

Try harder.

"It's going to be just us for the next year and a half, then you'll go off to college and I'll be all alone."

I hadn't thought about that. Now I really feel like a brat. I've been throwing the ultimate one-person pity party, not realizing she's going through the same thing. "You won't be alone."

She swirls the wine in her glass, staring at the liquid as if transfixed. "This is not where I saw my life going."

"Me neither," I admit.

She smiles at me over her glass, and it's the closest to a genuine smile I've seen since all this started. "Quite a pair we've become."

This time I get up and clink my glass against hers.

*****

Walking into school on Monday, I'm more nervous than I've been since the day after my arrest. And not because of Kenzie. She can power trip all over the school for all I care. No, after all the times I've made fun of snowboarding, I hate not knowing how people will react now that I'm one of them. And yes, I realize that of all the things I could be worried about, this is beyond superficial, but you can't take the self-absorbed pretentiousness out of the girl overnight.

No one looks at me differently as I walk through the halls, and I even get a couple smiles from kids I saw Saturday, but I brace myself when I get to History. Sitting next to Kenzie at the beginning of the year made sense because we were still inseparable, but now I feel like I'm walking into a viper pit.

Is this how I used to make other people feel?

Kenzie stalks into the room with her head held so high it's likely to flip off backwards and roll down the hall. She rolls her eyes at me and opens her mouth to speak, then closes it and shakes her head like I'm not worth the effort. Which is fine with me.

When class ends, I take my time gathering my things. I don't rush out with the first kids, and I don't dawdle so I'm the last. If Kenzie thinks she's got the upper hand, I need to prove to her that no one controls me. We end up walking out with only one person between us, her long black ponytail swinging in front of me, and I hold my head as high as hers. A thousand scenarios play through my mind—the most appealing is me pushing her from behind and screaming about what a bitch she is—but she turns the corner to her next class and my adrenaline falters.

Mike's waiting for me in Ethics with a tentative smile.

I slide into my seat and smile back.

"When did you start snowboarding?" she asks. Her eyes are curious, and her lip catches between her teeth like she's unsure if she should be asking.

"A few weeks ago." I can't fight the smile that curls my lips, and she shakes her head.

"I have to tell you, I never in a million years thought I'd see you on a board."

"You and me both."

She picks at an invisible spot on her desk. "Does this have anything to do with the guy you were with?" Her gaze meets mine, and for a second the past year falls away and she's my best friend again. No drama, no fights, just the one person I've trusted since sixth grade seeming happy for me that I've met a boy. I'm tempted to ask if she's seen him with Cally and Blake, but she'd bring it up if she had, right? I search her eyes for the Mike who used to curl up at the end of my bed and talk for hours about her dream date—always outdoors, always doing something active—but then I blink and the moment is gone.

I clear my throat, still smiling, but it's forced. "I'm still not sure how he convinced me."

"His smoking hotness probably had something to do with it."

I laugh through my nose and the tension in my chest loosens. "Yes. That had a lot to do with it." We share a smile and I remember her boyfriend. "And who were you with? He's no Evan but he's—"

She cocks her head, the smile slipping from her face.

If I could suck my words back into my mouth, I would. "I didn't mean it like that. Really. I'm sorry."

She shakes her head as I hold up my hand.

"Mike. I swear. I'm happy for you. You seem happy and you deserve that."

She turns away so I try one last thing.

"What's his name?" Because what girl doesn't like to talk about her boyfriend?

"Don't worry about it," she says, staring straight ahead.

Is she accepting my apology or refusing to tell me his name? Either way, I've totally screwed up my first chance to make things better with her. And now Miss Simpson is starting the lecture, ending any chance I have of fixing this.

After class, Mike hurries to the door without looking back. I'm tempted to skip lunch and just gnaw on the giant foot in my mouth, but I refuse to let Kenzie think she's intimidating me.

In line in the cafeteria, a few people look my way and whisper to the people next to them, but they seem more curious than anything else. Austin and Evan are at their usual table, surrounded by a mix of soccer players and kids from the snowboarding team, and it's like a punch in the gut. Kenzie's always been a bitch, but I actually liked the guys and I miss hanging out with them.

I scan the room for an empty table while paying and just as I lift my tray, a voice stops me.

"I saw you boarding Saturday. Do you want to sit with me?"

I never thought my savior would come in the form of a sophomore girl with a straight brown bob and braces, but that's who's standing in front of me, offering me refuge.

"I'm Becca," she says with a smile. She's got pink rubber bands on her braces and her clothes are a little sporty for my taste, but they're name brand.

Not that that should matter, I scold myself.

"Are you sure you have room?" My campaign smile is in full force, and she beams back.

"Follow me."

And that's how I end up sitting with a group of sophomores who, from the way they talk, will all be on the snowboarding team next year. They have an easy rapport that's nothing like my circle of friends—correction: past circle of friends—and I'm envious of how they seem to have it all figured out. It takes all my self-control to sit back and listen, to not monopolize the conversation and charm them into adoring me, but eating alone has been miserable and I don't want to screw this up.

I've barely said two words by the time they're picking up their trays. When most of the group has left, Becca gives me a curious look.

"You're not like what I expected."

My hand lifts to toss my hair over my shoulder, but I catch myself and trace the edge of the table instead. My nail catches on something sticky and I yank my hand away. "What do you mean?" I have a pretty damn good idea what she means, but I'm curious if she'll say it.

She looks over her shoulder, but no one is sitting close enough to hear. "No offense, but my friends all thought you were a total bitch."

I stiffen. Even though that's what I wanted people to think, it sucks hearing a stranger say it, especially one who I'm starting to like.

"They didn't want me to ask you to sit with us." She laughs nervously. "They thought you'd pull some mind control hocus pocus and turn us into your slaves."

"Your friends seem really nice. And you, too," I add quickly. This shift in power makes me feel off balance but I'm desperate to be invited to sit here again tomorrow. "I know I have a reputation for being a bitch, but a lot has happened and..." I shrug. "I guess that doesn't seem as important anymore."

She smiles so hard the fluorescent lights bounce off her braces. "I'm glad to hear it. You're welcome to sit with us again if you want."

We both stand, and even though I'm several inches taller than her, I feel like we're on equal ground. "Thanks, Becca. I mean it."

Now if only the rest of my problems can be solved that easily. Because I still have twenty-six hours of community service to complete by Dad's deadline and zero ideas how to get it done.

twenty-seven

Soup kitchen. Nursing home aide. Or slave labor.

Slave labor is really an option? Drea asks.

We're texting while I try to figure out a community service option that will give me maximum hours in the next couple weeks.

Seems like it from these descriptions.

In truth, none of them seem that bad, especially after the Chain Gang, but it's the thought of starting over with all new people—people who might ask why I'm there and judge me for my stupidity—that has me ready to hide under the covers and never show my face again.

Why are you in such a hurry anyways? Don't you have like 6 months?

For as much as I've bragged about traveling to Switzerland in the past, I don't know why I haven't told Drea. *My dad promised a fancy spring break trip if I finish by Christmas.*

Ooh nice. Where?

I bite my lip before replying. Drea's safely tucked in this new image of myself, and I don't want the two mixing. But if I go, she'll find out eventually. *Switzerland. To ski. But it'd be with his new family.*

Bummer.

I also haven't told her about meeting The Seconds. *Piper is pretty cool but it'll be more babysitting than partying.*

But still, Switzerland...

Suddenly thoughts of Pierre aren't as appealing, not when Xavier is twenty minutes away. *I do love it there.*

Wait. You've already been?

Last year. And the year before that, and before that.

Then I guess you better find a way to finish your hours.

A little while later, I'm still no closer to choosing anything and sleep sounds more and more appealing. I'm thumbing through my homework in bed, barely able to keep my eyes open, when Xavier texts.

Miss you.

Mondays aren't the same without the Chain Gang.

But it wasn't on Monday.

No, but I looked forward to seeing you.

He doesn't write back right away and I break out into a sweat. Should I not have said that? He knows I like him but—wait. I shake my head. Since when do I stress over what I say to a guy? We may not have said the exact words, but I'm ninety-nine percent certain we're exclusive so it shouldn't shock him for me to say that I want to see him. And he texted first saying he misses me.

Sweat beads on my upper lip. What is wrong with me?

Me too.

See, I was overreacting for no reason. *When can I see you again?*

Tomorrow?

Not soon enough. I'm still sweating, even though I'm no longer worrying, and my head feels like it's filled with lead. I drop to the pillow and thumb a reply. *Perfect. Want to come over after school?*

Yes.

My phone dings with more texts, but it drops from my hand onto the pillow next to me. My fingers reach for it, but it slides off the pillow and onto the floor. What is wrong with me? It takes all my energy to roll to my side and stretch my arm toward where it fell, but I can't reach.

It's like my phone drifted to another dimension and no matter how hard I try, I can't reach it. The heaviness in my head grows, forcing my eyes shut, and sleep overcomes me.

"Brianna." Mom's voice breaks through the fog that shoved me headfirst into sleep. "Dinner's ready."

"Mom?" My tongue feels thick and my voice is scratchy. Xavier. I never answered his texts. I lift my head but it's like a vise is wrapped around my skull, holding me down.

She brushes my hair from my face and touches my forehead. "You're burning up." She runs her hand over my cheek and rests it on my neck. "How long have you been feeling badly?"

"I don't know," I mumble into the pillow. "My phone." My hand opens and closes, still unable to reach it.

She sets it in my hand, and the bed sinks beneath her weight as she sits next to me. "Tell me what hurts."

"Everything." And it does. My entire body aches, chills sweep through me, and I'm still sweaty. At least that explains my mental meltdown earlier. I'm not losing it—I'm sick.

"I'll bring you some soup and aspirin. Do you need anything else?"

I try to shake my head but it's too much effort.

"Be right back." Her hand trails over my forehead once more, then I'm alone again.

My head refuses to budge, so I rest my phone on the pillow next to my face and with one eye, read Xavier's texts.

Should I bring more hot chocolate?

I can show you how to make it.

Or not....

Brianna?

Hello?

My eyes fight to close, but I manage to type out a message. *Sorry. Passed out. Think I'm sick. Talk soon.* I throw in a heart emoji so he doesn't think I'm blowing him off before dropping my phone onto the bed.

When Mom returns with a tray bearing tea and soup and aspirin, none of which sounds good, I'm still in the same position. She sets the tray on the nightstand next to the bed and helps me out of my jeans and under the covers. "At least take the aspirin," she says, holding the glass and pills.

As I'm swallowing the pills, a new text comes through. Mom glances at the screen and raises an eyebrow. *Oh crap.* "Who's sending you hearts?"

"What? Oh, no one. They're sarcastic hearts."

The urge to tuck my phone where she can't see it is probably just as strong as her urge to snoop in my phone, but neither of us move. Me because I can't, and her out of some intrinsic sense of decency or respect for my privacy.

"It's just my friend Drea."

"I thought perhaps it's the boy you don't seem to want me to know about."

This time I successfully shake my head, but immediately regret it. "Can we do this later?"

Her lips press in a tight line. "Text if you need anything. And no school tomorrow if you're still feeling like this."

Two days later, I'm finally able to crawl to the shower to wash off the sickness funk. Xavier promised not to come over until I was less achy, which I'm hoping will be tomorrow, and my teachers have all emailed my assignments so I have plenty to help me fall asleep to get that rest Mom insists I need. The only thing I don't have is the one thing I really need: a new community service option.

Since I missed yesterday, Dad texted to find out why I hadn't checked in. He was kind enough to say "feel better," but it was immediately followed by a reminder of how little time I have left to meet his deadline.

Drea offered to come over bearing soup, but I fended her off under the guise that I didn't want to get her sick. Really I don't want her to see the house. In a couple weeks we'll be in our new condo and I can start fresh. Until then, I don't want her over here.

By Thursday, I'm so sick of being sick that I beg Mom to let me go to school, but she refuses. "One more day won't kill you. Besides, you already have your assignments, right?"

Having and completed are two very different things, but I nod. "Can I have a friend over after school? I'm going stir crazy." I hadn't planned to ask her permission, but if she knows someone will be here, she won't feel the need to come home early. At least I hope not.

She eyes me like she suspects I'm planning something, so I smile weakly. Finally, she nods. "Not for too long."

"Okay." As soon as she leaves for work, I text Xavier. *My house this afternoon?*

His reply is almost immediate. *Yes querida.*

It's a good thing Mom's gone, because there's no hiding the flush that colors my cheeks.

By three o'clock, I've showered, cleaned my room, and even attempted some homework. But none of that has eased the nerves and excitement over having Xavier in my house. Part of me has the same hesitation that I do with Drea, but he's already seen the outside, so what difference does it make? I'm also going to ask him to the winter formal. Kids already saw us together last weekend, so we may as well make it official.

At five minutes past three, he texts. *I'm here.*

I smooth my butter-soft leggings over my hips and adjust my oversized sweater so it's falling off one shoulder. Whoever brought that back in style is a genius. My hair is down and my face is bare except for a touch of mascara, and when I open the door, the look on his face tells me I made the right decision.

He steps forward and I'm in his arms, the cold air from outside only tickling my bare feet because the rest of me is wrapped up in him.

"Hi," I whisper near his neck, unable to stop my lips from brushing over his skin.

He responds by squeezing me tighter. "I missed you."

I could stand here all day, but it's freezing outside and while the landscaping is extensive, it doesn't shield the front door from the road. "Come inside." With his hand in mine, I lead him to the living room, where I've already set out sparkling waters and popcorn.

He shrugs out of his jacket and sets a reusable grocery bag on the floor. "Hot chocolate," he says when he sees me look.

"Maybe in a little bit." I sink onto the couch, tucking one leg beneath me. "Come here."

He's at my side in a flash. His hand moves over the soft fabric of my leggings and pulls my legs so they're draped over his. Every touch makes me feel alive and I curse myself for being sick.

"How are you feeling?"

"Mostly better. I wanted to go back today but my mom made me stay home again." It's been pleasantly weird how motherly she's been. In the past, she barely noticed if I wasn't feeling well, but the past couple days she's been practically doting.

"How'd you get sick?"

"Probably the nastiness on the lunch table." I shudder, remembering the unidentifiable goop that stuck to my hand. "I probably shouldn't kiss you..." I push out my lower lip in a practiced way that usually gets me kissed. His gaze drops to my mouth and his eyelids lower, and it's nice to know I've still got it, even in my sickly state.

"My immune system is pretty strong," he whispers, leaning close to kiss my bare shoulder. My eyes close and I lose myself in the feel of his hands on me. Too quickly he pulls away. "But if you're not feeling well...."

I tuck my head against his chest, willing my immune system to catch up to his. "I'd hate for you to get this."

He holds my gaze, smiling tenderly, and I want to melt into him. "You promised me a movie." He lifts my legs and moves out from beneath me. "I'll get the hot chocolate going while you get it ready."

"Do you care what we watch?"

The look he gives me tells me he doesn't plan on watching much of the movie, and I get all swoony inside.

"Kitchen is down the hall. Be there in a second." I point down the hallway and pick up the remote and scroll through the categories. As much as I'd love to keep him on the couch with me as long as I can, Mom will be home in two hours. I hit play on a recent comedy, then pause it and join Xavier in the kitchen.

His back is to me and he already has a pan on the stove. I pause in the doorway, shaking my head at how life works out. Two months ago I never would have imagined our paths crossing, and now I can't imagine my life without him. He has a way of making me want to be a better person that, if anyone else had said it, I'd say was a load of crap. Yet here I am, trying to change.

"You going to stand over there or come learn how to make this?" His voice is light, teasing, and it pulls me to him.

I slide my arms around him from behind and rest my cheek against his back. His hand covers mine, holding it against his heart, which is pounding as fast as mine. His lips graze my knuckles and I'm starting to think hot chocolate isn't going to happen when he moves me to his side.

"The trick is the chocolate." He opens a yellow box with a grandmotherly-type woman on the front and takes out a solid piece of chocolate. "You have to melt it in milk. That powdered stuff is for amateurs." He winks at me. "No offense."

"After tasting how good this is, I understand."

He pours milk into the pan and sprinkles cinnamon on top. "Now we wait."

"That's it? I expected, I don't know, something more complex."

"Just time." He leans against the counter and I magically end up in his arms. I meant what I said about not wanting to get him sick, so instead of kissing him, I nuzzle into his neck, breathing him in. For a second, I imagine we're at the dance, swaying to a slow song, him in a suit and me in something with a low-cut back. As if reading my mind, his hand trails up and down my back, each time dipping lower until he's grazing my hip, then my butt. Score two for the super soft leggings. My fingers trail over his shoulders, finding their way to the back of his head, where his hair tickles my palm. I pull him closer, stretching my body to feel him fully pressed against me. He turns his face so his lips are on my skin and I exhale softly. When his kisses move closer to my mouth, I pull away.

"No kissing."

The corner of his mouth lifts in a smile, making my heart pound even harder. "Anything else off limits?"

And now I really want to drag him upstairs. "Probably for a couple more days." Like after the dance.

He buries his face in my hair. "It's a date," he whispers.

I'm not one hundred percent certain what I just agreed to, but I can't wait to find out.

He loosens his grip on me to stir the chocolate, and minutes later we're back on the couch, steaming mugs in hand. I hook one leg over his and sit as close to him as I can without actually sitting on him, even though I really really want to, and hit play on the movie. We don't talk much, but our hands roam over each other, and by the time the movie ends I'm second-guessing my no kissing rule. I hit stop on the remote and when I face Xavier, the look on his face makes everything else fade away. It's like I'm the only one in the universe, the only one he sees or wants or thinks of, and now his mouth closing in on mine. "Wait," I say as he presses his lips to the corner of my mouth. If I part my lips—no. I'm holding strong on this. I angle my face away from his and his tongue sears my neck. My willpower is barely holding on by a thread when the alarm on my phone goes off.

Mom will be home any minute. And I still haven't asked him about the dance.

I cradle his face in my hands and kiss the same spot next to his mouth where he kissed me. "That's the warning bell for my mom."

It's like I threw cold water on him. He sits upright, adjusting his clothes, then mine, before smoothing my hair off my face. "Don't want her to think we've been doing anything but watching the movie."

Shit. He thinks he's going to meet her? "Actually, I was thinking it might be best if you leave before she gets home. Since I've been home sick..." I trail off, hoping he can fill in the rest. That my mother's a judgmental bitch who will not approve of him.

He clenches his jaw and his eyes harden, but then he kisses my cheek and the moment passes. "If that's what you want."

I run my hand over his chest. "What I want is to hide you in my room and have my way with you, but that will have to wait."

He laughs softly. "I'm glad I'm not the only one thinking that."

With a heavy sigh, I extricate myself from his arms and stand. "I'll grab your stuff in the kitchen, and then I need to ask you something." I'm putting the yellow chocolate box in his bag when the front door opens.

No no no no no.

"Oh, hello," Mom says from the living room. I hear Xavier's voice but can't make out his words. He's no doubt introducing himself like the respectful guy that he is, and I can only imagine what's going through Mom's head.

I need to get him out of here before she says something I won't be able to fix. Because with Miranda Vines it's not a question of if, but when. I burst into the room with the bag in my hand and the perfect line evaporates with my breath. It's worse than I thought. On the surface, she looks as polite and polished as ever, but the tick in her eyebrow and the way she's clutching her hands tells me I have exactly twenty seconds before she loses her shit.

"Mom, hey. This is Xavier." I hand him the bag, careful not to let my hand brush his or do anything that will alert her that something's going on between us.

"Yes," she says through gritted teeth. "He told me."

"I was just leaving," he says, looking from my mother to me like he's unsure why she's pissed.

She gives him a once over, and it's not subtle. Her gaze scalds him from head to toe, then back up again before focusing on me. "This is who you're dating?" Emphasis on the word this, like he's not standing right here. "Oh, that's right. You said you're not dating anyone."

Xavier stiffens next to me.

"That's not what I said—or meant." He moves away from me and I reach for his arm, but stop before making contact.

Her eyes jump from his tattoos to his earrings and back to his tattoo. "I think it's best if you go," Mom says, her voice clipped, but he's already stalking to the door.

"Xavier, wait." I hurry after him to the foyer, where he's yanking on his coat. "I'm sorry about my mom. I told you she's a bitch."

He whirls on me, eyes flashing with anger. "Are you ashamed of me?"

"No!"

The look he gives me is one I've never seen from him, not even with that dickweed from community service. It's a combination of disgust and hurt and I'll do anything to make it go away.

"Then why did you tell her nothing's going on with us?"

"It—it's complicated."

He zips up his coat. "No. It's not." He moves to the front door and opens it. "You've met my friends. My family. I didn't lie about what you mean to me."

My eyes fill with tears but if it has an effect on him, it doesn't show. Asking him to the dance now is pointless.

"I'll make this easy for you." With a final glance over my shoulder, he turns away and walks out of my life.

When I push the door closed, Mom's watching me from the living room, arms crossed.

"Why would you do that?!" My scream echoes off the walls and she blinks, startled.

She smooths the front of her blouse. "I can't believe you'd let him into our house, let alone your pants."

"You are unbelievable."

"I'm just looking out for your best interests."

"Well don't." I push past her, but turn back at the bottom of the stairs. "And he hasn't been in my pants." *Yet*, I silently add. Although from the way he just looked at me, he may never speak to me again.

"Thank goodness for small mercies."

"You know what?" I yell. "He's the sweetest, most considerate boy I've ever met, but you're so hung up on appearances that you'll never understand that." I take a step toward her but falter when her eyes narrow. "And his mom could teach you a thing or two about being a mother. She was nothing but nice to me. But you..." My eyes close as I take a deep breath. "You have no idea what makes me happy."

She moves closer. "I just did you a favor if you think that boy will make you happy."

"Keep telling yourself that." I take the stairs two at a time and collapse in a heap on my bed, fighting back tears.

You knew it would end this way.

But that doesn't make it hurt any less.

twenty-eight

Xavier won't return my texts. I've broken Old Brianna's rules by continuing to reach out because I refuse to let this be the end. After I told Drea what happened, she insisted I tell Xavier the truth, and I've tried. I really have. The number of unanswered texts surely qualifies me for Desperate Loser of the Year.

The winter formal came and went—the first dance I've ever missed—but from what I saw online, no one missed me. My only saving grace is now it's winter break so I can pout in private.

Drea and I have been texting more, and she admitted that she's not happy with Colton. After a lot of back and forth, she decided to break up with him over the holidays because they won't have to see each other at school, and while I hate that she's struggling with this, I'm hopeful she can finally be happy.

Yes, I'm actually concerned about another girl's feelings.

And I haven't spoken to Mom in a week.

As Christmas approaches, we continue to tip-toe around each other. I was able to get regular breakfast hours at the food kitchen, and while it's less crowded than it was on Thanksgiving, that pissy guy has been there every time. With each encounter, his anger toward me seems to grow. The director assures me it's not my fault, but I can't help but wonder if this is my penance for years of treating people like shit.

If being his verbal punching bag will set things right with the universe, I'll take it.

Dad's pissed that I still haven't finished my hours, even though I'm on schedule, and he's not-so-lovingly reminded me that there won't be an extension. Today makes seventeen hours remaining, but if I don't complete my hours by next week, no Switzerland for me. After some serious time with my calculator, I figured out that if I work four hours every day until Christmas, I'll finish on time. Unless they send me home early.

I text Dad during an especially boring morning shift. *When you said Christmas, did you mean Christmas Day or Christmas break?*

His response comes as I'm driving home. *This is not a negotiation.*

So Christmas Day. Which is five days away.

My blood chills as I turn onto our street. Two moving trucks the size of a small country are parked in the driveway.

My driveway.

Deep down I knew this day was coming. Well, I knew on every level because everything we own is shoved in a box, ready for "the next stage in our lives." Mom's words, not mine. And while she reminded me half a dozen times that they'd be here today, I guess I was still holding out hope that it wouldn't happen. That we'd get to keep the house and hang onto this one thing from when things were good.

Or at least okay.

I park next to the truck closest to the house and scowl at the man holding a clipboard near the back of the truck. His uniform sports a logo that matches the decal on the truck, and a thick leather belt is cinched around his waist. He gives me a nod and smile, and I feel a twinge of guilt for not doing the polite thing and smiling back. He may be doing his job, but this is my life.

Inside, hulking men in matching uniforms carry boxes down the stairs. My name is scrawled across the side of several and my stomach plummets.

"Please be careful with those," I say.

"Don't worry, Miss," says the man holding all my belongings. "We'll take good care of your things." They march by in a depressing caravan, emptying the house of all evidence that I've lived here my entire life.

"Oh good, you're here." Mom comes down the stairs between two men who could pass for professional linebackers. "As they clear out each room, I need you to double check that nothing was overlooked."

My head nods, but it's like my mind and body are no longer connected.

Mom pauses, her checklist hovering between us. A glimmer of compassion crosses her face. "I know this is stressful, but I need you firing on all cylinders. You can wallow tonight."

Tonight. In our new condo. Where we'll get our fresh start and birds will chirp outside our window and little faeries will help me unpack. Right. "Sure, Mom."

She rests her hand on my arm and for a minute I'm ten years old, before status and appearances and the need to be idolized took over. "We'll order from Coast, okay?"

Tears burn my eyes, and I'm surprised to see her eyes watering, too. A lump catches in my throat, making it hard to speak. "It's a date."

She heads outside and I wander from room to room, committing each detail to memory, but everything that made this our home is already gone.

The men dismantle our lives in record time, then we're standing on the front porch, the cold air swirling around us. "Looks like it might snow," Mom says, and I raise an eyebrow. "I know, talking about the weather. But it does." She points at the heavy clouds rolling over the treetops. "Hopefully they can get everything unloaded before it hits."

The trucks back out of the driveway, their high-pitched beeps shrieking in time with my thoughts.

Don't go.

Come back.

This can't be happening.

Mom watches them for another moment before turning to

me. "I've already done my final walk-through, but if you want to check once more, I can meet you at the condo."

"Thanks." I wish I could say more. To tell her how grateful I am for this act of kindness. To acknowledge that underneath her steely appearance, she really does have a heart. "I won't be long."

She walks down the path to her car while I step inside one last time. Grief nearly knocks me to the floor. This is it. We're really leaving the only home I've ever known. The last thread to when our lives were complete has finished unraveling and all that's left to show for it is an empty house.

The day of my arrest, when Dad announced he was leaving, feels like eons ago. And yet it's barely been a few weeks. So much has changed that I almost don't recognize my reflection in the French doors. I seem older somehow, more grown up, and I'm both excited and scared for the future.

I don't go upstairs. The house is completely empty—I've already idiot-checked every room—and seeing my room will only make this harder. Despite what Mom said, I've never been one to wallow. Turning off the light in the foyer, I pick up the shoebox I saved for last, whisper "goodbye," then close the door on my past.

Maybe this move won't be all bad. I've hit rock bottom in every way possible, so the only way left is up.

Mom's expecting me at the condo, but I make a detour on the way. My fingers drum the top of the shoebox in the passenger seat, and I try not to think about what's inside. What it represents.

In a perfect world, I'd return the jewelry I stole to the stores, but A) I don't want to get in more trouble, and B) I honestly don't remember what came from which store. Carrying a shoebox around downtown Boulder and asking store owners to pick what belongs to them doesn't sound like the best idea, so I'm bringing it to the women's shelter Bruno mentioned. Bracelets and necklaces may not be as important as toiletries and clothes, but everyone likes to look pretty.

I'm not sure what I was expecting, but the metal door beneath a sign that says "Drop Off" is locked. A couple bags of clothes sit beneath the overhang, so I unceremoniously set the shoebox on top, giving it a final pat before heading back to my car. A weight doesn't lift my shoulders, and I don't breathe a sigh of relief.

Because I took the easy way out. But it's a start.

By the time I get to the condo, the truck is half empty. The second truck went to a storage unit, where furniture and wedding albums and vacation mementoes will sit until Mom's ready to get rid of them—proving she is human. My bed is assembled and boxes sit along the wall, ready for me to reinvent my life.

We eat sushi while watching a DVD since the internet won't be connected until tomorrow, and when I fall asleep in the strange room that doesn't yet smell like mine, an unfamiliar feeling settles around my heart.

Hope.

twenty-nine

On Christmas Eve morning, my alarm wakes me from a restless sleep—the rainbows and cotton candy I hoped to dream of were replaced by Xavier's look of hurt and betrayal and Dad's disappointment that I still haven't finished my community service hours.

But today's the magic day. Four more hours in the food kitchen and I'm done. With no time to spare.

I dig my phone out from beneath my pillow and my breathing stops when I see a text from Drea.

I need your help.

And she sent it over an hour ago.

I scramble to a sitting position. *Where are you?*

At a motel near the highway.

Shit. This can't be good. *I need an address.*

She gives me the name and which highway. I have no idea where it is but that's what GPS is for. *I'll be there as soon as I can.*

I throw on jeans and a dark hoodie—the same outfit I'd planned to wear to the food kitchen—and pull my hair into a ponytail. Old Brianna makes me hesitate for a moment. If I go, I won't finish my hours by Dad's deadline.

No Switzerland.

And Dad's eternal disappointment.

But I have to help Drea.

Downstairs, boxes line the kitchen but the coffeepot has

already been put to use. I fill a travel mug and call out, "Mom, I'm heading out."

A light dusting of snow covers my 4Runner—I lost the argument for the one-stall garage before we even had it—and while I wait for the windshield to defrost, panic sets in. What am I doing? I don't know how to help Drea. Sure, I can go find her, but then what? Will she need to go to the hospital? Or the police? If she called me it must be bad.

My hands tremble as I pick up my phone and check the location. The motel is half an hour away. Maybe longer if the roads are slick. Is she safe? What if her boyfriend's there?

The phone slips into my lap. I can't do this alone.

Before I can overthink it, I call Xavier. He's gotten so good at ignoring my texts that I wouldn't be surprised if he's blocked my number. When he doesn't answer, I switch to texting.

This isn't about me. Drea needs help.

The windshield starts to clear but I stay in the driveway. If her boyfriend is still around, it'd be stupid for me to go by myself.

Xavier, please. I'm scared to go alone.

Sixty long seconds later, my phone rings. Xavier's name displays on the screen.

I hit answer, my heart in my throat. Part of me wants to take advantage of having him on the phone and tell him how sorry I am and how much I miss him, but this isn't about me. "I know you hate me, but Drea texted that she needs help. She's at a motel and her boyfriend..." I trail off. She didn't give me specifics so I can only imagine what he did to her. And my imagination doesn't hold back. "I'm scared to go there alone."

"Subie's in the shop."

My stomach drops. He isn't going to help.

"Text me the address." Those four words wrap around me, easing my sadness, if only for a moment.

I do as he says.

"Can you pick me up? The motel's about ten minutes from my house."

"I'll be there as fast as I can." The back of the 4Runner fishtails as I whip into the street, and I grip the steering wheel with both hands.

Twenty minutes is a long time to imagine what your friend's boyfriend did to her. I'm so scared of what we'll find that I don't have the headspace to think about seeing Xavier, and when I pull into his driveway and see him waiting in front of the garage, everything inside me falls apart. A sob escapes my throat. I knew I missed him, but my entire being yearns for him. He stops next to my door and I roll down the window, fighting back tears.

"You okay to drive?" he asks. He's clenching his jaw and his eyes focus on my tears for half a second before he looks through me like we never meant anything to each other.

I nod and hit unlock, then the scent of his body wash fills the car and he's sitting inches from me. The pain from the past two weeks lessens, and I try to focus on the fact that he doesn't hate me enough to block my number. He's here now, and that has to mean something.

"What's wrong with Subie?"

He stares out the window. "Finally getting the door replaced."

"Oh."

We're there too soon. Not because I'm trying to milk this time with Xavier, but because I'm terrified of what we're going to find. I park near the office of the brick, two-story building.

I text Drea. *I'm here. Where are you?*

Room 212.

I show Xavier her text and he gets out of the car. We fall in step up the concrete staircase that cut the building in half, me slightly behind him. He hasn't touched me—heck, he's barely looked at me—but when we come to a stop in front of room 212, he stands so he's shielding me from whatever lies inside.

"Do you know if she's alone?" His voice is rough and scratchy, and I realize he's probably reliving what happened with Lily. I reach out to touch him but stop inches from his shoulder.

"I don't."

"Text her that we're outside and she can come out."

I'm outside your door with Xavier. Can you come out?

Her response is immediate and terrifying. *No.*

My stomach drops and it's like everything stops moving. The sounds of traffic fade away and all I can hear is the blood pounding in my ears. "Try the door."

He grips the knob and the door swings open. The lights are off, the bed unmade. Light from the open doorway falls upon clothes and what looks like everything from inside her purse scattered across the floor.

"Drea?" I whisper into the darkness.

A whimper sounds from deep inside the room. Xavier meets my eyes, and the look of terror in his nearly undoes me. "I think you should stay here," he whispers.

Everything in me to argue, but this is why I called him. As he steps into the darkness, panic grabs my chest. What are we doing? We're just teenagers. Shouldn't the police handle this? "Wait."

He reappears in the shaft of light. "Get ready to call 9-1-1." Then he disappears again.

The seconds tick by, each filling my head with what he'll find. Finally, he calls out, "It's safe."

I find them huddled in the narrow space between the bed and the wall. Drea's bare legs are pulled tight to her body, her arm cradled against her chest. Her curly hair is loose, covering her face. "What can I do?"

"Call the police," Xavier says.

Drea shakes her head. "No." Her voice is raspy, barely a squeak. So different from the strong, confident girl I've gotten to know.

I drop to my knees next to Xavier and reach across him to touch her leg. She flinches at the contact, and I yank my hand back. "Drea, where's Colton?"

"I don't know."

"We need to get you out of here," I say.

"I just want to go home."

"We can take you home," Xavier says. His jaw ticks. "But you need to see a doctor."

"Can you bring me?"

Xavier and I lock eyes in the semi-darkness. Our first priority is getting her away from this place. "Of course," I say.

He pushes up from the floor and steps over me to stand near the end of the bed. "You'll need to help her." He gestures at the floor. "Her pants."

Right. I squat next to her and resist brushing her hair from her face. "Is it okay if we turn on the light?"

She nods, tucking her face into her knees. Xavier turns on the light on the nightstand, then moves across the room to close the door and leans against the far wall. A pair of leggings are on the floor near the TV, along with her Chucks.

Her purple Chucks.

Seeing them on the floor of this dingy motel room connects this broken girl in front of me with the sarcastic, funny girl who's become my only friend and I can't stop the tears that slide down my face. I grab the leggings and hold them in front of me, unsure how to do this. "I need you to help me."

She lifts her face and the room tilts on its axis. Her eye is nearly swollen shut and a cut runs down the length of her cheek. Her lower lip is split, blood crusted along the edge, and angry red marks ring her throat.

"Oh my god."

"Who the hell are you?" We jump at the voice booming from the doorway. Drea curls even tighter against the wall. This must be Colton. I vaguely remember her telling me he plays football, and it shows. He's handsome in a conventional way—tall, blond hair, built—but nothing about him is attractive. He's gripping a fast food bag and his other fist flexes and unflexes at his side. A sneer darkens his face as his gaze bounces between the three of us.

Xavier reaches the door in two strides and blocks the entrance. "The question you should be asking is why the hell you came back." Xavier is several inches shorter but that doesn't seem to scare him.

"That's my girlfriend. I brought her breakfast."

My blood chills. It's like he doesn't realize she's been beat up.

Xavier doesn't back down. "She's not hungry."

Colton's jaw clenches. "Don't tell me what she wants." He peers in our direction over Xavier's shoulder and his voice softens. "Baby, you hungry? I got you hash browns."

Drea's hand finds mine and squeezes like her life depends on it. Her leggings are still in my other hand, so as discreetly as I can, I untangle them and nudge the opening over her toes. Without looking away from Colton, she relaxes her leg so I can tug them up her shins. We get them to her knees before Colton realizes something's going on.

"What are you doing? You can't leave."

"Hurry," I whisper.

"Back off," Xavier growls. "You are not coming in here."

I look up to see them toe-to-toe, the paper bag forgotten on the floor. Rage rolls off Colton like it's a second skin and he's staring down at Xavier like he wants to rip his head off. In that moment I realize Xavier isn't just protecting Drea.

He's protecting me.

We need to get out of here. "Drea, you have to help me." My hands tremble as I yank the leggings farther up her legs. She braces herself against the wall to pull them over her butt, then collapses against me.

Now what?

My phone! I can call the police!

It's on the bed within arm's reach, but I don't know what Colton will do if he sees me reach for it. It's like we're frozen in a stand-off, the three of us against Colton, and I'm terrified to make the wrong move.

"Get out of my way before you regret it." Colton steps forward until his chest bumps Xavier's, and I grab my phone while they're glaring at each other. But there's no way I can call with him standing here.

"Text," Drea whispers.

I've never called the police and I've certainly never texted them, so I don't know what to say. I enter 9-1-1 and type *Help. My friend's hurt and her boyfriend won't let us leave.* I add the name of the hotel and hit send.

A reply comes immediately, the ding loud and clear in the small room. I flip it to silent but it's too late. Colton focuses on me like he's seeing me for the first time.

"Who are you texting?"

I shrug, hoping it comes off as casual. "It's just my mom asking if I want a latte." I roll my eyes. "Obviously I said no."

Confusion flashes across his face, and Xavier takes advantage of the distraction. With both arms folded like he's a linebacker, he shoves Colton out of the room and slams the door. He leans his weight against the door and I scramble to my feet to help. The door thumps like Colton's throwing his body against it, my teeth rattling with each thud, and Xavier fumbles with the chain lock. It slips from his fingers once, then a second time. It feels like the entire room shakes as Colton pounds on the door, and finally Xavier gets the chain to catch.

"I texted 9-1-1," I say, hurrying back to my phone.

There's a string of replies.

Do you need an ambulance?

Can you lock yourself in a room?

We're on our way.

Colton keeps throwing himself against the door and Drea whimpers with each blow.

The flimsy lock in the handle finally gives way in a burst of splintered wood, but the chain holds. Barely. His red face fills the small opening, his eyes unfocused.

I type out a reply. *We locked him out of the room but he's still trying to get in.*

"Drea! Let me in! You know I didn't mean to hurt you. I love you. I want to spend the rest of my life with you." He lowers his voice. "Baby, think about our future. Everything we have planned."

Drea shakes next to me.

"Stay here," I whisper. "Don't talk to him."

Her eyes fill with tears. "I tried to break up with him."

Xavier shoves the door closed and leans against it. The pounding starts back up but it's less intense, like he's switched to his fists rather than his entire body.

"The police are almost here," I say. "They won't let him hurt you ever again."

Her eyes grow wide. "I don't want my parents to find out about this." Her gaze flits back and forth between me and the closed door.

I rest my hand on her foot as sirens pierce the air. "You won't be able to hide this from them."

She touches her cheek and winces. Her good eye closes, and tears slide down her face. "Is it that bad?"

"Yeah. But I'm here for you. And I swear I'll do everything I can to make sure he never hurts you or anyone else." I don't know what I can actually do, but the fierce protectiveness sweeping through me has to mean something.

The sirens grow louder, and moments later shouts come from outside the door. There's another thud against the door. "I didn't do anything!" Colton's voice sounds almost manic. "Drea! Baby, tell them I didn't hurt you." There are sounds of a scuffle, then silence, then a knock on the door.

"Boulder PD. We've secured the suspect. It's safe to come out."

Xavier slides the chain lock that kept Colton out and opens the door. Two cops Colton's size stand in the doorway, their hands hovering near the guns holstered on their hips. "We need an ambulance," Xavier says.

"No," Drea squeaks. "Please no."

"I can ride with you," I say, but the fear in her eyes makes me wonder if she even heard me. "Drea, it's gonna be okay." No one can know that for sure, but I have to hope that it will.

The cops enter the room, stalking through the small room like they're predators tracking their prey, and finally stop near the foot of the bed. "Did he do this to you?" the one on the left asks Drea.

She doesn't answer at first, but the tears streaming down her face seem to be enough of an answer. For now.

The cop squeezes the radio strapped to his chest. "What's the status on the bus?" He raises his eyebrows at me. "You hurt?" I shake my head, and he presses the button again. "Just one."

The other cop approaches Xavier. "What happened here?"

Xavier fills him in while I help Drea out of the corner. Her legs tremble as she stands, and she's still clutching her arm to her chest, so I guide her to the bed and grab her shoes.

Our cop squats next to the bed so he's looking up at Drea. "Can you tell me what happened?"

Her eye closes, a fresh wave of tears rolling down her cheeks and wetting the dried blood on her lips. "We come here sometimes to..." she waves her hand at the bed like she doesn't want to tell the cop they have sex here, "but I tried to break up with him instead."

"Has he hit you before?" he asks.

She nods, and I flash to the bruise on her back on trash duty. It seems like so long ago. How many times has he done this? She touches her cheek and sucks in a breath. "But this is the first time he's touched my face."

The cop's jaw ticks as he takes notes. He inhales deeply, then lets it out slowly, like he's practicing a technique to calm down. "The ambulance will be here in a few minutes and they'll take good care of you. We'll get your full statement at the hospital."

"Great." Her sarcasm isn't lost on the cop.

"We'll also need to call your parents."

If it's possible, she shrinks even more inside herself. "If they even care."

"I'm sure they care," I say. But I don't know that. From what she's said her parents are never around and don't seem very involved in her life, but I can't believe they wouldn't care that Colton beat her up. I rest my hand on her shoulder, but quickly pull back. Seeing what Colton did to her—has been doing—it makes sense that she seems terrified of physical contact.

The cop looks her in the eye. "If you're under seventeen, we have to call them. And we have to wait to get your statement until one of them is present."

"I've never been so happy to have a fall birthday. I'm eighteen."

"They still need to know," I say.

"Fine." She closes her eye and takes a deep breath like she's pulling energy from deep within herself. "I think my phone's under the bed." The cop retrieves it and she gives him their numbers. "If you can keep the details to a minimum, I'd appreciate it."

The cop stands and tucks his notebook in his front pocket. His already stern face deepens to a frown. "We'll do our best to make sure he never hurts anyone ever again."

Her lips wobble like she's trying to smile, but can't. "Thank you," she whispers, and he joins the other cop who's still talking to Xavier. She leans her head on my shoulder. "I don't know what would have happened if you hadn't come."

"I'm glad you trusted me to help."

"Is he gonna get arrested?"

"I think he already has been."

"What will this do to his future? To his football career?"

"Don't think about that. He deserves whatever's coming to him, and then some."

She lifts her head, tears shining in her eye, and stares out the open door like she can see him outside. "He used to be so sweet. I thought I was the luckiest girl in the world because Colton Rogers liked me." She shakes her head. "If I could go back and tell fourteen-year old me to run away screaming, I would."

I cover her hand with mine. "I'm so sorry this happened. But I'm proud of you. I know how scared you were to end things—rightfully so—but you did it. Things can only get better from here."

"We'll see."

Words of encouragement are not my strong suit, and this doesn't feel like the right time for it anyway, so we sit in silence until the ambulance arrives. Two paramedics strap her to a board, but because there isn't an elevator, they have to carry her down the stairs. She looks so small and alone that my heart breaks for her all over again. Once she's settled inside the ambulance, I start to climb in, but she stops me.

"Can you—" she closes her eye for a moment. "I need to be alone. Just until the hospital. Is that okay?"

I rest my hands on the edge of the gurney, wishing I could channel my strength to her. "I'll meet you at the hospital."

"Thank you, Brianna. Seriously. I don't know what would have happened if you both hadn't come." She looks over my shoulder like she's looking for someone. "Will you thank Xavier for me?"

"Of course."

The paramedics close the doors and I step away. Xavier's lingering near my car, alone. I start to move toward him but the cop from the motel room stops me. "I'll need your statement, too." He hands me a business card. "Can you come to the police station with one of your parents?"

There's no way in hell I'm setting foot in another police station. "Can we do it at the hospital?"

"Can one of your parents be there?"

I close my eyes, already imagining Mom's reaction when I call her. But I nod. "Yes." Because while she may not be the ideal mother, I believe she'll be there when it matters.

He tells me the name of the hospital and walks over to the other officers. Now nothing and everything is stopping me from talking to Xavier. If he'll even listen. He's still here, which has to mean something, but I can't get my feet to move. We stare at each other from across the parking lot, neither willing to take the first step.

Finally, after what feels like an eternity, I walk toward him. He doesn't stiffen or recoil as I get closer, but the hard look that's been on his face since he shoved Colton from the room is still there. I stop a couple feet away, lean against my car, and dare to look him in the eye.

thirty

"Thank you for waiting," I say.

"You're my ride."

His words hit me in the gut. He doesn't care. Whatever we had is in the past.

"Oh."

He lets out a breath and leans against the car, still keeping his distance. "I didn't mean it like that." He cracks his knuckles and his body seems to relax a little. "Are you okay? That was pretty intense."

"Intense is a good word." I take a quick inventory of myself, and despite my broken heart for Drea and a slight tremor running through me, I feel reasonably normal. "I seem to be okay."

"It'll probably catch up with you later."

"Awesome."

Our eyes meet, then we both look away, the silence dragging out between us. I could let this be the end. Drive him home and never see him again. Or I could tell him the truth—the whole truth—and try to rekindle this thing between us with whatever pieces are left. I clear my throat. "There are some things I need to tell you."

He watches me, waiting.

"Not here. Can we get coffee before going to the hospital? Or do you need to go home?"

"How about hospital coffee?" he asks.

"That works. Let me call my mom quick." He nods, and I pull out my phone. How do you tell your mother she has to come to the hospital so you can give a statement to the police without completely freaking her out? The fact that I rarely call her—we always text—will probably tip her off before she even answers.

She answers on the second ring. "Are you okay?" Her voice is a little breathless.

"I'm okay. But my friend was hurt and I'm on my way to the hospital to see her and I need to give a statement to the police." I pause to catch my breath, expecting a tirade on making bad choices and how busy she is, but the line is silent. "Since I'm a minor, I need a parent there."

"I can leave in five minutes. Text me the address."

"Okay. Tha—"

"Are you sure you're not hurt?"

I look up to see Xavier watching me. "Just a little freaked out."

"I'm glad you're okay. I'll be there soon. And Brianna?"

"Yeah?"

"I love you."

"O-okay. Bye." I hang up and get in the car, feeling like the wind's been knocked out of me. I can't remember the last time she told me she loves me. I text her the name of the hospital and get in the car. Xavier slides in next to me, but we may as well be on different planets.

Once on the road, the silence almost kills me. But I want to wait until I can look him in the eye and see his reaction. We both deserve that.

I park near the emergency entrance and he leads me through the maze of halls to the cafeteria with a confidence I admire, and it reminds me how much I still don't know about him. And may never know.

We get our drinks—hot chocolate for him and a latte for me—and face each other across a small table. Nothing is stopping me from talking, yet I can't get the words to come out. He watches me with a mixture of skepticism and curiosity, so I take a deep breath and begin.

"First, I'm really sorry for the way my mom treated you. She and my dad are..." I want to use his "cómo se dice" line, but I don't want to offend him. I look into his eyes, and my gaze drifts to the tattoo on his neck that my lips have touched, and despite everything, heat warms my belly. "They're really into appearances. The simple fact that you look different from them is enough to make you not good enough." I hold up my hands. "In their eyes. Not mine."

His eyes lower. "Is it because I'm Mexican-American, or because I have tattoos?"

"Honestly, I hope it's just the tattoos. But I don't know. Mom and I haven't talked much since the day you came over."

He looks up, surprised. "How do you not talk to each other when you live in the same house?"

A sad smile lifts the corner of my mouth. "Years of practice?"

He frowns. "You should try to talk to her."

"It's not that easy."

"Nothing worthwhile ever is."

I'm tempted to leave it at this and use his sympathy to convince him to give me another chance. But it can never work between us if he doesn't know the truth. "That's not what I want to talk to you about."

He takes a drink and sets his cup on the table. Everything inside me screams not to do this. To keep my secret safe. To hang onto this thread of whatever is still between us that will surely be destroyed once he knows who I really am.

My heart races. "Remember the Saturday we did trash duty at the park?" He nods and I pick up my latte, but set it down without taking a drink. "I didn't tell you what I know about when Cody died."

His eyebrows shoot up. "You knew him?"

My gaze drops to my cup. I can't watch his reaction when I say this. "I was there." My voice comes out a whisper, but from his sharp intake of breath, I know he heard me. "I'm the evil bitch Blake told you about."

He leans back in his chair and studies me like he's trying to fit what he's heard about me from Blake with what he knows firsthand. I've come a long way in the past few months and I cling to the hope that he won't be able to make the pieces fit. Then his face hardens. He opens his mouth to speak, closes it, then his eyes close too, like he's wishing me away.

"If I could take back what I did, what I said, I would. But I can't. There were too many emotions that day and anger won. I lashed out at Blake, and I've lived with that every day since. And I'm trying to change. I—"

His eyes snap open. "Blake has to live with the memory of watching his brother die, and you want me to feel bad for you?" The anger in his eyes burns up any hope that we can get past this.

I blink away tears. "No. I don't want your sympathy. I just want you to know everything so maybe..." I trail off.

"So maybe what? We get back together? I wouldn't be here today if it wasn't for Drea. My need for self-preservation is too strong to waste another minute on a stuck-up, calculating..." he pauses, like he wants to say bitch.

"You can call me a bitch."

He shakes his head. "I thought you were a different person."

"I'm trying to be. Instead of apologizing for what I said that day, I turned being a bitch into a life goal and I've wasted years trying to make everyone respect me, when really they just hate me. When I met you and Drea, I realized I finally had the chance to just be myself." My fingertips slide back and forth on the table between us. His mask of anger is starting to crack, and while I'm not stupid enough to think he'll come around, the need to make him understand pushes me forward. "I want to make things right. With you. With Blake and Cally. I know it might not change anything, but I'm trying."

"I can respect that."

A glimmer of hope shines in my heart.

"I accept your apology, but that's it."

My head drops. This is what I expected, but it still hurts. "Okay."

"Are you going to tell Drea?"

I look him in the eye. "She already knows."

He watches me like he's putting the pieces together. Drea knows the truth, and she still called me for help. Which means she trusts me. Emotions flick across his face, like he's trying to decide if he could learn to trust me again, too.

His hand reaches across the table, but he pulls it back before touching me. "Are you sure you're okay after this morning?"

I straighten my shoulders, relieved for the change of topic. "It's starting to hit me that we were actually in danger, but I'd do it again."

The corner of his mouth lifts in a smile. It's not the heart-melting smile I long for, but it's a start.

"How are you?" I ask. "This had to bring back everything with Lily and..."

He rubs his fist. "I kept reminding myself that I'm still on probation. I wanted to kick his ass but I couldn't." His eyes close for a moment, and when he opens them, his gaze is serious. "There's no way I was letting him back in that room to hurt either of you."

My heart skips at the ferocity in his voice. Maybe a tiny part of him does still care.

He takes another drink before pushing back from the table. "We should probably go find Drea."

Disappointment anchors me in my chair. This could be the last time we're alone, if you count sitting in the middle of a half-empty hospital cafeteria alone. I'm desperate to keep him here, to keep him talking, but he picks up his cup and carries it to the counter with dirty dishes. My feet drag as I follow him, and even though he waits for me at the entrance, my brain starts to accept that this is over.

But at least I told him the truth. As much as it hurts right now, I can move on knowing I gave it my best shot. We walk side by side to the emergency room, the distance between us the consequence of my years of bad behavior.

The woman behind the counter doesn't want to tell us where Drea is, and I'm about to lose my shit on her when I see the cop from the motel room standing outside a closed curtain.

"Hey," I call out, lifting my hand to wave.

He nods and walks toward us. "They just moved her to a room, so you can see her there. In the meantime," he looks between us. "I need to get your statement."

"My mom's on her way."

He leads us to an elevator and I ache to fill the silence, but there's nothing to left to say. Xavier's back to ignoring-me mode and I'm sure the cop has better things to worry about than my neuroses. We stop at a closed door. "I'll be out here. Grab me when your mother arrives."

I nod, and he pushes the door open. Drea's tucked into a bed covered in white linens, dwarfed by the machines surrounding her. A bandage covers the cut on her cheek. Pillows prop her in a sitting position, and another rests under her arm, which hangs from a sling around her neck. I rush to her side and grab the hand on her good arm. Xavier trails behind me, seeming uncertain, but she smiles at both of us.

"My heroes."

"Hardly," I say.

"I'm serious." Her voice is stronger than it was at the motel, more like the Drea I know. "I've seen him mad more times than I can count, but never like that. If you hadn't come when you did..." she shakes her head, and tears burn my eyes. She's already been through so much yet she seems ready to take on the world.

"I'm just glad we could help you," Xavier says from the foot of the bed. His voice is thick and scratchy, and when I look at him, his eyes shine in the fluorescent light.

"Have you talked to your parents?" I ask.

She nods. "They weren't supposed to be home from Dad's work trip until later tonight, but they left early." She touches her cheek. "I've only got a couple hours to make this look less horrific."

I try to smile but it comes out wobbly.

"Are you both okay?" Her gaze lingers on mine with unspoken questions. We nod, the tension between Xavier and me filling the room. I squeeze her hand again as my phone buzzes in my pocket.

Mom's here.

"I have to go give my statement, but I'll be back as soon as we're done." I brush her hair from her face and my heart feels fuller than it has in a very long time. This is the first time I've put someone else before myself and I don't know how to handle these emotions.

I glance at Xavier as I leave the room, but he doesn't look up.

Mom's pacing near the entrance to the emergency room, the automatic doors opening and closing with each turn. The panic on her face eases when she sees me and she pulls me into her arms. "I know you said you were okay, but my imagination went a little wild on the drive here." She grips my shoulders and pushes me back to look in my eyes. "I want to know everything that happened, but I suppose I can hear while we talk to the police, right?"

A woman coming through the automatic doors catches my eye. She looks like Xavier's mom, but before I get a good look at her, the cop from the motel interrupts my thoughts.

"We can talk in an office down the hall."

Once we're settled in the glorified closet, he pulls out his notepad. "Walk me through what happened. There's no right or wrong, I just need to hear your version of the events this morning."

Mom grabs my hand and I take a deep breath. I start with the text from Drea and the call to Xavier. If Mom's irritated he's involved, she doesn't let on. The cop's pen keeps pace with me, and as I tell them what happened, Mom's grip on my hand grows tighter and tighter. When it's finally over, he closes the notepad and shakes my hand. "Your friend is lucky to have you. In the future, call us first."

I nod, and he leaves us alone in the office.

Mom touches my cheek and her eyes fill with tears. "I'm so proud of you."

"You're not mad?"

"I'm terrified that you put yourself in that situation and would never wish that for you again, but you may have saved that girl's life."

Irritation prickles me. "Her name is Drea."

"Yes, Drea." She drops her hand and a frown tugs at her lips. "I know I haven't been the best role model, and I know I've often made things more difficult than they need to be." I open my mouth to object, even though she's right, but she holds up her hand to stop me. "Let me say this. Your father leaving was a wake-up call. I realized I can't keep living my life like no one else matters, because eventually there won't be anyone else. My marriage may be over, but you will always be my daughter and I can't let you slip away, too."

"So what does this mean?" She's saying the right things, but years of disappointment have taught me to be wary of Miranda Vines' promises.

"It means I'm going to stop worrying so much about what other people think and focus on what makes me happy. And that includes what makes you happy."

My mind immediately jumps to Xavier. Why couldn't she have had this revelation two weeks ago? "That's great, Mom." I'm not convinced she means it, but I've been trying to be a better person, so maybe there's hope for her, too.

She stands and I follow her into the hallway.

"You probably need to get back to work, huh?"

She faces me. "I've got a little more time."

This might not be the right place, but when has that stopped me? "Mom?"

She meets my eyes, her face relaxed. Calm.

"Something else has been bothering me and..." I wave my hand at the sterile hallway. "No time like the present?"

She adjusts her purse on her shoulder. "What's going on?"

My mind drifts upstairs to Xavier. He's probably doing his best to distract Drea from what happened, from what she's facing moving forward. "I know you have your reasons for not liking Xavier, but…" Just spit it out. I level my gaze at her. "I think you're wrong."

Her shoulders stiffen and her eyes narrow, but she doesn't erupt. She doesn't say anything.

Just once I wish she wouldn't make this difficult. That she wouldn't dismiss my opinions with a sneer and make me doubt that what I'm feeling is right. Because I am right. I've faithfully emulated her my entire life and now it's like the curtain's been lifted, revealing a flawed woman desperate to hide her true self from the world.

Her jaw ticks and I swallow past the lump in my throat. Things might be over with Xavier, but my feelings for him haven't gone away and if she really wants to change, I should help, right? "He's the sweetest boy I've ever met and you treated him like something I pulled from the trash." Poor choice of words. I can already hear her say, "Technically, you did."

Because that's what Old Brianna would say.

Her gaze softens and her arms cross tight over her chest like she's shielding herself, but she holds her chin high.

"I hope it's just his earrings or tattoos or crappy car, and not the color of his skin, but I honestly don't know." I take a quick breath. "And I need to know if my mother's just judgmental, or if she's also a racist."

She takes a tiny step back, and to her credit, looks shocked. She grips her purse strap like it's all that's holding her here. "I—I couldn't care less what color he is." Her eyes dart around the hall as if she's making sure no one is listening. "Yes, I judged him based on his appearance, but that's only because I was protecting you."

"From the scary Mexican?"

She shakes her head. "I only want what's best for you. Maybe I haven't expressed that well, but—"

"You would like him if you gave him a chance."

She catches her fingernail between her teeth, but jerks her

hand away as if scolding herself and rests her hand on my arm. The contact feels foreign, forced. "I'd like that."

"Me too." Never mind that he's no longer speaking to me.

"Maybe he could come over for dinner this weekend?"

My heart leaps, then crashes just as quickly. "Doubtful." If there's anyone he wants to see less than me, it's probably her.

Her forehead creases. "But you just said..."

"Today is the first time we've spoken since you..." She didn't exactly kick him out, but it had the same effect. "Since you met him."

Her face crumples and the next thing I know I'm in her arms, her perfume invading my senses. It's awkward and we don't fit together like a mother and daughter should, but she's trying. "I'm sorry. I promise I'll try to be better." She pulls back and looks me in the eye. "Is there anything I can do?"

My smile is shaky. "I think this one's on me."

We linger for a few more minutes, then I walk her to the exit with promises that we'll talk more tonight. I'm not naïve enough to believe things will change overnight, but this feels like a turning point. Like a new Before and After.

Mom's determination to change fills me with hope as I head upstairs to see Drea. As the elevator rises, I pull out my phone and scroll to the picture. Miss Simpson is smiling at Cally's dad like there's no one else in the coffee shop, and he's reaching for her hand. My gut twists. What was I hoping to accomplish with this? Aside from making Cally feel stupid and pissing off one of the nicest teachers in school, the high would be short-lived and I'd feel even worse.

With a quick breath, I hit delete and put my phone back in my pocket. A weight lifts from my shoulders and I straighten my neck.

I can do this. I can be good.

I step off the elevator into an empty hallway and fluff my hair. Xavier may think this is over, but I have to give it one last try.

But when I open the door to Drea's room, Xavier is gone.

thirty-one

ONE MONTH LATER

"You sure I can't convince you to try?"

Drea shakes her head and takes a sip of her coffee. I've been trying to get her on the slopes for the past two weeks but so far she's refused. "I don't like to move any faster than my feet can carry me." She nods at her arm, which is still in a sling. "Plus my doctor might have something to say about me damaging his work."

Colton didn't just break her arm—he shattered the bone in her upper arm and they had to put in steel rods to hold it together. The rest of her has healed, at least physically, and while she's gotten the all-clear to return to her normal life, it's like Colton broke something inside her that day. We've been spending a lot of time together after school and on the weekends, and I'm slowly starting to see the girl I got to know on the Chain Gang. I'm hopeful she just needs more time. She'll have to see Colton at his trial in a couple months and I've promised to be by her side for the whole thing.

"Do you need to get going?" Drea asks. I'm heading to Eldora, alone and with my brand new snowboard. After the drama at the motel, Mom's made a bigger effort to talk to me and I told her I've started snowboarding. It was under the tree in our new condo a couple days after Christmas, shining in its pink and white gloriousness. There were also hot pink snowpants and a matching jacket, but I exchanged them for something less flashy.

Maybe I really am changing.

We hug goodbye and I promise to come over tomorrow, then I'm in my 4Runner heading to Eldora. It snowed overnight and tomorrow is a government holiday, which means the entire school will be there. And it's Sunday, which means the ski team kids could be there too.

Which is what I'm counting on.

I still haven't had an actual conversation with Blake or Cally. I've cornered Blake a couple times between classes and while he usually looks right through me, the last time I said hi they didn't chased me away. Mike seems to be coming around a little faster. We met for coffee last week and I think I've convinced her that Old Brianna is gone for good. Now that she's with her boyfriend Mica she seems to have an ease about her that was always just beneath the surface. I don't know if it was me that held her back before, but I made her promise to put me in my place if my old controlling self reappears.

As for Kenzie, she's taken whatever power-trip I used to be on and multiplied it by a thousand. She's got an army of underclassmen who do whatever she tells them, and I'm a tiny bit afraid she's plotting something to humiliate me. But whatever it is, I can handle it. After being arrested, having Dad walk out, working on the Chain Gang, then facing down Drea's crazed abusive boyfriend, I can take whatever Kenzie dreams up.

Besides, she was never the creative one.

The parking lot at Eldora is already packed, so I park near the back and change my boots at the car. It took me awhile to admit it, but everything about boarding is easier. The falling still hurts, but before I'd have to carry my gear and change in the lodge, while now I can walk in my cushy boots with nothing but my board resting on my shoulder. My season pass is attached to my jacket, so I walk straight to the chairlift and attach my front foot.

The first couple runs are a little rough—it's not the same without a smoking hot instructor who gives you kisses when you do a good job—but I'm learning to love the way my board responds to the slightest movement of my body. My core has gotten stronger and to anyone else, it looks like I actually know what I'm doing.

I'm trying not to care what other people think, but I can't stop cold turkey.

The line for the lift is longer than when I first arrived, so I slide into the singles line. It sucks because you get paired up with a random, but at least the line is shorter.

When it's almost my turn, a low voice startles me.

"Is this seat taken?"

I see his board first—blue with navy swirls—then my gaze slowly moves up his body until I'm looking into Xavier's eyes.

An uncertain smile plays on his lips.

"That's why I'm in the singles line." His smile fades and I wink. "I'd like to say I planned this, but I didn't know you were here."

The pair in front of us gets in the chair and we move forward as the next one swings around. Once we're seated, I'm at a loss. He's never far from my thoughts, but he hasn't reached out a single time since we talked at the hospital. So why now?

As the chairlift carries us higher into the air, a sense of calm washes over me. Up here, it's just you and nature. Life and all the drama that comes with it is far below. It'll still be there when I come down, but for now, I soak in the quiet.

That said, I'd really like him to say something.

Sitting six inches away from him on a bench twenty feet in the air is a special kind of torture. Especially if he's not going to talk. Maybe he didn't plan for us to be in line together and rather than let someone else go, he figured he'd be polite. When we get to the top, we'll go our separate ways and pretend nothing ever happened between us.

My heart's slowly breaking all over again when he clears his throat.

"I've missed you."

I've imagined him saying those words so many times that at first I don't realize he actually said them. I shift my body to look at him—peripheral vision's a joke with a helmet and goggles—and he's watching me. "I've missed you, too."

"Drea told me you've been hanging out a lot."

"Yeah. Her arm is really jacked up but the rest of her seems to be getting better." My gaze drops to his gloved hands, which are gripping the guard rail. "Thank you again for helping that day. I don't know what would have happened if I'd gone there alone." I've imagined it a lot and every scenario ends with me in the hospital alongside Drea. Because I would have fought to protect her and I'm not stupid enough to think it would have made a difference. He would have tossed me aside like a rag doll—or worse.

"I've thought about that. A lot. And that's how I realized...." he trails off and my heart flutters. I don't want to get my hopes up but he's already said he misses me and why else would he be here with me now? "I still care for you," he says. "I'm still pissed about the whole thing with your mom, but you can't help who your parents are."

I smile. "She's actually gotten better. I think that day snapped her out of whatever self-absorbed haze she's lived in for most of my life and she actually seems to care."

"I'm glad." He looks out over the trees. "How's the new place?"

"It's not so bad. It's smaller and I don't have a spot in the garage, but Mom's tried really hard to make it feel cozy." She even found whatever combination of products our former cleaning lady used and it smells like vanilla and lemons.

Like home.

He sighs, and my fingers itch to reach for him. But it's too soon.

"I've also been thinking about the thing with Blake and his brother," he says.

And just like that, all hope of getting back together disappears. "Yeah?"

"I can't say I like how you handled it, but like you said, you're trying to change. You have changed." He holds my gaze and smiles. "The person Blake described to me wouldn't have done what you did for Drea. And she wouldn't come boarding by herself on the busiest day of the season."

"I'm done worrying what people think. Especially since most of them hate me. At least this way I get to enjoy myself."

"They don't all hate you."

I laugh through my nose and my goggles fog up. "You haven't been to my school."

"No, but I am friends with some of them." I cock my head and he points in the direction of the terrain park. "I talked to Blake. Told him what you said about that day with his brother."

Terror and nerves and a tiny bit of excitement swirl through me. Xavier talked to Blake for me? "What'd he say?"

"You were right. He really doesn't like you—"

My elation crashes.

"—but he's willing to listen."

"That's all I want."

He smiles. "Want to kill two birds with one stone?"

"That depends on who's throwing the stones."

He laughs. "I'm gonna guess you haven't been on the terrain park."

"Just once last year. On skis. It didn't go well." Back then, I was beyond irritated that Cally had waltzed into school and captivated everyone—including my friends—but decided she didn't want to be friends with me. I convinced Kenzie to go down the big jumps on the terrain park and while we didn't fall, it wasn't our best showing.

"Blake's there now. If we go, I'll coach you through the run and you can talk to him."

"Now?" Wanting to make things right and actually doing it are two entirely different things. The same nerves I feel when I'm about to start a run ripple through me. And it doesn't help that we're almost to the top of the hill. I still haven't mastered exiting the chairlift and I really don't want to fall in front of Xavier.

He shrugs. "Or you can stay here and things will never change."

"When you put it that way." I lift the guard rail and slide forward on the bench. "Ready?"

Our arms bump as we coast down the ramp and my edge catches, throwing me off balance. He grabs my arm, steadying me, and we come to a stop with his hand still on me.

"What's it gonna be?"

I don't know if I'm more afraid of the terrain park or talking to Blake, but having Xavier this close after so long makes it a little easier. "Let's do it."

We cut across trails to get to the terrain park, but when we're standing at the top of the hill, it's not as terrifying as I remember. The steepest parts are on the three mammoth jumps, but the rails and other obstacles are spread out enough that I can ride around them. Boarders and skiers maneuver past each other, flipping and twisting and making their bodies do things in the air that seem inhuman. I'm sure at least a few of them are people I know.

"Do you want to try the jump?" His eyes practically twinkle behind his goggles.

"Not a chance. But I'll meet you at the bottom so you can." I hop forward before he can object and cut from side to side across the hill. Since I'm not going near the tricks I don't have to go around anyone, and I reach the bottom while he's still in line for the big jump.

A boarder in gray crests the top of the first jump and touches the back of her board while spinning in a three-sixty. The next jump she spins the opposite way, and on the third she soars so high that I'm convinced she'll break her legs when she lands. She coasts to a stop not far from me and I realize it's Cally's friend Amber.

Which means the skier coming over the first jump must be Cally.

She crosses her skis behind her so they form an X, then disappears when she lands. The next jump is a backflip, which she makes look completely effortless. And on the third, she combines the two.

"No way!" Amber shouts.

The move looked impossible, but it all looks impossible to me. The one time I attempted these jumps I went so slow I barely made it over the incline. I glance at Amber, hoping she'll explain why she's so impressed, but Cally's already coasting to a stop next to her.

They high five and Amber gives her a hug. "That was awesome!" she shouts, even though they're right next to each other.

"Yeah," I say, not meaning to join their conversation but the words have already left my mouth. They both look at me like I've sprung a second head, and I smile.

Cally gives me a puzzled look, then turns back to the jumps as Blake does a twisting backflip. He does it again on the third jump and she bounces on her feet. He's still moving fast when he lands, but instead of showering them with a spray of snow, he leans forward on his front edge and spins in a huge circle on his belly.

Once he's back on his feet, Cally taps her helmet against his and says something too low for me to hear.

Then Blake looks my way.

She must have said something about me.

"Xavier's next," he says to me.

I'm so shocked he spoke to me I almost miss Xavier's first jump. He does a backflip similar to Cally's, and my jaw drops. Based on how muscular he is, I shouldn't be surprised he can move like that, but I am. Blake whoops as Xavier copies his twisting move, and on the third jump Xavier grabs the back of his board and arches his back, soaring so high that it seems like he's held up with string. He lands gracefully and slides toward the group, but when he sees me standing a few feet away, hops over.

"I'm impressed," I say.

His smile's so big it nearly splits his face. "That was fun. You sure I can't convince you to try it?"

I shake my head. "Maybe next season. I'm still happy when I don't face-plant."

"Fair enough." He looks over his shoulder at the others, who are moving toward the chairlift. "Hey, Blake. Wait up."

I think he's going to leave me standing here, but instead Blake peels away from the group and comes our way.

"Now?" I whisper, fear gripping my chest. All the times I called Blake a Ski Bum or Snow Rat and hurled other insults at him flood back to me. He has every right to hate me, and zero reasons to hear me out. Yet here he is.

Xavier touches my arm. "I'll catch up with you after the next run." And like that, Blake and I are alone.

His jaw clenches, like he's waiting for an insult or god knows what else, and he crosses his arms over his chest.

Standing in front of each other, I remember why I liked him all those years ago. And why it hurt so much when I screwed up our friendship. He has a calmness about him that draws people in. I take a breath and start talking.

"You have every reason to hate me and I don't expect that to change, but I want to tell you that I'm sorry." The words feel too small for how much I've hurt him.

His jaw ticks but he holds my gaze.

"That day with Cody..." I look down and my eyes burn with tears. "It haunts me to this day. I did absolutely everything wrong and instead of apologizing, I attacked you. Lashing out was the only way I knew how to handle my feelings, and by the time I realized I was wrong, it was too late."

"My brother died, and you turned into this monster bitch determined to make my life miserable."

"I know. And I know I can't take it back, but I can try to make it right." I take a breath. "I'm trying to make it right."

"The only reason I'm standing here is because Xavier asked me to. You somehow got him to believe that you actually give a shit about other people."

I silently thank Xavier, and can't help but hope there's still a chance for us.

"But you can't just erase the past four years."

"I know. And I'm sorry."

"It's gonna take some time for me to believe that." He shakes his head. "Mike's already convinced you've changed—she and Cally have talked about you—but I'm not that easy."

"Thank you, Blake."

"Don't thank me. Follow through on your promise." And with that, he turns and heads for the chairlift.

I wait at the bottom, feeling like a thousand-pound weight has been lifted. The muscles in my shoulders ache, but it's like when you stretch after a long workout.

I can finally breathe again.

It's not long before Xavier is flying over the jumps, and I join him on the chairlift. He doesn't touch me, but he stays by my side on the terrain park and even walks me through the big jump. I don't get air, but he makes me feel like it's possible.

When we head inside for a break, the lodge is packed. Mike and Cally are sitting at the primo table in front of the fireplace, and Mike waves us over. Xavier heads toward them, but I hesitate. The last time I was in this lodge with Cally we had a huge fight, and while she seems willing to forgive me, I don't want to go where I'm not welcome.

Maybe I should just leave.

"Bri, are you coming?" Xavier turns around and gives me a look that makes me weak in the knees. It's gone in a flash, but I didn't imagine it. He still likes me.

I follow him to the table, anxiety building with each step. When I reach the table, the girls both smile.

"Mica and Blake are getting drinks," Mike says. "But we have room for you."

My heart surges.

"I'll get in line with them," Xavier says. "What do you want?"

I pull cash out of my zippered pocket. "Hot chocolate, obviously."

His smile makes everything else fall away and for a moment, we're back in his kitchen, kissing next to the stove. "It won't be as good as mine."

"Nothing is."

He walks away and I sit, heat burning my cheeks.

"So you and Xavier, huh?" Cally asks. "Can't say I saw that coming."

I smile. "Me neither."

"So Bri," Mike says. "Switzerland for spring break?"

"Nope, not this year." Dad was pissed I didn't finish my hours by his deadline, and even though he said he was proud of me for helping my friend, a deal is a deal. But I'm okay with it. Switzerland will always be there, and no matter how much I like Piper, I'm still getting used to the idea of him being with The Seconds. Going would crush Mom, and we're finally getting to a place resembling friendship.

But I am taking Piper boarding before the season's over.

"Wow, you're not going to Switzerland AND you're still smiling?" Mike teases. "You really have changed."

"I'm trying."

She and Cally chat about the ski team and soon the boys return with trays loaded with drinks and snacks. The conversation is light, and for once I keep quiet. The truce with Blake feels too fragile, too new, to risk screwing it up. They're all so comfortable together that I can't help wanting to be a part of it, to have a group of friends who genuinely like each other and aren't hanging out for appearances.

When the drinks are gone and nothing but empty wrappers litter the table, I stand. "Thanks for letting me crash your party. I'm gonna get going."

"You're leaving?" Xavier asks.

"I'm getting tired. And the last time I kept going when I was tired I got a face full of snow." I laugh, and they laugh with me.

Not at me, with me.

"Text me later?" I ask him before I realize I gave him the opportunity to reject me in front of everyone.

But he smiles. "Okay."

I wave at the group. "See you." Then I weave through the crowded room and step outside, breathing in the cool air. A sense of calm fills me from within. This must be what happiness feels like. It's crazy to think how much has changed in just a few months, how the things that my world once revolved around no longer matter. I don't want people to worship the ground I walk on—I want them to like me for who I am.

It feels like it's already starting with Mike. We'll never be best friends again—too much has happened for that—but I'm okay just having her in my life.

And at least I know if I see Cally and Blake, I can say hi without worrying I'll start World War Three. I'll forever be grateful to Xavier for talking to Blake, regardless if things work out with us romantically.

Even though I really hope that they do.

I pause near the fire pit and look up at the mountain, at the people criss-crossing the slopes. Each one of them has their own drama, their own friends, their own dreams. I hope that some of my friends are back there in the lodge, but if I have to find new ones, I know I can.

I turn to head to the parking lot and freeze. Xavier is standing ten feet away, watching me. I move toward him, my heart racing. His eyes lock on mine and that same look from earlier is on his face. We stop inches from each other, and he smiles. "You left before I could do this," he says, his fingers grazing my chin. He takes my helmet from me and tosses it to the ground. My hair blows in the gentle breeze, but I barely notice. All I see and feel is him. His hands slide through my hair and he looks into my eyes a beat longer, then lowers his head and kisses me.

It's like the world resets on its axis. Being in his arms, knowing he's here after everything I've done, confirms the most important Edge Rule: When choosing a side, choose the one that makes you happy. The rest will fall into place.

to you, the reader

I've said it before and I'll say it again: you are why I do this. I've always loved telling stories and being able to entertain people with my imagination, so thank you for spending time with me.

Want more of Xavier?

If you write a review on Goodreads and the bookseller website where you bought this, email the link to MelanieHooyenga@gmail.com and as a thank you, I'll send you bonus scenes from Xavier's perspective.

One final note.

Boulder, Eldora, and Monarch High School are real places, and while I did my best to research them (thank you internet!) any factual errors are entirely mine.

author's note

I lived in Zihuatanejo, a fishing village on the Pacific Ocean in Guerrero, Mexico, for three years and it's exciting to finally include snippets from that part of my life in a novel. Everything about the way I describe the town is true—at least it was when I left in 2010:

• Lilies really are EVERYWHERE. I had a pair of nightstands with them carved into the sides, and you could go into almost any restaurant and see them.

• The in-home restaurants I ate at weren't nearly as fancy as the one Brianna and Xavier visited, but the food was just as good.

• I ate so many tortillas when I first moved there that the locals thought I was pregnant. Yes, I had a tortilla baby. (I quickly cut back after that.)

• The Spanish phrases Xavier and Fernando use are ones I said—or heard—every day. I had Xavier's family come from the town where I lived since so much of dialect is regional, and I wanted it to be accurate.

Now for a story. When I first moved to Mexico in March 2007, my ex and I were living in his parents' house, which had no running water and zero privacy, and no one except us spoke English. I had minored in Spanish in college, but I hadn't practiced in the ten years since I'd graduated, so I didn't talk much those first couple months. Tortillas were served at every meal, and were eaten in the same way Xavier teaches Brianna:

fold it in half and tear, then tear those halves in half so you have four pieces. Then you use a piece to scoop up your food. It's tricky to get the hang of if you've only ever used utensils, and needless to say, it took me a lot of tortillas to get through a meal (see the earlier comment about my tortilla baby). About three weeks after we arrived, I commented that I didn't want to eat as many tortillas (because people thought I was pregnant), and my ex said, "oh, did you want a fork?" My jaw dropped and my eyes went wide. I believe my words were, "WE HAVE FORKS?" My tortilla baby quickly went away and I learned to limit myself to three (or five) tortillas per meal.

I've been gone almost nine years, and I still miss the food. Bringing it to life for you—gambas con ajillo and molé con pollo were my favorite—was a pleasure.

acknowledgments

Writing is a private, quiet thing, and as an extrovert who likes to be around people, it can be challenging to find a balance. That's why I'm so thankful for my writing friends who understand what I'm going through, and my non-writing friends who still think it's cool that I share my imaginary friends' stories.

I'd like to thank a few people for holding my hand over the past year:

My online writing groups for providing suppport and laughter, and knowing which I need when.

My beta readers Bridgid Gallagher, Patrick Hodges, Sarah Emery, Ann Marjory, and my mom Judy Hooyenga, for making Brianna's story better than I could on my own.

Nancy Matuszak for continuing to challenge me. I'm a better writer because of you.

Nadine Nettmann and Sara Carlson, my best friends and real-life wonder women. I can't remember what my life was like before you, but I'm sure it was severely lacking in inappropriate hashtags, Friends gifs, and T. Swift lyrics.

And finally, my husband Jeremy for not batting an eye when I said I wanted to write—then publish—two books in one year. Your love and humor shine through Xavier's eyes, and I couldn't be more grateful.

Keep reading for the start of Flicker, *the award-winning first book in Hooyenga's* The Flicker Effect *trilogy.*

chapter 1

Sunlight pulses across the dashboard—light, dark, light, dark—and catches the dust dancing on the imitation leather.

My eyes stutter, but I blink it away. My heart jumps around in my chest. I stroke the grainy piece of cement stuck between my back teeth with my tongue. The orthodontist swore he got it all, but that was as true as his promise that it wouldn't be uncomfortable.

Uncomfortable. Right.

A tingling sensation pricks the tips of my fingers. I press them together, watching the blood shift beneath my skin. The tingling turns to those sharp needles that remind me of anything but sleep.

I press harder and my toes start tingling too. What the hell?

The dancing on the dashboard gets faster. The trees here are taller, straighter, and the sunlight strobes through the branches. My breath catches and a sudden heaviness pushes me deep into the seat.

I glance at Mom but she's concentrating on the road, humming along with golden oldies or whatever the hell it is she listens to, oblivious to the fact that something very weird is happening to her daughter.

To me.

I close my eyes. The heaviness lifts. Too much. Now I'm floating and—

"But Mom, I'm fine."

Mom crosses the kitchen and leans against the counter. "Biz, you're going. The dentist said your face will change if you don't get braces. Your entire face could look different..."

A sense of déjà vu slams me over the head. I've had this argument. Next Mom is gonna grab the stack of mail that Dad left on the counter and toss it in the basket.

She does.

"Biz?"

The words tumble out of me. "Mom..." The déjà vu doesn't lift. This isn't a memory. I'm not in the car anymore.

I've gone back to yesterday.

*****

Find all of Melanie's books at melaniehoo.com, and sign up for her newsletter at melaniehoo.com/hoos-letter.

about the author

Multi-award winning young adult author Melanie Hooyenga writes books about strong girls who learn to navigate life despite its challenges. She first started writing as a teenager and finds she still relates best to that age group.

Her award-winning YA sports romance series, *The Rules Series*, is about girls from Colorado falling in love and learning to stand up on their own. Her YA time travel trilogy, *The Flicker Effect*, is about a teen who uses sunlight to travel back to yesterday.

When not writing books, you can find her wrangling her Miniature Schnauzer Gus and playing every sport imaginable with her husband Jeremy.